William Golding
The Man and his Books

William Golding
The Man and his Books

A Tribute on his 75th Birthday

Edited by John Carey

faber and faber

LONDON · BOSTON

First published in 1986
by Faber and Faber Limited
3 Queen Square London WC1N 3AU

Filmset by Wilmaset Birkenhead Wirral
Printed in Great Britain by
Butler and Tanner Ltd, Frome and London

British Library Cataloguing in Publication Data

William Golding, The Man and His Books: a tribute on his 75th Birthday
1. Golding, William—Biography 2. Authors,
English—20th century—Biography
I. Carey, John
823'.914   PR6013.035Z/

ISBN 0-571-13901-9

Acknowledgements

The editor and the publishers are grateful to the following for permission to include copyright material:– the Eliot Estate for lines from 'Gerontion' and 'Little Gidding' in *The Complete Poems and Plays of T. S. Eliot*; the British Council for extracts from Literature Study Aids; the author's estate, The Hogarth Press and Harcourt Brace Jovanovich for an extract from *Moments of Being* by Virginia Woolf; Mrs Laura Huxley, Chatto and Windus and Harper and Row for an extract from *Antic Hay* by Aldous Huxley; the Wells Estate for quotations from *The Outline of History* and *A Short History of the World* by H. G. Wells; Allen and Unwin for a passage from *Portraits from Memory* by Bertrand Russell; Sigmund Freud Copyrights Ltd, The Institute of Psycho-Analysis, The Hogarth Press and Basic Books for a quotation from *The Complete Psychological Works of Sigmund Freud* translated and edited by James Strachey.

Contents

CONTENTS

Illustrations

Preface

JOHN CAREY

Lord of the Flies is the *Robinson Crusoe* of our days. Partly through its appearance on 'O' and 'A' level syllabuses, it is known to thousands of children (and to thousands more who were children, and have grown up to discover other Golding novels). Despite this fame, Golding himself remains virtually unknown – as shadowy, almost, as Defoe. That seems a deliberate choice. He has resisted the temptation (if there ever was one) to become a cultural personality or a TV guru – as, with his commanding presence, and that beard, he surely might have.

On the principle that if you are celebrating a birthday it is best to know whose birthday it is, I decided, when Faber invited me to edit this 75th birthday tribute, that I would have, whatever else, contributions from people who were, or had at some time been, close to Golding, and could tell us about him.

So four of the first five essays are memoirs. Their authors have known Golding as schoolteacher (Anthony Barrett), as mentor (Stephen Medcalf), as friend (Peter Green), and as author seeking publisher (Charles Monteith). The first of the five, Peter Moss, goes further back in the search for Golding, portraying the father whose personality, Golding has always acknowledged, shaped his own.

Then come the literary critics – again, five in number. They were given little in the way of editorial briefing, beyond the implicit request to be as interesting as possible. Despite this lack of directive, their contributions circle around a single point – the search for Golding, or at any rate for his precise imaginative imprint and allegiance, in the books. John Bayley finds no intimate sense of the writer's self in Golding's novels and treats that as one of their distinctive marks. Mark Kinkead-Weekes, Ian Gregor and Barbara Everett focus on disparities between different facets of Golding – between the visual and the visionary; or between fable and felt reality. Anthony Storr, approaching Golding as a psychologist, as well as a friend, concludes that he, and the novels, remain, in the end, mysterious.

For five of the remaining contributors I decided to choose from among Golding's fellow authors. I asked them to be as idiosyncratic and personal as they liked – not to compose 'essays' on Golding, but to think about Golding and then write around their thoughts. The result, as I hoped, is suggestively miscellaneous: a poem from Seamus Heaney; a meditation on baboons from Ted Hughes; new light on Golding's sources from Craig Raine; acknowledgement of Golding's literary parenthood from Ian McEwan; a declaration of imaginative allegiance from John Fowles.

At the end of the book is an interview which Golding was kind enough to give me last year. On the way down to Cornwall in the train I started reading his (just published) *An Egyptian Journal*. Finishing it on the way back to London, I came upon (p. 132) Golding's golden rule: 'Always treat an interviewer as a guest, but remember always that he is not a guest.' I felt glad I had not read that before I met him, but his and Ann's hospitality would probably have made me forget it, even if I had.

Talking to him, it occurred to me that he was essentially the product of two factors in twentieth-century English social history: firstly, the Second World War, which changed his view of man's nature, and from which *Lord of the Flies* was born; and secondly the English state-system Grammar School, as it was before Comprehensives killed it. It was that workaday, ink-stained, serious institution, with its hand-to-mouth intake of 'culture', its disdain for frills, its social unease, its respect for brain – and its stubborn retention of Latin and Greek – that Golding came from, and that his father helped to create. It might seem an odd breeding ground for a great writer; but any breeding ground can seem odd for that, whether a muddy market town on the Avon, or a scrivener's house in London's Bread Street. The English Grammar School will produce no more Goldings: now we must wait for the Comprehensives to come up with their first Nobel Prize winning novelist.

Meanwhile this book is offered to William Golding as a tribute, in consciousness that what we write cannot be good enough, but in hope that respect and affection will piece it out.

Alec Albert Golding 1876–1957

PETER MOSS

I doubt if a schoolboy has any real insight into the character of a master, however much admired and imitated, who is forty years his senior. At the time the great gulf of age and status is impossibly wide, and it is only in the light of adult experience that the significance of so much that was accepted without question in the narrow years of schooling becomes apparent. Certainly I feel this is very true of Golding père, who taught me science in the 1930s and who now comes back to me in a series of brilliant flashbacks as one of the most remarkable men I have ever met. As I look back over my own life and teaching career I am very conscious of just how important an influence he was on me both in his advanced, free-ranging ideas and the warmth and humour with which he presented them. I am quite sure that this richly liberal atmosphere obtained even more strongly in his own closely-knit family circle, and must have played an important role in shaping William Golding's work.

Alec Albert Golding was born into a working-class Quaker family near Bristol, and in his early teens became a pupil teacher – one of the very few paths in the nineteenth century which allowed poor children of vision to fulfil at least some of their potential. After some years of exhausting apprenticeship, teaching by day and studying for the equivalent of 'O' level in the evenings, he moved on to formal training, and became a 'certificated' teacher. In 1902, armed with this passport to a then sub-professional world, he took a post as science master at Marlborough Grammar School, a very ancient establishment which after centuries of vicissitudes had been reorganized as the grammar school for the small market town and its surrounding villages. It was here that he spent virtually the whole of his teaching career, finally retiring in the 1940s. In this time he took an external degree (1916) and gained qualifications in music and architecture, as well as being appointed a Fellow of the

Royal Geographical Society. Perhaps this is the key to the whole of AAG's personality: despite his academic excellence and his amazing versatility, which could have taken him to a very senior position in the educational world, he chose deliberately to remain in this rural backwater, teaching the rudiments of science to the rather stolid children of local tradesmen and farmers – and enjoying life to the very full in his individual way.

But AAG was no bumbling Mr Chips: he was a man whose influence must have been as strong with hundreds of other, now ageing, men and women who studied under him during those forty years, as it was with me. In his breadth and versatility, in his delightful sense of humour and his free thinking, he was a true Renaissance figure.

AAG was essentially very private, and the core of his life his family. Although he was such a warm person, I suspect that he was extremely shy with most adults with whom he had to have anything more than formal contact. Certainly his relationships with colleagues at the school seem to have been correct and cordial, but not intimate, and I believe that in general the family made few close friendships, though, of course, many acquaintances, in the town.

But with children the situation was quite different, as if they were almost an extension of his own family. His inhibitions and diffidence fell away; he was so childlike himself that in class he was a *primus inter pares*, the teacher-taught relationship being a strange amalgam of equality and authority. One obeyed instinctively out of respect and affection, and only once did I see him enforce discipline physically and then, in the prevailing mores, justifiably. One boy, assuming that AAG had left the room, connected the rubber tube of his bunsen burner to the water tap and sent a jet across the room to soak a girl on a distant bench. AAG leapt from the podium, cuffed the offending boy round the ear and then, with gown swirling in indignation, stalked back to his place. But I think that even then it was likely that the rage was simulated, and that secretly he was highly amused at the boy's ingenuity.

When I first met him he was already an institution in the district, now teaching the children of former pupils, as I myself was. My mother, who was a student under him between 1904–09, remembers that self-containment and privacy were his strongest characteristics, even as a young man.

In appearance, at least in the 1930s, he had something of the tourist's concept of a pixie from the Cornwall he so much loved – short, slight, with a round cherubic face topped by a bald pate that gleamed whatever the weather, and a tonsure of white hair. The gold-rimmed glasses which should have rested on the snub nose were more often pushed up on the forehead as he peered short-sightedly at a book, or into a microscope muttering like an incantation, 'Paramoecium . . . vorticella . . . volvox . . .'

Apart from its intrinsic interest there were two characteristics that made a Golding lesson unique – the frequent use of biblical quotations for almost any situation, critical or complimentary, and the stream of personal anecdotes to illustrate a scientific point, or often just for fun, as if he had become a little weary of formal instruction and wanted to play.

The biblical quotations were the more surprising as he was a dedicated atheist. Perhaps expressions such as 'Go to the ant thou sluggard; consider her ways, and be wise . . .' for minor lapses of attention were in a way a practical gesture of support for his non-belief by, as it were, totally secularizing the scriptures. This rejection of doctrinaire religious belief was completely rational and never flaunted: it was for him, like his socialism and his pacifism, a passionately-held personal opinion which concerned no one but himself. The only time I heard religion mentioned in the classroom was when in reply to a question he tried to explain the difference between agnosticism and atheism, and on that occasion he claimed to lean towards the former rather than the latter. But I suspect that in view of his strict Quaker upbringing his fierce disbelief went very deeply into the soul he would have denied, and that there were agonizing conflicts between reason and emotion. It may have been coincidence, but on the only two occasions I remember AAG, as deputy, taking the morning assembly in the absence of the headmaster, he collapsed and had to be helped from the hall. On both days he managed to get through the opening hymn, even if with what I now see as some distress, but broke down completely, once in the scriptural reading and once in a prayer. A man of total integrity, he had obviously had to face a terrible battle between intellectual honesty and professional duty. I am certain that he would have given a great deal to avoid what he knew would be an ordeal; but having decided that it was his responsibility, he would have given as much to be able to carry it through. In the event his body took the decision out of his hands with a compromise of which I am sure he would not have approved in his heart.

His personal anecdotes were altogether more lighthearted. After a little experience a class could detect when one was germinating: the eyes twinkled, a boyish grin of delight spread across his face, and it was only a matter of time before the usual opening 'I remember . . . I remember . . .' Generally the anecdotes were relevant to the lesson: sometimes they were a comment on local or even personal issues: sometimes, as in the case of the motor car accident, they managed to combine all three.

In the mid-1930s he determined to learn to drive a car. He seems to have had problems, and during one of the lessons in Savernake Forest he knocked a man, while passing him, from his bicycle. There was no harm done to either of the participants, though AAG reported with great amusement the remarks of the cyclist whose dignity, if not his machine, had been a little dented. However, the police decided to prosecute. AAG, I believe, pleaded guilty – though he did not offer the extenuating circumstances he described in the anecdote – and was fined. Shortly after the case had been settled, there came the twinkle in the eyes in the middle of a dynamics lesson – a subject for which even he could not rouse much enthusiasm. 'You may have heard . . .' he began, and then chatting as if to friends he explained, without attempting to exculpate himself, the rational scientific explanation for the accident. He drew on the blackboard the vectors of the relative velocities and lengths of car and bicycle, worked out the times and distances, and then said that he had imagined himself a point in space. He had forgotten that there were ten feet of car behind him which he had not taken into account when passing. That I remember such a trivial incident after fifty years gives some idea of the effectiveness of his teaching methods which were far ahead of his time – a true Comenius of the science lesson.

In another physics lesson – thinking back, it seems to me that anecdotes came more frequently in physics than in the other sciences – he had been demonstrating the refraction of light with the usual pencil in a beaker of water, when the impish smile spread across his face. 'I remember . . .' he started, and chuckled to himself at the memory. 'I remember when I was a child . . .' He then told of two notorious Gloucestershire poachers whose practice was to shoot fish in the local river – the scientific link was the difficulty of knowing precisely where an object under water really was when viewed obliquely from above. The marksman walked slowly along the bank, and if he made a kill, his companion, who was completely naked, leaped in the water to retrieve the prey. 'Once,' said AAG, 'the man with the gun shot a fish, which was carried down with the current. The other man rushed along the bank, keeping his eye on the floating body and did not notice a clump of nettles four feet high in his path. His language, when he came through, was not very polite . . .'

Many of AAG's stories appealed to us so strongly because we as country children had seen the same phenomena, but unlike him had done nothing about them: it was at the same time a clever and exciting way of inculcating a strong interest in science and of establishing a deep personal relationship. 'I remember . . .' he began once as he prodded with a pipette for a specimen of a hydra in the tank of stinking, green and slimy water that putrified gently on the end of his desk, and released a stream of bubbles from the mud at the bottom. 'I remember as a boy I thought the gas which came to the surface when I poked a stick into the ponds was carbon dioxide. So I took a gas jar with me the next time and collected some. I brought it back home to prove my point by doing the tests for carbon dioxide . . . and what are they, Collins? Yes . . . extinguish a burning taper. So I lit a match and pushed it into the jar, but instead of going out, it exploded, burning off all my eyebrows, my eyelashes and much of my hair. It was a very good way of discovering that the gas in question was marsh gas, or methane . . .' From here it was a short step for him to go on with remarkable frankness to discuss the gases produced in the intestines by a similar breakdown of organic material. It was one of the great secrets of his success as a teacher that he was always ready to turn off the main highway of the lesson into any side road that seemed to offer interesting views, whether of another branch of science or of the broader issues of life. He was creating whole people, not merely teaching a subject.

The sheer exuberance of AAG as a boy finding out about his world with the minimum of formal instruction and the maximum of curiosity was contagious, though some of our experiments could have been more disastrous than his with the exploding gas jar. I cannot remember whether it was electricity and magnetism, or the nervous system of the frog, as it could have applied to either but suddenly came the story of the chapel fête. 'One of the stalls,' he said, 'consisted of a large copper vessel filled with water and with many sovereigns scattered on the bottom. You paid sixpence and took as many sovereigns as you wanted . . .' Pause for effect while the implication of sovereigns for sixpence sank in. 'But,' he went on, 'the vessel was connected to one side of a shocking coil, and as soon as the person's hand touched the water, the circuit was completed and the victim received a violent electric shock. The pain was terrible, and the nervous system was paralysed so that the muscles would not respond . . .' It all sounded very scientific and logical, and all over the room I knew plans were being made with large metal vessels and mains electricity figuring largely in them. Then came the Parthian shot which so often made these reminiscences so delightful. 'There was the manager of the local mine,' he went on,' a very devout man. He paid his sixpence, plunged his hand into the water and removed all of the coins in handfuls – but he did put them all back afterwards. He explained that he never felt any pain at all under any circumstances . . .' As this miner occurred in several stories all connected with absence of pain sensations, I imagine he was genuinely suffering from some degenerative nervous condition, but why his muscles were not paralysed puzzled me even at the time.

AAG's passionately held pacifist and socialist views were as well known as his atheism: perhaps the combination of all three was a factor in his not advancing in the educational field, at least in strictly conservative and Conservative Wiltshire. But I believe that had he been rigidly orthodox in all his views he still would have found the sheer fun of living as he wanted far more important than ambition. Life was for living, and neither that nor, more especially, his family was to be sacrificed on the altar of material advancement.

Though socialism was so important to him, and though his lessons were so wide ranging, politics was almost never mentioned. The only comment on the subject I remember him making in class was immediately after the election of 1935. I cannot recall whether it was the theory of inclined planes or the reproductive system of the earthworm that led to the question, but at one point in the discussion a pupil asked, 'Whom did you vote for, sir?' AAG beamed: 'I'm not going to tell you whom I voted for,' he said, 'but I will tell you that in the whole of my life I have never voted for a candidate who was elected.' In the traditional two-horse race for the Devizes constituency, which Labour did not contest until 1945, this left little room for doubt, though I am sure he would have registered a protest vote.

AAG's relaxed, enjoyable and, judged even by that awful criterion of examination results, successful teaching was not, I now realize, the effortless exercise it seemed at the time. Apart from his encyclopaedic knowledge which could find some fascinating sidelight about almost any subject that cropped up, there was an immense amount of sheer hard work and preparation. Perhaps the only visible sign to us was the science text books; the school bought none at all. AAG wrote, illustrated, printed and bound every copy himself. Each one was laboriously written on a jelly hectograph and copied page by page in slack moments. When a year's supply of page 1 had been completed, the jelly was melted, and page 2 begun. The booklets, each of several dozen pages, were filled with experiments, line drawings and ways of analysing the results; they needed only the minimum of oral explanation to make a very satisfactory elementary course, which is probably why he could spend so much time on his illustrative stories, which were infinitely more valuable than formal elaboration. The books were sewn into manilla covers, and each one titled by hand with the initial letters of the subject and a number for the year. There were C1-C5 for chemistry; P for physics; B for biology; and, for more advanced pupils, H, L & S (Heat, Light and Sound); M & E (Magnetism and Electricity) and, the pinnacle of the academic attainment in the school, D & H (Dynamics and Hydrostatics). Even though there were fewer than 200 pupils, to produce textbooks for each of them – and for the first five years everyone took chemistry, physics and biology – was an incredible feat.

Much of AAG's charm was that in many ways he never grew up, but with his brilliant adult mind and experience still looked through the eyes of a child, seeing what they wanted and needed. And if this came through to us, his pupils, one can only guess how much more intensely it was felt by his own sons. Perhaps nowhere was this trait more obvious than in his joy in making mechanical devices of which Heath Robinson himself would have been proud. But like the anecdotes, these toys were both playthings and immensely instructional. There was, I remember, the treadle sewing machine which had been converted into a bizarre dynamo, with a giant horseshoe magnet some two feet long and a pair of whirling, handwound coils the size of small jam jars. When pedalled furiously, the whole equipment vibrated violently, the flash-lamp bulb lit up feebly, but nowhere else have I seen the whole process of the generation of electricity reduced to such basic and easily comprehended elements.

In similar vein was the water turbine, a truly magnificent Golding device. Seventy or eighty teaspoons were fixed by the tips of their handles into a cylindrical wooden core which turned on an axle. Jets of water played into the bowls of the spoons, setting the whole thing revolving at high speed. Yet despite a massive tin cover over the whole apparatus, water blasted out all over the room at a dozen places, much to the delight not only of the pupils, but also of AAG himself who was invariably soaked in adjusting it.

But the *pièce de resistance* was the wireless set which, apart from its single thermionic valve, was made entirely from scrap materials – the kind of challenge that AAG enjoyed so much. Handwound coils and chokes were, of course, mere child's play: lower value resistors were carbon rods taken from discarded dry batteries and filed down until the right value was reached: resistors in the megohm range were made by rubbing a soft pencil on a piece of card. Capacitors were manufactured from long strips of metal foil from cigarette packets interleaved with waxed kitchen paper and rolled into cylinders. But the most ingenious component of all was the tuning condenser, which was made from two sheets of brass separated by waxed paper. The upper sheet was bent upwards into a curve, and was pressed into greater or lesser contact with the lower by means of a sliding wooden shutter. Crude though it was the set would receive on its crackling headphones the more powerful British stations, and it certainly reduced the principles of electronics to something the dullest pupil could understand. At the time – and the BBC was only a dozen years old – radio still had a strong element of magic in the minds of many people: by creating a wireless from such everyday materials as kitchen paper and cigarette wrapping, he put the whole new world in context. How he must have wished he could expose so easily what he saw as the fallacies in other superstitions.

But these fine set pieces of scientific equipment were only the more spectacular ones, and orders from Marlborough Grammar School to the suppliers of laboratory apparatus must have been almost as meagre as those to publishers of textbooks. Everything that it was possible to make, AAG made himself from the most unlikely materials – though in what time stolen from time I do not know. He encouraged this in his pupils, making science a reality and not a string of abstractions to be learned for the next examination. Every child in the second year, for example, made his or her own thermometer, starting by making the file mark on the stock capillary glass tubing and breaking off a ten inch length. This was sealed at one end in the Bunsen flame, the bulb blown and filled with dyed alcohol. The other end was then sealed: the thermometer was calibrated in ice, and water of varying temperatures, and finally mounted. All the while AAG scurried round the class of some twenty-five pupils advising, correcting lopsided bulbs and even providing the puff for a few girls whose genteel upbringing would not permit such undignified activity. It was a *tour de force* I did not see attempted in a mixed class in twenty years of teaching.

Music was very important to AAG, as it was indeed to the whole family: people using the path that passed the Golding house would hear on many, many evenings the sound of quartets or sonatas floating across the churchyard. He himself was a fine player on the violin, viola, cello and piano: 'My father,' he once explained, 'would let me learn any stringed instrument, but would not allow me to touch any wind lest it damage my lungs. And, of course, I have always wanted to play wind instruments.' He was, I believe, a very competent flautist.

Musical anecdotes tended to appear in the 'H, L & S' class, but the highlight of this half year was the making of flutes as part of the study of vibrating columns of air. Lengths of bamboo about the size of broom handles appeared in the laboratory and were cut into fifteen inch lengths, one end of which was tapered. A cork was inserted, and then AAG himself began the task – which went on concurrently with his teaching – of making a dozen 'flutes'. A sound

23

hole was cut, and then the first finger hole. He blew a tentative blast, tapped the tuning fork, and then busied himself with a rat-tail enlarging the hole until it gave the correct note. This continued until a set of twelve instruments – with nominal assistance from the class – had been produced. Some breathy collective sessions of scales and, I believe, 'Rousseau's Dream' followed briefly before the class passed on to vibrating strings.

In school his real musical abilities came into their own at the annual parties which each of the three 'sets' into which the school was divided for competitive purposes held immediately before Christmas. These gatherings, which had strong echoes of the Victorian nursery junketing, consisted of games and decorous dancing – the Boston two-step, the valeta, the military two-step, the Lancers, an occasional polka and, as a daring concession to modernity, one foxtrot and waltz in each half of the evening, which was divided by sandwiches, jellies, cakes, and powdered lemonade. For all of these dances he thumped the insensitive school piano, but then came Sir Roger de Coverley, when he took up his beloved 'fiddle'. He sawed out the tune faster and faster, his face getting redder and redder, his pate shinier and shinier, but everyone was invariably exhausted long before he was.

AAG was a kindly man and, though my mother reports that he could be sharply sarcastic, I saw none of this; perhaps he had mellowed in the thirty years between our experiences of him, or perhaps Victorian girls had different values. His kindness is typified by the fact that he allowed two or three of us who were particularly interested in science and who intended at that time to make it a career – though in the event none of us did so – to stay unsupervised in the locked laboratory all through the lunch hour. Generally we did not abuse his trust, which I am sure was without the headmaster's knowledge, but I can recall two instances when his confidence must have been shaken. When he returned from lunch, which unlike most of the staff he invariably took at his home, he normally asked what we had been doing, and we were delighted to show him the microscope sections we had cut or the apparatus we had made. I think it must have been during the Italian invasion of Ethiopia when the news was all of the mustard gas bombs dropped on the defenceless villages, that one of the popular scientific magazines contained an article showing how easy it was to produce this appalling liquid. The chemicals, we noted, were all on the laboratory shelves, and one lunchtime we set about producing our own gas. Perhaps the instructions were not complete, perhaps we missed a step, perhaps we were just incompetent, but fortunately we failed to produce anything. When AAG returned he asked with what I am quite sure was sincere interest, what we had been doing: when we told him, he did not blink an eyelid, though our militaristic leanings must have been totally repellent to him – to say nothing of the appalling danger we had so narrowly avoided. He commented mildly, 'You should not really do that, you know, but if you must, you should do it in the fume cupboard . . .'

On another occasion we had made a 'telephone' from a pair of discarded headphones and batteries. A wire was taken through the laboratory window to the changing room below and a tiny tinny communication established by alternately speaking into and then listening to the headpiece. A few exchanges had been made when AAG returned from lunch: in his usual way he wanted to share in the fun, and took up the instrument. He spoke briefly into it and then applied it to his ear. The coarse youth below, not recognizing the voice and still believing he was talking to his friends above, replied with some rustic obscenities audible to all, though whether electronically or by simple sound conduction through the walls I do not know. AAG smiled, put down the apparatus and said mildly, 'Well . . . it seems to work all right.'

Although full class lessons were a delight, it was smaller gatherings, whether the half dozen pupils who would invariably gather round AAG's desk at the end of a session and with whom he would chatter happily right through the break period, or the tiny sixth form science groups, that felt the full impact of his personality. I suspect that he rather dreaded the public aspects of school life, the most important of which were the annual sports day and the prize giving. On sports day he reached a compromise between personal feelings and his sense of duty as head of 'C' Set: for the majority of the afternoon he remained in school, filing flutes, hectographing textbooks or making some new apparatus, but always turned up in time for the final excitement of the relays and presentations.

Prize day was an altogether more serious occasion: on sports days he could always have been in odd corners of the field watching the various events, but absence from the platform among the assembled governors, local dignitaries and staff would have been very obvious. It was a lavish evening ritual, and in my own time as much a reunion of old scholars, now parents, as a presentation. On the morning of prize day AAG had his own ritual; for the only time during lessons his gown was removed, and was spread carefully over the demonstration bench. A large stone bottle of Indian ink and a small brush were produced, and the year's chemical stains, bleachings and spatterings were carefully painted over to present a more or less even black. Usually there was an amused commentary as he disguised one mark after another, first on the reasons for the activity, and then turning it to teaching advantage, explaining the properties of the substances which had caused the discoloration.

I remember Alec Golding with deep affection – and gratitude, for in my own teaching career I often smiled as I caught myself quite unconsciously using some of his techniques. His own home must have been a wonderful environment in which to grow up, and one wonders perhaps at the black pessimism of many of William Golding's characters. Perhaps it is that when one has such a secure and happy background one can explore the darker sides of human nature with more objectivity than someone who has had bitter early experiences of them. But I am certain that had AAG been on that island, there would have been a very different story of Jack and Ralph and Piggy.

Memories of Golding as a Schoolmaster

ANTHONY BARRETT

In appearance the William Golding who returned to Bishop Wordsworth's School at Salisbury in 1945 was not exactly what we boys had been expecting. He had taught there briefly before the war and his reputation for untidiness and the nickname which it earned him had survived the intervening years. We viewed with some astonishment this white-collared, perfectly turned out, former naval officer who addressed us with crisp and well chosen words of command.

It did not last. He grew a rather straggly beard; his trousers lost their creases, his jackets lost their shape and his tie its correct position in the collar: but his love of the sea did not desert him. He took command of the school's Combined Cadet Force. The training of this formidable body of adolescents had formerly been biased towards the air force, but under Lieutenant Golding RNVR it assumed naval uniforms and devoted itself to the study of knots, semaphore and seamanship in general. Most important of all it acquired a dinghy or two and under Golding's instruction some of its members were taught to sail in Poole Harbour. Of course, his love for the sea was coupled with a proper respect, amounting to awe, which is evident in *Pincher Martin* and, more explicitly, in the essay 'The English Channel'. This respect was no doubt reinforced when he was himself shipwrecked in a sailing boat in the Channel several years later.

My own acquaintance with him was confined to the CCF and to the numerous other non-academic activities in which we were both involved. Perhaps even acquaintance is too strong a word, but at least for my part I was in a position to observe him in the casual way that schoolboys do observe their masters. Whether he was aware of me I do not know, but the author of *Lord of the Flies* must have been observing schoolboys much more profoundly. In any case, conversations with people who were taught by him suggest that in class he was rather reserved. This was probably owing, at least in part, to the fact that he was required to teach his main subject, which was English, to those middle and lower forms which were least interested. He may have found this something of a chore, and not always succeeded in disguising the fact. It must not be thought that he was aloof, however. There is a story that once, when he was supervising an examination, the noise of his heavy shoes as he paced the wooden floor so distracted one of the examinees that he was driven to protest. Whereupon Golding immediately removed his shoes and spent the rest of the time walking up and down in his stockinged feet.

If he showed any lack of enthusiasm inside the classroom he more than made up for this in other activities. For example, when he decided to learn the oboe to play in the school orchestra he gave up smoking to improve his breathing. He was both fond of music and very musical. He played the piano and his slightly throaty tenor was a mainstay of the chapel choir. He was a useful soloist and in 1945 took the part of the innkeeper in a broadcast of a musical nativity play written by the then headmaster. It would be interesting to know whether a recording of this still exists in the BBC archives.

His connection with the school chapel seems to have gone deeper than singing in the choir. My contemporary Otto Plaschkes has recounted elsewhere how Golding would retire to the chapel from time to time for private prayer and meditation.

His other contribution to school life at that time was in the field of drama. Rumour had it that he had at one time been a professional actor. Whether this was true I do not know, but certainly both he and his wife Ann were excellent performers. Masters were not allowed to act in school plays, but I remember him producing an English version of Aristophanes' *The Frogs*. He was not content merely with showing the young players how to interpret the text in front of them. Perhaps finding that 'Bre-ke-ke-kex koax koax' was not a sufficiently punchy lyric for 1948, he himself wrote words and music for some additional songs. Four lines have stuck in my memory:

> This is the only kind of music we can understand;
> Syncopated four-in-a-bar, especially if it's canned . . .

and

> This is the only kind of dancing we know how to do;
> Shuffling around in a sweaty hall with you and you and you . . .

No doubt some scholar will one day unearth the rest.

Of course, these superficial recollections date from before the publication of *Lord of the Flies*, and long before Golding's fame as an author had spread throughout the world and achieved the recognition of a Nobel prize. His pupils at that time had no reason to set him on a pedestal, even if they ever felt disposed to do so. But in a staff which included several outstanding teachers and not a few 'characters', he made a particular impression. Not because he was a great teacher; I doubt if he would claim that distinction. Not even because of his wide range of accomplishments and the prominent part he played in the life of the school. When one recalls him, the person who springs to mind is not the extrovert sailor or producer but an observant, reflective, thoughtful man apparently brooding on problems which he did not seem to share with anyone else. This is not said with hindsight. I am sure that even if he had never published a single book, my contemporaries would still have retained the same impression of him; an impression formed as they saw him carrying on a humdrum existence in that small school, under the vaunting spire of the cathedral, with the sea not far away, and all around cheerful jostling schoolboys, with all their potential for cruelty.

Bill and Mr Golding's Daimon

STEPHEN MEDCALF

I have stood alone in Stonehenge in winter quiet not long after dawn while the low red sun gave a touch of warmth to the rough pillars on the head of each of which – or so it is in my mind's eye – an immense black rook was sitting.

It seems a good way to have begun a Sunday the rest of which was spent drinking cans of beer with Mr Golding. I protested impotently that my upbringing constrains me to go to church on Sunday: he protested genially that we all have these difficulties with our upbringing but must learn to overcome them. It was that day that he said – swearing me, since 'the discovery should go to him who published it', to a secrecy which with his permission I now break – that he had seen the carving of a Mycenaean dagger on one of those stones before it was noticed and generally proclaimed. And didn't he remark that the moving thing about Stonehenge is that while its proportions, its entasis and geometry make it a piece of architecture, the rain has worn runnels in it and turned it back to nature? I think he did – and it matches another remark of his about the possible etymology of Arthur, *artos* a bear, something black, animal and inarticulate which seems to convey one dimension of the Arthurian stories, crossed at right angles by the white light of the Grail – 'that's what all my novels are about, only no one has seen it.'

I suppose it is what he is about too. He looks somewhat like a bear – only a small bear. It is the hardest thing to hold in one's mind about him and indeed about his whole family that with a force of personality that makes one remember them all as huge, they are actually all – Bill, Ann, David and Judy – short: a series of painful knocks from the timbers of their cottage, under which they pass easily enough, has driven it into my head. And again when Bill was working in the watergarden he made there in Wiltshire he looked like a smallish Proteus arising from the deep.

It was after he rose from the deep – though that's a frivolous expression for a hurtful experience – that I met him first. I had taught his daughter Judy at the University of Sussex, and in the summer of 1967 she showed me in Shoreham harbour the boat, called the *Tenace*, in which she, her parents and two friends were going to explore the canals of Europe – a lovely rounded boat with tiled walls, though one did crack one's head on the beams. I lent her a Wodehouse to read on the voyage. On the third of August she sent me a letter:

I expect you won't have heard our stroke of melodrama. All six of us were (and are) quite safe, but unfortunately (minute word) *Tenace* was run down and sunk on Friday 14 July . . . Some primitive superstition prevented me from salving any of my worldly goods when I could have done – so amongst other things I much regret your kind opportunity to develop a liking for Wodehouse . . . It is in quite stunningly good company, that of Homer and Joyce. Papa wishes me to infer that *Tenace* only sank because she had two copies of *Ulysses* on board . . . : despite such seeming levity he is rather upset, as also my mother. Neither of my parents, I am glad to say, saw *Tenace* actually sink. The Japanese (on the tanker that ran us down) would not let them stay, but took them away and supplied whisky and coffee at a rate – I was going to say of knots but will leave sentence affectingly unfinished . . . Too much of water – quote employed by mournful father as he reflected on farcical situation – when the tanker returned to scene of crunch to find small battered yacht two feet lower down than previous, Papa found his throat a trifle dry. Calling upon his wife, he requested a glass of water, which my mother then fetched, wading thigh deep through the main cabin to get to the galley. [My friend] Paulette thought such a literary view of disaster unhealthy – she does not share the Golding security in classification or somewhat . . . I . . . found myself muttering . . . as *Tenace* wallowed and wallowed –

& still the sea came in

Talking of *Tenace* wallowing, I detect the same emotional behaviour in myself, and will therefore conclude, with the only bright result of the whole ghastly business. I lost forever my beastly Dr Scholl sandals.

When I wrote back, Judy suggested I come to stay at the cottage at Bowerchalke in Wiltshire. I was to be brought down from London by Mr Golding, who had gone up to see his tailor: and I went in awe. Awe is appropriate but not needful. As Bill's small height is to his immense personality, so is his immense, and immensely companionable personality to what erupts in his books. And I'm not sure that he regards that eruption as exactly something about himself so much as something of which he is, amazingly, capable. When he conceived *Lord of the Flies*, he said in 1977, 'I even thought to myself (this will show you how certain and silly people can be), before I put a word on paper, I thought of myself winning the Nobel Prize for Literature because of *Lord of the Flies*. Now I didn't, ever, but it was not impossible. I discovered what I was about, d'you see?' But when he saw Peter Brook's film, he thought, amazed '*I* imagined this'.

But in any case, as the parrot in Don Marquis's *Archie and Mehitabel* says about Shakespeare 'what poor Bill wanted was to be a poet'. He writes novels, he says, because he can't write poetry. And I think he regards T. S. Eliot, on whose trousers he once spilt champagne, with at least as much awe as I approached him with, in that London square in 1967.

The difference (and similarity) between what he is and what Eliot was can perhaps be best understood through their relation to silence.

In Eliot's poetry there are silences like

> . . . In the juvescence of the year
> Came Christ the tiger

> In depraved May, dogwood and chestnut, flowering judas,
> To be eaten, to be divided, to be drunk . . .

in 'Gerontion'; or the one which follows

> . . . So, while the light fails
> On a winter's afternoon, in a secluded chapel
> History is now and England.

in 'Little Gidding'. Different as these silences are, they are all

1. Mildred and Alec Golding, parents of William, at the Well, Holywell Bay, Cornwall

2. William (*right*) with his elder brother José

meditative, and are to be dwelt on. They are so much part of the movement of consciousness that one could say that the rest of the poem is there to give the meaning and emotion which fills them, or that the poem is formed round them. There are silences in Golding's novels too, conspicuously the ones which come at the shifts from one consciousness to another near the end of a novel, which are one of his most familiar characteristics. But in contrast with Eliot's, these come at the climax of violently accelerating or intensifying movements of consciousness, and signal a change away from one person's consciousness to another. They are not themselves full of emotion or meaning. There is one case, the silence in *The Spire* which follows Jocelyn's dying words, 'It's like the apple tree!' where you could feel that the silence suggests the state beyond words into which Jocelyn passes, that is, if you do feel that Jocelyn passes into a positive state. In that case the silence might be like the one from 'Little Gidding'. But that is an interpretation chosen by the reader, who is just as likely to make nothing of the gap in the text except a change of person, and read straight on into the last sentence, where the consciousness is that of Father Adam watching Jocelyn's death.

The silences in Eliot express something beyond the words on either side of them, the silences in Golding signal a change from one kind of consciousness to another. I wonder if it follows that Eliot, as he makes very clear, needed to distract his everyday intelligence for something else to happen, while in Golding's writing the 'something else' makes his everyday intelligence accelerate until it rises to a crescendo and stops or changes direction?

Something related might be that while no one ever had much from Eliot about his poetry beyond a stone wall, Bill will talk with great interest and understanding – but to what degree the same understanding that wrote the books? – about any of his novels except *Darkness Visible*. And *Darkness Visible* feels more than any of his novels like an overtaking flood.

What has struck me most in talking to him about his novels is that it is impossible to forecast what he deliberately designed and what he did not: or what indeed, as he remarked about Ralph's remembering in *Lord of the Flies* in his moment of frantic despair Simon's prophecy 'You'll get back', he actually designed to come up 'like a spring whose course has been so deeply buried that it has not been felt'. His surface is intimate with his depths, and to him the writing of a novel is 'a single activity . . . like the apple tree growing out of a seed'.

And yet there is a great distinction between Bill and his daimon, his ka, his genius, and no doubt it is the distinction which makes it a pleasure, like eating a good meal, to talk to him, whereas it would be terrifying to address the author of *Pincher Martin*. The man one talks to has all the interests and capacities of the writer of the novels. He is fascinated by technical contrivance (and in the case of the wooden structure that weights the *Spire*, explained it better for my capacity in the car in 1967 than the author of the novel had, who is closer to, more sensuously involved with the thing); by historical speculations that take one into the thick of experience, as whether Shakespeare might not have first travelled to London by water, not by road; by the evolution of mankind; by the sea; by the depths below our consciousness; by God. The modes of consciousness are there; even, like Jocelyn and Pincher Martin, when he hears sounds he sees them. The quickness of consciousness, and the changes of direction are there too – a quickness in his responses as long as he is paying attention at all, then a quick shifting away, or weariness; something inclusive, urgent, Celtic, almost febrile, is it, coming through the calm of his slow English voice?

What I suppose is the work of his daimon, his ka, is just that acceleration which is not quite the same as what Eliot's daimon does; these interests, these modes of consciousness coalesce and take on a driving force. Perhaps it's because of that intensification that William Golding's daimon has little or no sense of humour; Bill is all humour. The fact about the daimon is not a necessary one; in the film of *Lord of the Flies* a boy actor did what Golding's daimon avoided, made Piggy funny without changing the sense or diminishing the tragedy. Perhaps only a small boy could have done it – the director, Peter Brook, on the contrary intensified the cruelty, the black and white – perhaps as part of the twist he gave it by stressing the corporate organization of the choirboys as the source of the blackness and evil. Bill remarked both of the making of the film and of Brook's production of *King Lear* that Brook doesn't understand poetry. The daimon of *Lord of the Flies*, the book, obviously does understand poetry: the grief, terror and wrath of that and of all William Golding's novels coexist with an enjoyment of the process of things and an ecstatic apprehension of beauty.

Yet with all that somewhere close to his surface, all that constantly appearing in his conversation, Bill has the humour which his daimon eschews. His conversation flows with pun, sardonically humorous anecdote, and a quite unsardonically humorous presentation of himself. And any aspect of his apprehension of the world is quickly checked by another. I remember one visit when he had been rereading *Ulysses*, and remarked in the evening on a phrase he'd found uncharacteristic of Joyce and sympathetic in its distance from the cerebral and verbal, its closeness to worship and fact – 'the heaventree of stars hung with humid nightblue fruit'. Next day he took some friends round Salisbury Cathedral – pointed out a stone cadaver in the choir, whispering almost furtively, 'You remember Jocelyn in my book wishing to be portrayed as he really was' – and then a tomb in the south nave aisle of which he told a terrible story – that it was rumoured that the person buried there had died of a poison that would accumulate in the head – and that when many years later the tomb was opened a rat was found dead in the skull. I was reduced to a quotation from *Ulysses* – 'History is a nightmare from which I am trying to awake' – all unaware that I was giving Bill opportunity to grin and declare triumphantly, 'On the other hand, think of the heaventree of stars hung with humid nightblue fruit.' It wasn't long after, that Bill felt that we'd had 'too much culture' and we went off to do something else. (But who knows what else was going on in his head when he said 'too much culture'? When I had read Peter Green's essay 'In the Shadow of the Parthenon', which describes a rainy day on the acropolis with Bill anonymously voicing misgivings on culture, and asked if it was really he, he said, 'The odd thing is that I remember it for a quite different reason. As the huge raindrops fell, splat, splat, splat, they struck a smoothed bit of the sacred rock between my feet, and I saw at once why it was sacred – it became (because it *was*) translucent like a quartz pebble in a pool, and I saw that the whole rock was a semi-precious stone. I haven't dared go back lest they should have changed it (THEY, I mean) into a dreary old lump').

35

No doubt humour is among other things a defence against what one finds most painful. The foundation of Bill's considerable admiration of C. S. Lewis seems to be a remark in *The Problem of Pain* that the sum of pain felt is not increased by the number of people who endure it – the maximum amount of pain felt is that felt by one person – a remark which read in the thick of the Second World War enabled a great many people to carry the weight of the time. And that is only one instance among many of the impact of the war on Bill. But the subjects of his anecdotes are likely to be concerned with the war, the navy or related matters like his *Boy's Own Paper* brother-in-law. And when I thought of planning a course on the impact of the Second World War on English literature, Bill suggested a professional soldier's book, John Masters' *Bugles and a Tiger* which has a good deal of professional humour. The daimon does not concern itself with such defences.

Again the daimon presumably has not to concern itself with the manipulation of persona which perhaps in its awareness is what Bill is. How else but through a certain humorous play with persona could a man go on being ordinarily human while – alas – having essays like this written about him? Besides, Bill has been an actor and a schoolmaster, two professions which endure the problems of fame day by day. He once gave me a relevant piece of advice about schoolmastering – be first to arrive at the classroom so that the boys form a group on you as a centre instead of being already formed in a group over against you.

Actually what most surprises me about Bill is that he does not like P. G. Wodehouse nor, I think, read Max Beerbohm. His daimon might well not like either, because both live by an innocence which politely excludes crisis, the solitariness of moral action, treachery and death, while allowing a sort of pressure from these things to emerge in humour.

But no one knows more than they about style, about the handling of persona, about using a language instinct, as English is, with tradition, cliché and quotation. No doubt this skill explains why T. S. Eliot uniquely prized Wodehouse, and Evelyn Waugh accorded to both the title of Master. Bill's conversation has just the delight in turning a quotation which is at the heart of Wodehouse's play of language (I have even heard him use a quotation from William

Golding in this way – 'I do not see this picture'). True, as Ann once pointed out, more than anyone he avoids using cliché; but that is absolutely consistent with the Wodehousean turn on cliché. Bill's ordinary conversational tone is best expressed in his published works, apart from his essays, by his last three books, *Rites of Passage*, *The Paper Men* and *An Egyptian Journal*: all are humorous. *The Paper Men* is perhaps a presentation of the persona Bill would have if he wrote novels with faintly embarrassing Malcolm Lowry-like titles such as *All We Like Sheep* and *Horses at the Spring* rather than *Pincher Martin* or *The Spire*, and *An Egyptian Journal* has just the elegant way with the disasters of travel that you would expect from an amiable Evelyn Waugh – the Waugh of *A Tourist in Africa*. And Bill does like Evelyn Waugh. Why then does he not like P. G. Wodehouse? I do not see this picture.

His daimon, I think, is only concerned with innocence when innocence understands (Father Adam, Simon) or is otherwise brought into contact with guilt: and it purges language. Once, trying to think why God should make the world, Bill said he could imagine a need for absolution so great that it would bring one to create the universe. But then again on that first visit when we were talking about God and the existence of evil he said, 'Yes: there's something which can't be said in words. I don't know what can do it. Music perhaps.' And beyond even the feeling that he writes novels because he can't write poetry is the feeling that what he wants to do and cannot is to be a musician.

Actually he's a clever performer. I see I have instinctively pictured him so far with a can of beer and in a watergarden, and these probably are the first and second situations to envisage him, but behind a piano is certainly the third. (The fourth is carving the meat which Ann has brought in from the kitchen.) And Pamela Gravett, who is a common friend, remembers Bill and her husband, a don of New College and Balliol, in the small cottage at Bowerchalke at the grand piano, long after midnight, performing Stravinsky's *Oedipus* –Kenneth Gravett singing Jocasta and Bill, Oedipus – 'playing at a great rate – with lots of wrong notes – they didn't pause to get the notes right – they kept up with the rhythm – and it was brilliant! It was electrifying!'

But creation, which he wants to happen in music and poetry,

happens to him in words and prose. That it should be in words is – I suppose – inevitable because words have peculiar power, mystery and independent existence for him. Phrases from the Bible haunt him. He once gave me as an example, 'Day unto day uttereth speech, and night unto night sheweth knowledge'; a verse which takes the point further, because it suggests that there is a conversation going on in the world which we are not exactly excluded from, but are on the outside of – as if the world were words. Part of the fascination which Egypt holds for him seems to be that hieroglyphics express just this complex of thought – they are human symbols but they were made by people who thought they might come to life. And in the essay 'Egypt from My Outside' he quotes 'Day unto day uttereth speech, and night unto night sheweth knowledge', to illustrate the sense hieroglyphics have for him. When he first went to Egypt what struck him most was that 'nothing feels so secular as an Egyptian temple': but the writer who best expressed this for him was of all people the mystic who saw the signature of things, Jakob Boehme: Boehme said that when the children of Israel spoiled the Egyptians, they took away their wisdom and mystical power.

Moses in that story saw something corresponding to hieroglyphics in a sense, something that was the signature of God, the burning bush; and that is another thing that concerns Bill. I don't know how he envisages it outside the story. He has used it as an image, in *Free Fall*, of miracle violating the law of the conservation of energy, and in *Darkness Visible* explicitly of the blitz, and implicitly of a human body surviving the blitz, of victory over entropy. But I once was watching a biblical epic on the television with him, and the burning bush happened – a leafless tangled blackthorn bush in the desert with a white flame playing about it, petrol perhaps. It was unsatisfactory (I thought) because the bush was leafless and the flame not part of the bush; anyway, it didn't satisfy Bill. He does like nature to be allowed to go its own way and triumph in its gorgeousness over entropy. He was once shown Vita Sackville-West's and Harold Nicolson's white garden at Sissinghurst: at which he raged. Nature has, he said, been for aeons diversifying its colours – and these people on the fringe of Bloomsbury try to reduce it to white.

The Inheritors, I have heard him say, is his favourite among his novels, and is this because it portrays a people who think in pictures, and leave nature to go its own way without projecting their fantasies on it? (He *said* it was because it was about murder and cannibalism – 'a nice homely story' – but that was not offered to be believed.)

Projection – but then isn't that what one always stands in danger of when one finds the signatures in things? Worse, the more one understands the nature of things by any means, the more one finds in them the system of symbols by which one is understanding them, and so the more it seems that it is oneself that one contemplates. Bill began his life as a teacher at a school run by anthroposophists, who profess to have some resolution of this difficulty, but he thought there was almost none of them who had come out from the shadow of Rudolf Steiner; they were kept like children by his doctrines.

Jung has made another attempt in the same direction, perhaps more congenial because less abstract – for him Bill has a certain admiration as one of the 'great crumbs' who enable modern man to approach religion. But the very fact that Jung is talking psychology makes it difficult to find in him a breaking out of the sphere of subjectivity. For example, Bill admires C. S. Lewis's novel *Perelandra* and a passage in it which suggests how a man might know that what seems like a voice in himself is actually a voice from beyond himself: a professor of philology called Ransom, trying to decide whether or not to perform an action that may save a world but result in his death, hears the voice in his head with which he is arguing say 'It is not for nothing that you are called Ransom.' And Ransom knows that this cannot be a trick of his own mind, because, having trained himself for years to know that Ransom as a proper name is derived from Ranulf's Son, he could not have made that kind of pun.

Bill remarked that one of the effective things about that passage is that the unconscious does work by puns. Only of course – this is my comment and not Bill's – if that rather Jungian observation is true, there is no longer here any guarantee such as Lewis wished to provide that anything but Ransom's self is speaking. There is something similar but more effective in *Pincher Martin*. Pincher seeing a figure who may be only a reflection of himself hears it say, 'Have you had enough, Christopher?' and realizes 'I could never have invented that'. This involves a Jungian pun, Christ bearer, but I take it that what impresses Pincher is the questioning of his primary urge to survive as himself at any cost. What he is offered is the presence of what is utterly not himself: not nothing, not a silence into which to fall, but something questioning and creating.

Pincher Martin is a novel about imagining; but at this point there is at least the imagination of breaking out of the globe of imagining. 'How long,' a student once asked Bill, 'does it take Pincher Martin to die?' He said firmly, 'Eternity.' 'But in real time?' she persisted. He paused and grinned and said, 'Eternity.'

What Pincher Martin meets is God: and God is real, and eternal. But what is one doing talking about the eternal and real God in a fiction? Evelyn Waugh tried the paradox of writing his own kind of fantastic social satire as a historical novel, whose centre should be the Empress Helena finding the actual wood on which Christ was crucified, and whose theme therefore is the necessity of a religion based not on vision but on fact. Waugh thought it his best novel, and among Waugh's novels it is Bill's favourite; I guess because, all unlike as it is in style and in kind of belief to his own novels, it shares with them that concern with the impossible meeting place of imagination and the last irreducible object who is not imagination: God. I think Bill sees an analogy for what the writer does in the sacrament of the eucharist: he praises those lines of Shakespeare's of which he gives as an example

> Give me my robe, put on my crown; I have
> Immortal longings in me.

as 'moments no more to be defined than taking a Sacrament or bearing a child, or falling in love'. When Pamela Gravett asked him if he had ever received the communion he said 'I should be sick'. He is more likely, if asked, to say that he is not a Christian than that he is; but the balance of those two remarks is Christian enough. My colleague, Peter Stallybrass, once told me that there is a remark by St Augustine 'Woe be to me if I speak of God: woe be to me if I do not speak of God.' I quoted it to Bill who remarked 'Woe all round, in fact' and then later said that if I wanted an epigraph for a study of his writings, that would do.

For all Bill's fascination with the magic of the Egyptians, with their spiritual pragmatism, and with the Israelites who spoiled them of their magic, he is fascinated too by the Greeks who worked their way to doing without magic. His fascination with the Egyptians, indeed, he thinks goes back to reading Rider Haggard's *Cleopatra* – and Haggard's historical imagination is fired by just this interaction of the three nations, by the play of symbol and awe and intellect, by how much the symbolism of the Egyptians might mean the religion of Jew and Christian, and by the destruction of Egyptian tradition by the Greeks. But when Bill speaks of the Greeks in themselves, he slides into attacking them as clodhopping Squaddies, or equally clodhopping scientists: what keeps them a living force in his mind is the point where they have something close to hieroglyphics – their language as it is used by Homer and the tragedians, that marvellous organic, substantial and active language which is full with the going-on of things and with primitive fears and guilts.

For anyone brought up in England between 1920 and 1960 a sort of compromise between Egyptian, Israelite and Greek, a kind of child's nosegay of the conjoint tradition of wonder, morality and intellect, was Arthur Mee's magnificent *Children's Encyclopaedia* – all those maps and pictures and meditations and wonderfully succinct if not always satisfactory answers to all the questions one wanted to ask – 'Why do the leaves turn colour in autumn?' – and the just sense of personal values. Bill remembers from it, though I don't, a story of a man who greeted a friend just going to prison and of what the greeting meant to the prisoner – who though not named was clearly pictured as Oscar Wilde. I suspect that all those who could recognize a quotation from the Greek text of the sherd of Amenartas in Rider Haggard's *She* were also brought up on the *Children's Encyclopaedia* – certainly Bill is in both companies.

Someone once said of Bill that he has contrived to preserve in maturity all the interests of an intelligent English schoolboy – boats, treasure, islands, Rider Haggard, natural history, Greek (rather than Latin), geology, the Bible in the Authorized Version, machines, riding, Egyptian hieroglyphics, stained glass, *Paradise Lost*, Shakespeare, cricket. I suppose it is the peculiarly English form of Renaissance education; so one could equally well see Bill as the peculiarly English form of Renaissance man. I caught myself thinking when I discovered, from television, that Bill gave Jim Lovelock the word Gaia with its associations for Lovelock's near-mystical concept of the Earth's biosphere as a self-regulating

41

organism, 'Then Bill's *really* a great man.' I'd thought even my subconscious had alway recognized that; but evidently it was the unity of the classics and natural science that really struck home. I suppose his father might have done the same, and I have always gathered, whether from Bill, Ann or Judy, that Bill's father was *really* the great man of the family.

So there is Bill, deep rooted in an English tradition. On or off a horse, he recalls William Cobbett – a patriot, a radical patriot, a humorous indignant passionate grumbling mouth-filling radical patriot. I have a feeling that one of the causes of the eleven-year silence between *The Pyramid* and *Darkness Visible* was that that was a drab time to think oneself English. When he was watching television during that time (watching television with Bill is a rebuke to the glassy distancing with which it afflicts one – I remember his being moved to tears by the fate of Eleanor Marx, and at other times to wonder) he once vehemently burst out, at a conversation between Herr Brandt and Mr Callaghan, 'I never thought I'd see a British prime minister playing yes-man to a German one.'

About that time he was planning a novel about a ship in which after a mutiny there was to be a gradual breakdown of the substituted order and a drift to destruction – it was to be in some way an allegory of England. It did not happen, but one can see traces of it in what did happen, the pair of novels which seem to be almost night and day versions of it, *Rites of Passage* and *Darkness Visible*. *Rites of Passage* comes nearer to being the novel as planned and moreover nearer than most of the novels, in its particular temperature or degree of intensity, its humour, its sardonic observation of class and English history, its Greek quotations, and its one stupendous piece of sheer reportage – 'I have seen it at sea,' Bill remarked – the sight of sun and moon hanging level at opposite ends of heaven – to Bill's ordinary conversational self. Its obvious formal link with *Darkness Visible* is that both books happen round the journals of visionaries, different kinds of visionaries but both offering something eruptive, revelatory but uncomprehended by the narration outside. The contrast is like that between Bill whom one talks to and the daimon in the books. And the contrast between *Rites of Passage* as a whole and the unaccountable imagination of *Darkness Visible* is something similar again. (It is not, of course, a difference of literary value: which is the better of those two books? I do not know. But it is, I think, the contrast between the artist who more or less knows all that he is doing, and the artist who is doing much more than he can account for.)

I remember having dinner with Bill in Brighton and at a pause in the conversation his saying 'What is the most interesting thing in the world?' and to whatever was answered, responding 'No. The most interesting thing in the world is saints. I don't mean very good people. I mean people round whom miracles happen.' Later in Egypt, the colossi of Memnon, as he records in *A Moving Target*, gave him something he wanted to write about – faces 'struck away as if blasted by some fierce heat and explosion . . . an image of a creature maimed yet engaged to time and our world and enduring it with a purpose no man knows and an effect that no man can guess'. If that picture were seen in conjunction with the saint – and both with the burning bush – and these drawn to an idea of what was happening in England – it would help me to imagine distantly how Matty and *Darkness Visible* might rise from the mind's abyss and push aside the story of the ship, to be given its own life as *Rites of Passage*.

I guess something slightly different is happening in the imagining of these books from what happened in the novels up to *The Pyramid*. In those earlier novels one can trace, as an image for the point where the imagination confronts what it is to do before the face of God, the childhood terror of the darkness in the cellar by Marlborough churchyard which Bill has described in *The Ladder and the Tree*. I have fancied that this image was becoming unusable when he could describe the churchyard as a fact in daylight in *The Pyramid*. He said, in 1977, that though he still dreams of that house in Marlborough his dreaming self has moved away from the cellar – that the graveyard has become more friendly perhaps because more of his life lies there.

Instead of this darkness, it seems to me, he has become more willing to talk of human creativity, as he does in his lecture 'Belief and Creativity', as 'a signature scribbled in the human soul, sign that beyond the transient horrors and beauties of our hell there is a Good which is ultimate and absolute'. His feeling now seems to some extent a confirmation in our time of Coleridge's. But though I have heard him indicate approval of Peter Shaffer's *Amadeus* for raising the problem of the source of inspiration, and dissatisfaction with its actual dealing with the problem – and though in 'Belief and Creativity' he talks guardedly of human creativity as perhaps like the creativity of God, since we are said to be made in His image, he never comes near, as Coleridge sometimes did, any hint of pantheism. He values his daimon, 'the act of human creativity, a newness starting into life at the heart of confusion and turmoil.' But I do not think he values the human self: it's somehow attractive in him.

Of the immortality of the human soul he said once: 'You see, in what I conceive to be my one or two better moments I believe the only thing that matters *in saeculo saeculorum* is the existence of That not this. Really the profoundest happiness is the contemplation of the more-than-eternity (because outside eternity) of God. That's mixed and I can't say it straight: even the elders cast down their crowns so what should poor Tom do but throw himself?'[1]

---

[1] Those quotations in this piece which are referred to as happening in 1977 are from a tape-recording in the British Council's series *Literature Study Aids*.

King Fix: Bill Golding in Greece

PETER GREEN

When I and my family emigrated to Greece in the spring of 1963 my acquaintance with Bill Golding was polite, appreciative, tangential, and more than a little nervous: the creator of Piggy, and those disconcerting Neanderthalers in *The Inheritors*, was clearly a man to deal with cautiously at literary cocktail parties. We corresponded before we ever met, which was lucky. I had to lecture about him, and wrote with what I hoped were answerable questions. The answers were shrewd, meaty, and – something that then surprised me – witty. At a Faber thrash, slightly stunned by the baying of ambitious young poets in eager search of free food, booze, and publicity, we chatted desultorily for a little, but found ourselves defeated by the ambience. I also got a most vivid impression of Ann – sapphire eyes under burning dark Welsh hair, a peacock dress, a volcanic personality in equipoise. Later, Bill and I found ourselves fellow members of the Book Society selection committee. At committee meetings Bill was tweedy, countrified, and (as I now realize) on his best behaviour. Even so, between us we several times drove Tony Godwin, then the Society's brilliant but to us over-commercially minded Director, out of his mind, firmly picking eccentric novels as choices rather than the sure-fire non-fiction winners he thoughtfully put in our way. We lunched several times, found we liked each other's style. But the relationship remained intermittent, half formal, a product of literary London in the late 1950s.

Molyvos changed all that.

The move to Greece had been for me what Solon called a *seisachtheia*, a shaking off of burdens: I still remember the sheer exhilaration of sitting down and writing six or eight letters of resignation in one day, watching my various alter egos – fiction columnist, consultant editor, committee member, TV and film critic – being scribbled out of existence. *Na kai en' allo*, as I would learn to say from my Greek island neighbours: there goes another

45

one. The sixteenth-century house and the Mini-Cooper were sold. In my last column for *The Listener* I wrote, rather fancifully, about the prospect of sitting under a plane tree and reading mediaeval Greek epic, something which, during the best part of a decade in Greece, never quite came off. Anthony Burgess, who took over the following week, kept up the epic note in his valedictory: 'There he goes now, windswift over the wine-dark sea to Lesbos . . .' So he did, first in a Comet 4B, then by homely Olympic Airways DC3 to Mytilene. The children discovered the joys of mask and snorkel. Upper-Class Mytilenaean Greeks said: 'You can't possibly go to Molyvos, there's no one to play bridge with, why are you so determined that's the place for you?' Understandably, I was reluctant to admit that I'd been hooked by the description of Molyvos — once ancient Methymna, home of Arion, haven for Orpheus' singing head — in an eighteenth-century travel book. We made our excuses, hired a Datsun, and went. The first sight of the little town, as we drove over the last ridge above Petra, was breathtaking: a scatter of pink, white and red houses rising in a shallow cone from the harbour, and crowned with a crumbling Genoese castle. It was what I had been looking for all my life. I had come home.

Years later, old Greek hands now, bilingual and burnt nearly black, hair bleached by salt and sun, survivors of Greek primary and American secondary education, my children saw, to their utter astonishment, a Greek tourist board film about the joys of coming to Greece, and found they were watching themselves and their parents — younger, whiter, fatter, foreigners, Martians — arriving in the cobbled *agora* of Molyvos, being greeted by the uncertainly anglophone locals, what Osbert Lancaster once labelled the 'hullo boys', and recorded, all unawares, for posterity by some smooth Athenian *fonctionnaire* with a cine camera. Had we but known, this was a typical Molyvos happening. The town was never quite what it seemed. That same evening we all had dinner in the then one taverna. Lunch had produced only one other guest, who turned out to be Patrick White, the Australian novelist. Anything seemed possible, and was. The place rapidly filled with people in extraordinary dresses and hats — *could* that be a Chinese coolie? or a bullfighter? surely not? — whom by now, dazed by travel, cheerfully disoriented, and full of excellent local retsina, we assumed to be part of the local scene. But why were they mostly speaking English, French, or German? It was quite a while before we realized that Molyvos had a sizable colony of foreign writers, artist, deadbeats and eccentrics, who had chosen the night of our arrival to throw a fancy-dress party.

Acclimatization was rapid, and a long hot Aegean summer stretching ahead made the postponement of social and family problems all too easy. The children picked up Greek with enviable ease; they also had a keen ear for laid-back English locutions that buzzed over their heads in the post-prandial *kapheneion*, early bed for the young being unheard of in these parts. Sarah, at two and a half, riding my shoulders to the beach on a hot insect-laden afternoon: 'Bloody wopses.' Long pause. 'Fuck 'em.' And eyeing my wine, later: 'Piss-poor plonk, dad.' There was an on-going fantasy among the foreigners that Molyvos was in fact a minimum-security lunatic asylum, with them as patients, and the Greeks as staff. 'You may *think* you can leave,'said one old hand, darkly, 'but wait till you try it, is all.' A month or two of this and all our latent eccentricities rose seething to the surface, though at the time we'd have denied this hotly. But we did get some odd reactions from our guests – obviously we wanted to show off our new way of life, convince those we'd left behind how fuddy-duddy they were. There was the well known editor who wanted to know what time we'd be going swimming next day, and was out pacing up and down the balcony to the minute, towel in hand, while the rest of us surfaced from sizable hangovers; there was the lady writer for whom the drive from Mytilene was an experience akin to the African bush, and who failed to appreciate the casual passes, and comments, made at her and on her by colonists of both sexes. 'Molyvos,' we wrote to prospective visitors, 'does things to you.' And then, for the hell of it, we invited Bill and Ann Golding, and they came: the first of several long visits.

They appeared that first time on the quayside after gingerly manoeuvring a vast and shiny Rover 3000, weighing considerably more than a ton, out of the bowels of the *Karaïskakis*. This, we figured, was a sizable claim on English respectability; but by the end of the summer it was the only one left. Never did oddballs size up a scene quicker, or adapt to it with greater ingenuity and enthusiasm. In those days the colony was, for the most part, a working group; it was understood that calling on anyone before lunch was a no-no, and even Roger Furse, Olivier's former stage designer, who had obviously decided to spend his latter years as a high-class beach bum, was invisible till past noon, ostensibly painting, though no one ever saw any of his canvases. It was, in fact, a working summer for all of us: Bill was revising *The Spire*, while my then wife and I were both in the thick of novels of our own. We occupied a vast and sprawling house high on the hillside, with a view of the sea and the castle. Down below, in the little square, black-clad women would gather to exchange gossip as the sun went down. The platitudes flew to and fro: 'Life is hard.' 'Yes, life is hard.' 'What can we do about it?' 'That's the way life is.' Bill, whose novelist's ear picked up Greek clichés such as this with uncommon speed, suddenly said, as we observed this scene: 'And scholars argue about how the Greek chorus got started.' Unlike most visitors, but like the Greeks themselves, Bill made absolutely no distinction between past and present; a passionate Euripidean, he always hoped (I suspect) to find that lonely humanist's tomb where the sources said it was, beside the Athens–Piraeus road, somewhere among the (now) depressing flotsam of run-down junkyards, old tyre heaps, and sleazy garages.

For someone who took so dim a view of human nature and original sin, he turned out to be an extraordinarily cheerful companion: a great romantic too. His essay on the last stand of the Spartans at Thermopylae still moves me to tears every time I reread it ('A little of Leonidas lies in the fact that I can go where I like and write what I like. He contributed to set us free . . .'), even though I know, being reasonable, that Leonidas was a pigheaded and incompetent commander whose dispositions set him and his men up for an unnecessary sacrifice and the ruin of a fine amphibious battle plan. Even in the act of rejecting myth (whether *Coral Island*, or H. G. Wells's *Grisly Folk*, or, as I found out, the popular enskyment of the Parthenon), Bill would contrive to mythicize his anti-romantic stance. On a later visit, one rainy, wind-driven March, when we were living in Athens, the island now an ambivalent memory, I found myself, after an excellent and discursive lunch in the old quarter known as the Plaka, shepherding Bill by back streets up towards the Acropolis. When I'd asked him what he'd like to do that afternoon he said: 'See the bloody Parthenon, I suppose.' His voice was a fascinating blend of helplessness and suppressed resentment. So we plodded our way to the summit of that vast outcrop, eyes half closed against the stinging, dust-laden wind, passed through the Propylaea, and began picking our way across a wilderness of jumbled marble blocks towards the huge and too familiar temple, outlined now against a sky of grey scudding clouds. The air was mournful, oppressive; occasional rain drops plopped heavily groundwards. It was all very different from the travel posters.

A curious expression came over Bill's face. He stopped, blew his nose with a loud trumpeting sound, and stared, briefly, at the Western world's biggest cultural cliché, clearly resenting its long and all-too-influential shadow. '*Aaargh*,' he said. Into that curious noise he injected all the censorious impatience produced by years of peddling Greek culture to lymphatic schoolchildren. Then he found a comfortable block, and settled himself down in it – with his back squarely turned to the ostensible object of our visit. Little by little he relaxed, taking in the hazed industrial gloom of Piraeus, the squalid proliferation of sugar-cube houses creeping out to embrace the lower slopes of Mt Parnes, the big jets whining down past us on their approach to Ellenikón airport. His eyes focused, briefly and mistily, on the middle distance, where a dirty white mushroom cloud ascended from the Eleusis cement works, symbol of Demeter's final capitulation to the *deus ex machina*. 'Ah,' he said at last, 'now *this* is what I call the right way to look at the Parthenon.' He paused, then added: 'Did you know who invented that phrase about "the glory that was Greece"? Edgar Allan Poe.' As a pregnant conversation stopper this remark had decided merit.

While we were still sitting in silent (and, to tell the truth, mildly befuddled) contemplation of the Eleusis cement works – with an occasional furtive glance back over one shoulder to make sure Reason was still with us – what must have been the first cut-price conducted academic tour of the year came into view: Yeatsian bald heads, bulging alpaca jackets, baggy trousers, bifocals, gingham dresses and shapeless cardigans, sensible shoes, flat busts, and endless copies of the *Guide Bleu*. Camera shutters clicked neuroti-cally, like deathwatch beetles up a blind alley. Bill stared, and shook his head. At this moment (with true Homeric appositeness) there came a splendid clap of thunder, and the sky exploded with rain.

Bill, who looked then, and today looks even more, like a reincarnation of Zeus the Cloud-Gatherer (though I doubt if even he would describe those flowing locks of his as hyacinthine) beamed hugely, as though he had created this effect himself. We watched the torchbearers of culture scatter unhandily for cover: what had become of those eternal blue skies? 'Well,' Zeus said judiciously, 'it's a beginning.' From some hidden recess he produced a hip flask, and we sat there, laughing, nipping, sodden, Olympians in mortal guise, as the spring rain hissed down.

But that was in the future, when we knew each other much better; the days when we drove to Delphi and sunshine through a snowstorm, when Ann tried to explain to me, being a mathematician, the principle of the Kline bottle and the Mobius strip, with the result that whenever I travel along the section of the Corinth road where I learnt about these one- and two-dimensional paradoxes I still relapse into a spiralling neurotic frenzy at the mere thought of them. 'But you have to understand, Peter,' she explained. 'The bottle *swallows itself.*' 'Ann, for God's sake stop it.' 'But –' 'I'm serious. I'm driving. You want us to go over the cliff?' In 1967 Bill published an essay about this trip in *Holiday* magazine which compounded the agony by reminding me of all my *obiter dicta* about the oracle, and, worse, a sly joke if ever I heard one, making me claim that the answer to feeling flat on the site was a visit *to the museum.* Oh what libel: what we needed, wanted, and got, was a long and creative evening at the best *taverna* in town. All right, Bill, I swore I'd get you for that one and now I have.

In many ways those long incandescent evenings over wine (or brandy, or ouzo) were central to our relationship. As I reminded Bill in the Greek dedication of the novel I'd been writing that first summer, there'd been so many times that we'd 'tired the sun with talking and sent him down the sky'. 'That's all right,' came the immediate riposte, from someone who knew how the epigram went on as well as I did, 'so long as you don't think I'm dead'. What Bill discovered that first summer, along with grilled octopus and *tyropitakia*, was Greek beer: in particular the brand known as Fix, a Greek locution mangled from the original Herr Fuchs who accompanied King Otho's court as royal brewmaster, and made a success of it. 'Time for a Fix',' joked the American beach boys. In the early

1960s beer was a luxury drink in the Greek outback, and came accompanied by particularly splendid *mezes* – those infinitely varied titbits that always accompany Greek drinks, and for which *hors d'oeuvres* is far too formal a name. Bill had his favourite *kapheneion*, and from about noon began to work his way through ice-cold bottles of Fix. The empties stood on the table in front of him in a soldierly row. Yiorgo outdid himself with *mezes* – pairs of fried eggs, slivers of squid and octopus, tomato salad rich with good oil, crusty new bread, and, as Arnold Wesker has it, chips with everything. Companions and discutants would come and go. Bill's lunch time *Bierfest* became an institution. Every foreigner in the village had a Greek nickname, though not all of them realized it. Within a week Bill had become *O Vasilevs Phix* – King Fix, the Lord of the Liquid Feast.

But the mornings, as I said earlier, were sacrosanct, and recognized as such by Greeks and resident foreigners alike. Not so, always, by less permanent visitors. I vividly remember one bearded American intellectual who would walk into my study most days, unannounced, about nine in the morning, with some such introductory remark as 'I felt I should tell you the present state of my relationship with my wife'. 'Bugger off, Andy.' 'Now, Peter, you know you don't mean that, it's just that you're overworked, a break will do you good.' Short of physical violence there was nothing you could do about Andy and, as he was going blind, physical violence was ruled out. About the only thing I owed him one for was explaining – this was, after all, the 1960s – just why so many American transients hung around our front gate staring hopefully at the morning glory that grew thickly over it.

And then there was Freya Stark.

At that time we shared a publisher, and had met once or twice in London. News came that she was planning a descent on Lesbos *en route* for Turkey. I remembered her as a dumpy lady of immense charm and brilliance, addicted to picture hats, and with a knack of talking people into things. This, as things turned out, was an understatement. She arrived, she dazzled, she waved a casual hand to indicate that suitable lodging should be found for her. Greeks whom I had never before seen move except during an earthquake rushed to oblige. Then it was my turn. '*Peter, I know* I can rely on you to find a little man with two donkeys for me to go to Ephtalou at six o'clock sharp tomorrow morning, *can't* I?' 'Of course, Freya.' So that was how she'd worked it through the Valley of the Assassins. 'And Mr Golding – would you by any chance be free to drive me into Mytilene about noon on Monday?' Free, King Fix or not, was what Bill assured her he'd be. A house was found, the donkeys materialized, trips were taken. Two working novelists of reasonably mature years and standing found their whole schedule shot to pieces. In the end we actually took turns keeping watch, like a pair of schoolboys, for Freya's appearance on the horizon. At least one of us could be officially out. It was the only time I ever saw Bill at a total loss. 'It's those eyes,' he once said lamely. 'You just can't resist them. She's the Laughing Cavalier. She's living history.' So she was. The last news I had of her, she'd contrived, when well into her eighties, to charm her Intourist guide into letting her across the Oxus into what had been forbidden territory ever since the Revolution. The poor guy, we all agreed, hadn't stood a chance.

Later, when the Rover had been left behind in a proper Dorset garage, instead of, as at first, being bounced over what in those days were totally impossible roads, we took Bill and Ann for expeditions round the island in our own ancient Mercedes, known affectionately as The Rubber Car because we'd never succeeded in discovering the maximum number of warm bodies that could squeeze into it, being stopped by the police for overloading when we'd only, as my elder son said indignantly, got three fairly small Greeks on the bonnet. Bill had a marvellous eye for varieties of flowers and stones, and the omnivorous curiosity of a nineteenth-century polymath. He also, as we found to our astonishment, was scared stiff by heights. Many of the roads we had to take were winding rock-strewn tracks barely wide enough for a car to negotiate, and cut into the sheer cliff above a plunging ravine; Bill would huddle into a near-foetal position on the back seat, linen hat crammed over his face. 'Tell me when it's safe to come out,' he said once. But he came along all the same; even, once, when we were ferrying three large Greek ladies across the island to vote in their home town, and they spent most of the trip noisily throwing up into (oh misery!) transparent plastic bags. I have a blended memory of pinewoods, remote beaches, salt surf burnt into the flesh, the pleasure of sitting over chilled wine and fresh caught lobster, siestas in the cicada-loud afternoon, and always the bright kaleidoscopic flow of tumbling conversation.

Even when communication between them was minimal, the Greeks always recognized, instantly, the special quality of Bill's personality and mind. Twenty years ago beards were less common in Greece among the population at large, as opposed to Orthodox priests, than they have since become, but there was more to it than the sacerdotal element. A country of a mere nine million souls that has thrown up two Nobel prizewinners in as many decades has an eye for genius, however alien. I was never so conscious of Bill Golding's moral and spiritual strength as when I watched the way people reacted to him on the island. I remember one incident, small in itself, that illustrates this to perfection. We had been exploring in and around Aghiassos, a high town among mountains, with a strange dialect and a miracle-working icon of the Blessed Virgin, a place of pilgrimage in mid-August, a numinous centre of strong and primitive belief. While we drank in the taverna Bill climbed the long narrow street of stepped cobbles that led up to the great chestnut forest above the town. He wanted, he said, to get the feel of the place. It was almost dark by the time he got back, stepping down the street lost in a far away reverie, hair and beard blowing in the breeze, immensely dignified, somewhere private and quite different. And I could hear the quiet, breathless ripple of Greek voices accompanying him as he came: '*O yeros katavainei* –', 'the old man descends', spoken in the wondering tones that might have welcomed Moses back from Mt Sinai with the Tablets of the Law. You could almost feel the air crackle round him; over and above the drinking and talking, the sea and sun and work and good fellowship, there was an electric charge, sometimes static, sometimes branch lightning, that Bill Golding and Greece struck out of each other. The Greeks knew it, and so did he. Sometimes it was so strong the fuses nearly blew; and the result of that, on occasion, would be a bender to relieve the pressure. A fix for King Fix.

I remember one expedition, to Chalcis and Euboea, when we all decided to forego ouzo or retsina for the day – 'Clear bright heads at sundown,' said Ann, firmly. It worked fairly well during the morning, but by late afternoon a diet of *gazozas* was producing a collective case of spiritual wind. Still, we persevered. On the drive back we paused at a hilltop *kapheneion* for a rest and refreshment. 'Tea,' we told the waiter. 'For everyone.' Bill sloped off to the rest rooms. He seemed to be gone rather a long time. When he came back the waiter was setting out cups, sugar, a dish of lemon slices, and, I noticed, two teapots. 'Is ezpecial,' he said, pointing to one. 'For the *aphendis* – how you say, boss.' No question about who the boss was. Bill set about his tea with gusto. The conversation picked up wonderfully. Sitting there, staring at the table, I thought, puzzled: What's missing? And then I got it: Bill's tea had no steam. My nose twitched, a bubble of laughter rose inside me. Only one person in the world could talk a Greek waiter into filling a teapot with retsina, garnish the cup with lemon slices, and drink the entire contents while everyone else was letting virtue be its own punishment.

I realize that in this reminiscence very little has been said about Bill Golding's main *raison-d'être* in life, creative literature. Surprising though it may seem, this wasn't a topic we discussed all that much, feeling, I think, that it was best left to the professional critics whose business such analytical chat was, and acutely conscious of Hemingway's remark about solemn writers always being bloody owls. Something of Bill's attitude to Eng. Crit. professionals, a mixture of high amusement and even higher exasperation, comes out in that hilariously funny squib *The Paper Men* (a predictably damp squib for those it satirizes with such lethal accuracy). When he and I went fishing in the critical tank the results too often seemed comic, or embarrassing, or both. I remember Bill once calling me up in puzzlement about Iris Murdoch's *A Severed Head*, a book we both had to review the following week. 'Look, old boy,' he said, '*surely* she can't be serious?' I said no, I didn't think so, and in my view the novel was a raging send-up of Freudian psychoanalysis and liberal humanism. 'Good. Just what I thought too.' After our reviews came out we discovered that Ms Murdoch had, indeed, meant every word in deadly earnest: she was, according to rumour, even less amused than Queen Victoria. A well-meaning Athens hostess thought to make things go by introducing both of us to Kimon Friar, unaware that both of us had just savaged his translation of Kazantzakis' *Odyssey*, publicly and at length. The party was not a success.

But on the island there were moments of Molyviot serendipity. One night, about two in the morning, a late party was in progress at the Blue Fox taverna (now, alas, sacrificed to the hotel-building urge). Word came up from the harbour that some slightly bedraggled foreigner had appeared in a yacht and was on his way up, with a Greek boy in tow. Sure enough, a little while later a darkly handsome but unshaven, tousle-haired, and rednosed wreck of a reveller lurched in, plus boy. From the next table he brightened perceptibly at the literary gossip in progress at ours. We invited them over. Two brandies, and he snapped into focus. Three, and one of the most scintillating conversationalists I have ever listened to was launched and away. Four, and I'd figured out who he was, having been invited to review his last book by a mean literary editor ('Sounds like tedious author meets odious subject,' I ventured on the phone, to get the reply 'Tee-hee! We *hoped* you'd feel that'), but then, finding it by far the best he'd ever written, had said so: no more commissions from *that* quarter. The stranger, a stranger no longer, by now had identified both Bill and me, and was thanking me, us, everybody, for a splendid notice. The party went on till five. Then the stranger collected his boy and vanished into the dawn. When we woke there was no yacht in the harbour either. If anyone asks me if I've ever met Gore Vidal I never quite know what to say.

But the 1960s came to an end, and all our lives changed. I exchanged the expatriate's life in Greece for academic respectability in America; my first marriage ended not long afterwards. Bill tried sailing a Dutch barge across the Channel – he could only take Greece in limited doses – and got it cut in half by a Japanese freighter in a fog, not the kind of hazard liable to beset a good paid-up Molyvos eccentric in the normal course of events. My children, grown up now, talk wistfully of the island, of our old life, of 'the *real* Bill', the only Bill who, for them, qualifies. When the news of his Nobel Prize broke, I called him up, on impulse, in his quiet village – today neither quiet nor his village – near Salisbury. That incredibly springy, youthful, resonant voice came across the Atlantic, clear as the proverbial bell. 'Peter? Nice of you to call. Look, hold on a minute, there's a Spanish TV crew from Bolivia or somewhere all over the living-room –' I held on as instructed, reflecting that though Bill's, and my, Molyvos days may be over, something of the unique and tangential life we enjoyed there (I think of Forster's description of Cavafy, the man in a straw hat at a slight angle to the universe) has clung to us both, a delightful infection, ever since.

Strangers from Within

CHARLES MONTEITH

The typescript was unenticing. Bound between two pieces of cardboard, the sheets had a dog-eared, shop-soiled, down-at-heel look. The edges of the first dozen or so were yellowish, evidence that they, and they alone, had been read a number of times; the remainder were whiter but not pristine. Though I had been a publisher for less than a month, I could already spot a manuscript that had been the rounds and this was an obvious example. A short submission letter, written from Salisbury, was attached: 'I send you the typescript of my novel *Strangers from Within* which might be defined as an allegorical interpretation of a stock situation. I hope you will feel able to publish it.' It was signed 'William Golding'.

A Tuesday afternoon in late September 1953. As usually happened on Tuesday afternoons, three or four editors were weeding out the week's haul of manuscripts in preparation for Wednesday's weekly editorial committee, appropriately, if somewhat quaintly, called the Book Committee, at which decisions were made. *Strangers from Within* was in the pile pushed in my direction. Our professional reader – she read for a number of other publishers as well as Faber and also for a leading literary agency – had already given it one of her 'quick looks' and her verdict was in green ink at the top of the author's letter: 'Time: The Future. Absurd and uninteresting fantasy about the explosion of an atomic bomb on the colonies and a group of children who land in jungle country near New Guinea. Rubbish and dull. Pointless.' This was followed by a capital R enclosed in a circle, the symbol for 'reject'.

I opened it expecting nothing and after the first dozen or so pages was inclined, like so many readers before me, to abandon it at that point. They described a nuclear war. Remembering them now, more than thirty years later, my impression is that they were powerful, if occasionally over-written, and that they contained, initially, no characters at all. Later the focus shifted earthwards and to a hurriedly organized evacuation of schoolchildren destined, presumably, for the Antipodes. The planes in which they flew had detachable cabins, 'passenger tubes', which could be released by the pilot *in toto* to float to earth beneath giant parachutes. The focus altered once again to one particular plane, to a fierce air battle over the Pacific, to the release of the 'passenger tube', to the island and, at last, to some human beings. They were all boys.

As I read on I found that, reluctantly, I was becoming not merely interested but totally gripped. The island was vividly, brilliantly real and the boys were real boys: despite his half promise, Ralph's betrayal of the secret of Piggy's nickname; the appalling sycophantic laughter of the crowd; Jack's authority over his choir. A fat, spectacled boy at school myself, I squirmed for Piggy. I said that I would take the manuscript home to read properly and when I had finished it I found it unforgettable. Indeed, to anticipate a little, as I read and reread it over the next month or two, thought about it, discussed it with colleagues and with the author, it came to dominate my imagination completely. I found that, increasingly, I kept talking about it until friends began to hint that I was becoming a Golding bore.

But I realized that the novel had flaws which seriously weakened it and might, for some readers, make it a partial or total failure. Some were superficial – commas which studded the pages as thickly as currants in a fruit loaf, Piggy's 'common' speech – his 'ass-mar', 'them fruit' – laid on with too heavy a hand; but these could easily be put right. Two others were more serious.

The first was structural. In addition to the long description of atomic war at the beginning, there were two further occasions on which the scene shifted from the island to what was happening in the world outside: an 'interlude' occurring about halfway through and describing an air battle many miles above the island which culminated in the body of the dead airman, the 'Beast from Air', drifting down by parachute; and, at the very end, an outline of the lethal manoeuvres in which the 'trim cruiser', the whole fleet of which it formed part and the enemy fleet opposing it, were engaged – rather too clearly placed there, I thought, to show that what had happened on the island was a fable, reflecting in miniature what was happening in the adult world. These passages needed severe pruning.

The second flaw, more fundamental and much more difficult, was Simon. Simon was Christ; or, too obviously, a Christ figure. At times he would retire to a secret place in the jungle hidden behind a mat of creepers, where a Voice spoke to him from the green candle-buds as they opened in the scented dusk to reveal their white flowers; a vision assured him with prophetic certainty and he assured Ralph, at a moment of appalling doubt, that Ralph would get home safely; when the boys' fragile society began to fall apart and Jack and his blood-smeared hunters began their murderous dances, Simon led the boys, or some of them, on Good Dances on the beach. Alone and terrified he confronted and was not vanquished by the Lord of the Flies – a literal translation of Beelzebub, as Golding later told me. Simon alone, despite his weakness, the threat of epilepsy, taunts that he was 'batty', seemed untainted by an otherwise universal stain. In the end he was murdered.

To put it crudely and insensitively, Simon was not to me, and would not be, I suspected, to most readers wholly credible. I do not, in fact, think that I fully understood the problem at the time and it is only in the light of Golding's other novels and later discussions with him that I see it more clearly now. Simon is not only a boy, a fully and totally human boy; he is one of those rare people who are in fact – it is impossible to avoid these imprecise and difficult words – 'numinous' or 'charismatic'. Nathaniel in *Pincher Martin* and, most clearly of all, Matty in *Darkness Visible*, are later variations on the same mysterious theme. But Simon, as he first appeared, was not entirely successful. For the reader – or at any rate for me – the suspension of disbelief was a very unwilling one and the only idea I had was that any purely miraculous events in the narrative must be made ambivalent, eliminated or 'toned down' in such a way as to make Simon explicable in purely rational terms. At the same time his importance, indeed his centrality, must be preserved.

At the next Book Committee I reported that the novel was odd, imperfect but potentially very powerful and that I would like to discuss it with the author. There was general doubt, not unnaturally in view of the description I had given of it and the reservations I had expressed; and it was decided that it should have several more readings before any contact was made. Two editorial colleagues agreed with my verdict; Geoffrey Faber took it and was also prepared, though with doubts, to support me. The final hurdle was the Sales Director who, like our 'reader', was regarded as a real professional who could tell by instinct whether or not a book would sell. He kept it for a week or two but eventually brought it to a Book Committee meeting where we all waited for his verdict which he gave – he was a kind-hearted man – with a ruefully apologetic glance at me. The book, he said, was unpublishable. This led to a heated discussion at the end of which it was decided – this was chiefly due to Geoffrey who was unwilling to dampen too abruptly a young editor's enthusiasm – that I could meet the author and discuss the changes I thought would improve the book, but that I must make it clear that the firm was in no way committed to publishing it.

Golding and I first met in early December. I was nervous and so, I suspect, was he: he was the first of 'my' authors. In advance I had speculated a good deal about him and had decided that he was almost certainly a young, or youngish, clergyman, for the more I thought about the novel the more its theological sub-structure became apparent. Brought up a Presbyterian as I had been, with parts of the Shorter Catechism immovably embedded in my mind, I could recognize Original Sin when I saw it: 'the guilt of Adam's first sin, the want of original righteousness and the corruption of man's whole nature, together with all the actual transgressions which proceed from it'.

So the neatly trimmed beard – clerical beards were not as common then as they are now – the grey flannel trousers and tweed jacket surprised me; but when Golding told me he was a schoolmaster I realized that I had been stupid. Only a schoolmaster would know so intimately, and with such precision of detail, how awful boys could be. We talked at length and at the end I felt that a cautious trust and even liking had established themselves between us. I made my suggestions, rather nervously, and Golding, to my relief, promised to take the typescript back with him and, in the light of a rereading, consider them.

About ten days later he sent me

. . . some bits of the emended version of my novel – the beginning, the middle and the end. I've done away with the separate bits, Prologue, Interlude, Epilogue, and as you'll see, merged them into the body of the text. Furthermore, Chapter One now begins with the meeting of Piggy and Ralph and I'm allowing the story of how they got there – or all that is necessary of it – to come out in conversation. Simon is the next job, and a more difficult one. I suppose you agree that I must convey a theophany of some sort or else he won't be as big a figure as he ought. I'm going to cut down the elaborate description of it, though, and try to get the same effect by reticence. Then I'm distributing odd bits and pieces of 'Simonry' throughout the text, to build him up . . . I'm making Piggy's speech ungrammatical but not misspelling it . . . Rereading the novel as a stranger to it, I'm bound to agree with almost all your criticism and am full of enthusiasm and energy for the cleaning up process. In fact I'm right back on the island.

The changes were even better than I had hoped for. All that I had suggested was a drastic shortening of the 'nuclear war' passages but Golding's solution was more radical and totally successful. They had disappeared completely and the novel's new opening could not have been bettered. In my reply I congratulated him and suggested a few other, fairly superficial changes which he accepted in a letter a few days later with which he enclosed the redrafted 'Simon' passages. It is clear from my reply – which rereads, I fear, rather pompously – that I was still not completely satisfied.

Here are the 'Simon' bits back again, with my tentative emendations pencilled in. I think you have hit on the right approach to this most tricky of all the problems in the novel; and my emendations are again simply 'toning down' of emphasis. I think the danger to be guarded against now is turning Simon into a prig, a self-righteous infant who insists on saying his prayers in the dorm while the naughty boys throw pillows at him. In the early stages I feel it is enough simply to indicate that he is in some way odd, different, withdrawn; and therefore capable of the lonely, rarified courage of facing the pig's head and climbing the mountain top. The allegory, the theophany, is the imaginative foundation and like all foundations is there to be concealed and built on.

Before long, Golding returned the typescript in what was to be, by and large, its final form. He had been ill, running a very high temperature which was partly due to tonsillitis and partly to 'the effort of patching – so much more wearing than bashing straight ahead at a story'. With this version I was, by and large, satisfied, though I thought a few small changes might be made with advantage; and when I reported all this to the Book Committee it was decided, at long last, to accept the book for publication. I suggested we offer Golding what was then our usual advance for a first novel, £50, but in view of the author's patience Geoffrey Faber made it sixty. And so it was settled.

The next problem was the title. In our earliest exchange of letters I had said that *Strangers from Within* didn't seem to me right – both too abstract and too explicit – and Golding did not demur. Indeed, he began at once to suggest alternatives, 'A Cry of Children', 'Nightmare Island', 'To Find an Island'. Both I and my editorial colleagues offered suggestions – my own favourite hunting ground was *The Tempest* which is set on an island – but it was Alan Pringle, an editor rightly reputed to be good at titles, who eventually thought of *Lord of the Flies*. It has turned out to be probably the most memorable title given to any book since the end of the Second World War. Chapter titles were the next problem. Our Production and Design department was adamant that a decent looking novel must have chapter titles to be used as running heads; and Golding, though he said his instinct was slightly against them, accepted without further protest a list of suggestions I sent him.

The book went into 'page on galley' proofs, which looked like galleys but were half the length, and it was only then that I carried out a final editorial operation – cutting Ralph's hair. In the desperate chase at the end, when Ralph is being hunted down by Jack and his pack, his long, unshorn locks keep falling blindingly over his eyes, symbolizing effectively but perhaps too heavily the descent of irrationality, instinct, panic, over reason and intelligence. Golding was as patient as ever: 'By all means cut Ralph's hair for him. I had some doubts of it myself.' So I simply took out every other reference to it. The Production department completed its work and Sales took over.

Before publication we made various efforts to whip up some advance publicity but with only modest success. *John O'London's Weekly*, that forgotten literary periodical, was to make it 'Novel of the

Month' but ceased publication a week before the accolade was to be conferred; a committee set up by the first Cheltenham Festival did not even short-list it for their First Novel award – nor did it have any better luck with the Authors' Club's annual Silver Quill. The Book Society, then a very powerful body, promised a reference to it, though no more, in their monthly magazine.

On 17 September 1954 *Lord of the Flies* was at last published, by a curious coincidence exactly a year after it was first submitted. Its early reception by reviewers was usually good, and even, on occasions, enthusiastic. E. M. Forster and C. S. Lewis both praised it. Eliot, who had not read it before, was told by a friend at the Garrick that Faber had published an unpleasant novel about small boys behaving unspeakably on a desert island. In some mild alarm, he took a copy home and told me next day that he had found it not only a splendid novel but morally and theologically impeccable. The book began not only to be talked about but to sell and before very long we had to order a reprint. In the United States, where we had great difficulty in placing it, it made little impression at first, but after a year or two, a paperback edition began to spread like forest fire through university campuses, at first on the West Coast and then in the rest of the country. Personally, I was first alerted to what was happening when an article on Golding appeared in the *Hudson Review*. And finally the book began to be 'set' at university level, at 'A' level, finally at 'O' level, in Great Britain and then at equivalent levels abroad. By now there are translations of it into twenty-six languages, including Russian, Thai, Japanese, Slovak, Serbo-Croat, Catalan, Icelandic and Persian; and versions in Indonesian and Malayalam are in preparation. Sales of Faber editions alone total over three million copies but there is no record, so far as I know, of total sales throughout the world. They must be astronomical.

In December 1983 Golding invited me to accompany him and his wife to Stockholm for the Nobel ceremonies; and on the evening of the presentation there was a great ball at which the laureates and their entourages were presented to the King and Queen. Carl XVI Gustaf – a spectacled, serious looking young man – shook Golding's hand warmly. 'It is a great pleasure to meet you, Mr Golding,' he said, 'I had to do *Lord of the Flies* at school.'

The Visual and the Visionary in Golding

MARK KINKEAD-WEEKES

How do you know but ev'ry Bird that cuts the airy way
Is an immense world of delight, clos'd by your senses five?
                                        William Blake[1]

> In such strength
> Of usurpation, in such visitings
> Of awful promise, when the light of sense
> Goes out in flashes that have shown to us
> The invisible world . . .
>   William Wordsworth[2]

My task which I am trying to achieve is, by the power of the written word to make you hear, to make you feel – it is before all, to make you *see*. That – and no more, and it is everything.

                                        Joseph Conrad[3]

I have been asking myself which moments in Golding's fiction have most stayed with me, and time after time those that I remember most vividly turn out to be visual. 'He holds him with his glittering *eye*' – the birthday guest stands still. Of course one has always known that there was something compelling about the seeing of the not-too-Ancient Mariner whom these essays honour; that his imagination is remarkably visual; and that in the relation between the visual and the visionary, in *that* kind of 'glitter', lies something definitive about him. Yet the more I have come to wonder about the nature of his 'seeing', the more paradoxical and distinctive it seems. He is quite different from Blake and Wordsworth for whom, in their different ways, the concrete visualization of the ordinary is a barrier to vision, and for whom therefore the eye must be cleansed or put to sleep before the visionary can see. But he is also quite different from Joyce and Conrad for whom (again in different ways) there is nothing but the eye and the object; so that it is only the visualizing itself, the act of artistic perception, charged with individual

3. On the family's Whitstable Oyster Smack
Wild Rose. (Photo John Miller)

4. The *Wild Rose* in the Beaulieu River, Hampshire, 'affronting all the posh yachts'

response, on the rescued fragment of experience, that can capture the epiphanizing radiance, or 'through its movement its form and its colour, reveal the substance of its truth'. Golding is unlike the modernists in Blakean and Wordsworthian ways; and unlike the Romantics in Joycean and Conradian ways; he is both intensely 'sceptical' and intensely 'religious'; he uses the visionary *against* the visual and the visual against the visionary. So what and how does Golding mean, by 'seeing'?

Interestingly, the eye seems equally pre-eminent in Conrad's 'before all to make you *see*' and Wordsworth's accusations against 'the most despotic of the senses'.[4] No mere literary critic should tangle with the argument implied here, which is ultimately metaphysical – but it seems that whether one believes the physical universe to be all there is, so that the empirical making real of that 'all' to the senses becomes particularly important against the abyss of non-being and non-meaning; or whether one suspects that the physical universe is a mask for 'something far more deeply interfused', so that a Gloucester or an Oedipus can only 'see' truly when the vile jelly is out; it is the eye above all that conditions our view of 'reality' for good or ill. In our everyday language we may say (with Nick Shales or Sam Goodchild) that we will believe only what we see for ourselves, though that means we may believe more, the more that an author's power of language makes us visualize. Or we may say that sight is nothing without insight, and may deceive like words; that it is only when the physical eye is 'made quiet' by some deeper kind of perception that we can for a moment 'see into the life of things', wordlessly. Golding's fiction says *both*.

Certainly, from the earliest impulse to create a coral island more 'real' than Ballantyne's, the function of the eye in 'realization' was all important in Golding. *Lord of the Flies* is a remarkably visual fiction; physical realities come first for its author and must remain so for his readers; they must convince before what is revealed through them can earn imaginative assent. When Ian Gregor and I[5] began our account of the book with the finding of the conch, it was to insist that the episode worked through the physical senses first, and only secondarily through symbolic or interpretative intelligence. Hence the description of fulcrum and lever; the interest in how the thing is physically disentangled from the weeds, until it can be seen:

> In colour the shell was deep cream, touched here and there with fading pink. Between the point, worn away into a little hole, and the pink lips of the mouth, lay eighteen inches of shell with a slight spiral twist, and covered with a delicate, embossed pattern. Ralph shook sand out of the deep tube. (17)[6]

It is made 'real' in its context of salt water, brilliant fish, green weed; then in its own strange cream and rose spiral, embossed by an art other than the human; finally in the harsh otherness of the noise which shatters the peace of the island and terrifies bird and beast. The conch is no mere 'symbol' but a 'shining thing', visualized, realized, through which other meanings emerge (or are destroyed) as human breath comes through the spiral. The book proceeds by a series of revelations in which we learn to see more and more in what we have seen already; but the authenticity of each step depends on that of the one before, and all are grounded in the original undoctored sense perception.

So the first function of seeing is as the cliché has it, that it is believing. Or rather, as Sammy Mountjoy says – 'I do not believe merely, I see' (*Free Fall*, 193) – it is authentic precisely because it keeps at bay the idea-making patterning intellect so that all that lies 'in' the object and situation can come through. In *The Hot Gates* the author, talking learnedly about Thermopylae, sets out to climb the cliffs over which a traitor had led the Persians:

> I put out my hand to steady myself on a rock, and snatched it back again, for a lizard lay there in the only patch of sunlight . . . I began to grope and slither down again. In a tangle of thick grass, flowers, dust and pungency, I heard another sound that paralysed me . . . I saw a lithe body slip over a rock where there was no grass, a body patterned in green and black and brown, limbless and fluid. I smiled wryly to myself. So much for the map, pored over in the lamplight of an English winter . . . I stayed there, clinging to a rock until the fierce hardness of its surface close to my eye had become familiar. Suddenly, the years and the reading fused with the thing. I was clinging to Greece herself. (19)

Not the 'idea', the 'map', the mental scale over the retina, but imagination plus the bedrock of the thing-perceived-in-itself pro-duce the 'double power' that can put Golding behind Leonidas's eyes, as they can put us behind his.

It is indeed the reverse power of the human mind to *un*realize, so that what is before the eyes is converted to image for the ego's urgency, that is the root of evil. The end of the conch, as it shatters with Piggy, comes about because of eyes that can no longer see shining thing or boy, but only empty shell and pig, which stand in the way and fuel the power urge. And in *The Inheritors* we have both the most wonderfully imagined of Golding's fictions because it is the most inno-sensually realized (led by eyes wholly un-sapient, non-egotistic, at one with what they see); and also a terrible focus on the nature of our difference, through our ability to understand what those innocent eyes can see but never take in. Situation after situation comes extraordinarily alive as we see through Lok's eyes, but page after page we have to decipher, between the lines, what lies behind that other kind of seeing that turns him into an image of murderous and ravenous cruelty on the rock face.

But this brings us to the first of the Golding paradoxes. There can be no true seeing that is not primarily and simply visual, undistorted by our fallen nature; yet concrete seeing in itself is always blind at a deeper level, because unaware of the nature of things. It is only we who can really see in *The Inheritors*, by focusing Lok's eyes with our own.

> As he watched, one of the farther rocks began to change shape. At one side a small bump elongated then disappeared quickly. The top of the rock swelled, the hump fined off at the base and elongated again then halved its height. Then it was gone. (79)

It is only when we bring to bear *our* knowledge of suspicion, fear and hostility, which take not-self for enemy, and so turn looking-out into spying, that Lok's register of meaningless activity suddenly clicks into focus. We see-with-*in*sight, of which Lok is incapable, his first glimpse of man. But it is not only a matter of human 'evil'. There are whole dimensions of Nature (water, ice, the tiger, the flux of time and change), and of language (which works by differentia-tion as against the communal telepathy) which 'the people' cannot enter, however they may approach the brink. So if the wonder of the book is to be inside Lok and Fa, and its horror to discover thereby what it is to be us, the power of its vision is always *double*, fusing sight with insight. Only we can focus Fa going over the Fall with both Lok's grief and the perspective of history; only we can look over the artist Tuami's shoulder at the shape of Innocence-with-Experience. The central action of *The Inheritors* is to see through, and into, and past that purely concrete perception which is at the same time the rock and guarantor of vision. And it has become clear how and why the so-called 'gimmick' endings in Golding, making one look again, are never gimmicks, but structural necessity.

Pincher Martin reinforces the first paradox and brings to light a second one. It is above all the concrete realization of the rock that holds our fascinated, riveted attention – what a convincing world! – only to find that it turns out to be radically false and 'made up' because it not only lacks, but actively seeks to evade, an even deeper kind of 'insight'.

> He frowned at the stone. Then he worked his way down until he was hanging on the cliff by it with both hands and the crack was only a foot from his face. Like all the rest of the cliff where the water could reach it was cemented with layers of barnacles and enigmatic growths. But the crack was wider. The whole stone had moved and skewed perhaps an eighth of an inch. Inside the crack was a terrible darkness.
>
> He stayed there, looking at the loose rock until he forgot what he was thinking. He was envisaging the whole rock as a thing in the water, and he was turning his head from side to side.
>
> 'How the hell is it that this rock is so familiar? . . .' There came a loud plop from the three rocks. He scrambled quickly to the Red Lion but saw nothing. (124–5)

'Inside the crack was a terrible darkness.' However close the imagined rock to the 'eye', however loud the attempts by the mind to distract itself from becoming aware of what it is doing, inexorably the surface of Pincher's 'seeing' splits to reveal the reality and the hidden structure it has been his frenzied obsession to deny, by inventing out of his own mouth a world in which his ego can go on living. His world of concrete perception turns inside out in a Blakean way (though in horror not delight) when instead of being behind his eyes looking out, they become the windows of a room with reality trying to get *in*. For the Pincher Ego the design of the universe is a vast world of terrible darkness, closed by the desperate inventiveness of its senses five. So now 'insight' has to become metaphysical, forced to contemplate the signature at the heart of things, whether that be loving design, or 'black lightning', destroying the 'self' that sought to evade it by refusing to 'die'.

But the second paradox is that, while concrete seeing is now twice blind if it also lacks the visionary glimpse of what is preterhuman, the most visionary of Golding's heroes is the blindest of them all. Jocelin laughing with joy as the sun explodes in his face through the stained glass (*The Spire*, 1), or confidently remarking the optical illusion of the slanting pillars of sunlight in the dust-filled cathedral (9–10), cannot *see* either Abraham and Isaac in the window or that his great ship has indeed begun to go askew, because (so confident that his light is God the Father's) he cannot see 'sundust' either; how it is the dust that makes the sun so solidly visible, how 'God' (and the Beast) become visible 'between people'. Looking at the dumb man's carving of him, 'the gaunt, lifted cheekbones, the open mouth, the nostrils strained wide as if they were giving lift to the beak, like a pair of wings, the wide blind eyes', Jocelin nods. 'It is true. At the moment of vision, the eyes see nothing' (24). That, for this author, is the most dangerous blindness of all. So the action of the novel is precisely to bring home to Jocelin, by a series of sharply focused visual perceptions, how blind he has been to physical reality, to people, to relationships, to himself, to the nature of things, until, at the very last moment of his life – cleaned of himself – he can bring the two windows of his eyes together and focus that extraordinary mysterious *thing*, the spire, in a moment of wonder and terror fused with all the languages of explanation, but going beyond them all. The whole book is a preparation for that single moment of visual perception, that must be stone before it is anything else, that must be wholly 'objective', but finally holds so much in such fusion of opposites that it is beyond words and can only be caught, in a flash, by the eye.

So we begin to see not only why 'seeing' in Golding is so paradoxical, sight and insight, visual and visionary, but also why he must be constantly employing one way of looking *against* the other. To the visionary the sceptical concrete man must always say:

> Let your eye crawl down like an insect, foot by foot. You think these walls are strong because they're stone; but I know better. We've nothing but a skin of glass and stone stretched between four stone rods, one at each corner. D'you understand that? The stone is no stronger than the glass between the verticals because every inch of the way I have to save weight, bartering strength for weight or weight for strength, guessing how much, how far, how little, how near, until my very heart stops when I think of it. Look down, Father. Don't look at me – look down! See . . . (*The Spire*, 117)

And it is not only the sight of the earth stirring like grubs in the pit (79), or the horrified eye taking in the behaviour of the extra counter in the children's game far below, that tells of the tower swaying silently like a tree (133); the realizing concrete seeing must take in also, however belatedly, the tear splash on the dubbined boot, the sprig of mistletoe, all the human as well as physical realities of the 'lesson for each eight'. Only this can clean off the scale of the idea, the symbolizing, the religiose delusion, the ego. But equally, to the sceptic who believes only what he can see with his ordinary eyes, or the cynic who has seen it all, must be made to come home the extraordinary strangeness of things, the mystery of their beauty and their horror. So to Sammy Mountjoy in his salt obsession, lighting the nude body of his Beatrice with harsh electric shades to make his painting sear like *Guernica* (*Free Fall*, 123–4), comes the extraordinary revelation that what his brush has caught is blessedness. So to Wilf Barclay, cooling his hangover in the Sicilian cathedral with its fifth-rate Mafia glass, comes the horrific sight of the steely-silver Christ with the carbuncle eyes striding towards him – a vision that overturns his view of the world (*The Paper Men*, 123). So Sim Goodchild[7] ('all he believed in as real . . . was himself'), sees for the first time the hand that Matty is holding:

The palm was exquisitely beautiful, it was made of light. It was precious and preciously inscribed with a sureness and delicacy beyond art and grounded somewhere else in absolute health. In a convulsion unlike anything he had ever known, Sim stared into the gigantic world of his own palm, and saw that it was holy. (*Darkness Visible*, 231)

This is probably the most Blakean moment in Golding – 'to see a world in a grain of sand and a heaven in a wild flower, hold infinity in the palm of your hand and eternity in an hour'.[8] But it enables one to uncover a third paradox about seeing in Golding: that although its most powerfully imaginative revelations have come from perceptions supercharged, by intensities of wonder or of terror, so that his is an art of extremes; yet it is at its most extraordinary when ultimates are focused through the most ordinary things, and with the greatest impersonality. So Simon's vision of the Lord of the Flies, powerful though it was when one first read it, no longer seems among the most memorable glimpses of 'the horror' in Golding. In retrospect it seems too set-up, too symbolic, in both perceiver and perceived, to release what hindsight has taught one to recognize as his fullest power. Even Lok's terrible vision of a 'darkness' in the water – turning into 'a thing of complex shape, of sluggish and dreamlike movement', turning into a body rolling slowly with the current, until 'The head turned towards him with dreamlike slowness, rose in the water, came towards his face' (*The Inheritors*, 108–9) – though it has the authentic and universal rhythm of nightmare rising from the depths, and is one of the purest moments of horror in Golding, does depend for its fullest effect on the special world of Lok's innocence and non-violence, and the special sense of the sacredness of the Old Woman as the guardian of the mysteries. No, the most terrible scene in Golding will come from our world and be grounded in the experience of millions. I think everyone would agree that he has never written more powerfully than the visualizing of the burning city at the beginning of *Darkness Visible*, which takes the most ordinary eye and object (everybody has looked into a fire) and heightens them to Holocaust:

. . . the light of the great fire was bright as ever, brighter perhaps. Now the pink aura of it had spread. Saffron and ochre turned to blood-colour. The shivering of the white heart of the fire had quickened beyond the capacity of the eye to analyse . . . (13)

The same is true of the moments of the purest and strangest wonder, that they transfigure what everyone has seen into a vision that momentarily alters the world. Simon's candle-buds are wonderful, but 'tropical' in more senses than one (*Lord of the Flies*, 72). The vision of Johnny on his motorbike with his girl, taking off over the crest of the hill (*Free Fall*, 131), is an image of the purest zest and loving self-abandon, but that is what it is most: an image. But the tree in the general's garden . . . that is an experience of the ordinary become miraculous, that one does not forget.

The moon was flowering. She had a kind of sanctuary of light round her, sapphire. All the garden was black and white. There was one tree between me and the lawns, the stillest tree that ever grew, a tree that grew when no one was looking. The trunk was huge and each branch splayed up to a given level; and there, the black leaves floated out like a level of oil on water. Level after horizontal level these leaves cut across the splaying branches and there was a crumpled, silver-paper depth, an ivory quiet beyond them. Later, I should have called the tree a cedar and passed on, but then, it was an apocalypse. (*Free Fall*, 45–6)

Indeed all these moments are apocalyptic; beyond personality ('We were eyes'); making 'last things' suddenly visible in wonder or horror; a final Revelation of beauty and horror in the universe *through* ordinary 'reality' transfigured. But there is another kind of seeing that is no less intense, but altogether predatorily of the self. It was there in the ego-intensities of Pincher, of Sammy, of Jocelin, a hint of hectic in the eye (that is also a touch of corruption in the language – for after *The Inheritors* the language of the fiction is always coloured by the point-of-view). It is clearest of all in Sophy and the dabchicks.

Oh that bird all black with a white keyhole on the front of its head, and the tweeting, squeaking, chirping brood of fluffies climbing and scrambling and tumbling among the grasses at its back! They came out into the water, mother and chicks all ten on a string. They moved on with the brook and Sophy went right out into her eyes, she was nothing but seeing, seeing, seeing! It was like reaching out and laying hold with your eyes. It was like having the top part of your head drawn forward. It was a kind of absorbing, a kind of drinking, a kind of. (*Darkness Visible*, 107–8)

As opposed to a vision of evil this is an evil kind of seeing, that claws in unison with some force in the nature of things when Sophy finds the stone fitted to her hand and the perfect destructive arc, the fiercest satisfaction. It is exactly the opposite of Matty seeing the glass ball in the shop window fill with the sun.

It contained nothing but the sun which shone in it, far away. He approved of the sun which said nothing but lay there, brighter and brighter and purer and purer. It began to blaze as when clouds move aside. It moved as he moved but soon he did not move, could not move. It dominated without effort, a torch shone straight into his eyes, and he felt queer, not necessarily unpleasantly so but queer all the same – unusual. He was aware too of a sense of rightness and truth and silence. (47–8)

But this 'still dimension of otherness' (how much better Matty's simplicity than Edwin's language of mysticism), this revelation of golden peace, is the light whereby Matty sees his own darkness, and renounces. What meeting ground can there be between such opposite kinds of seeing? Golding's fiction seems continually Manichean, the vision always fracturing into separate worlds without a bridge. And yet, a final paradox, he seems as stubbornly insistent as the old folk song, 'I'll give you one, oh', that the many not only come out of, but must be drawn back into, the one. No seeing, it seems, can be truly human that is not split, or even multiple; but no human seeing can be true unless all things are made one, if only for an instant.

What bridges the two worlds is grief – and seeing through eyes that have been washed clean by tears is the deepest dimension of all in Golding, because that is a vision different both from innocence and guilt, which can fuse into it. I wish I could quote the whole passage where Sammy Mountjoy, emerging from the cell, sees the camp and its people through the tears that have sprung from terrible insight into his own being. Horror and wonder fuse, self-awareness longs frantically to escape self, grief and terror cry out and change what cries, so that 'dead' eyes can open on new seeing, beyond both innocence and experience. What he sees are both 'huts' and 'shining', both 'boxes of thin wood' and treasure houses full of sceptred kings.

> Huge tears were dropping from my face into dust; and this dust was a universe of brilliant and fantastic crystals, that miracles instantly supported in their being. I looked up beyond the huts and the wire, I raised my dead eyes, desiring nothing, accepting all things and giving all created things away. The paper wrappings of use and language dropped from me. Those crowded shapes extending up into the air and down into the rich earth, those deeds of far space and deep earth were aflame at the surface and daunting by right of their own natures though a day before I should have disguised them as trees. (*Free Fall*, 186)

This is more than Jocelin seeing sun and dust, and more than the infant Samuel's tree, not only because it has admitted both the wonder and the horror, but also because it insists that 'Everything is related to everything else' – though Sammy will go on worrying to the end of the book about the nature of that relation.

Moreover as Golding's art develops, it seems to become more and more important that this kind of seeing should not be described, but actually created in the reader. Grief must get into our seeing-for-ourselves, between the lines, and because of our involvement with what is not us. Since language warps or distorts reality, readers must be brought by the words to that point where vision can laser-leap beyond. Sammy's heartbroken seeing is beautiful, awe-ful, strange – but does it really move us? Much more disturbing to a reader are moments that come through language utterly deadpan and insentient by a sudden welling up of *our* response. A coldly objective anthropological eye reports from the outside the appearance and behaviour of a 'red creature', near the end of *The Inheritors* (216–22). The reader who has lived the novel inside Lok is nonplussed; cannot really *see* (any more than the narration) what is being described. Then suddenly, there is shocking awareness, actually something of the grief and love and horror that are Lok's . . . for suddenly one sees what the 'light poured down over the cheekbones' *is* (so that one's own eyes may begin to prick) . . . and then, with indescribable disturbance, one realizes the full horror of what Lok is weeping over. The effect is literally indescribable because it has renounced description; it can take place only through, and then beyond, the process of the text, with the whole experience of the book to power it. The same is true of Matty's farewell to Australia (*Darkness Visible*, 77). Apparently meaninglessly he shakes one foot, and then the other; he takes a last look at the continent; he goes hurriedly to a little pile of dust and strews a handful over his shoes. 'A single drop of water rolled out of his good eye, found a quick way down his cheek and fell on the deck. His mouth was making little movements, but he said nothing.' We have known Matty and have seen what has been done to him. But more and more, down under, we have been challenged to read between the lines of his wordless behaviour, while cobbers laugh at what they see as idiocy, and some readers turn off. Those that have eyes to see, let them see – and feel – for only that will guarantee the sense of the Mattyness of Matty and what he brings with him when we come to the final seeing. Those who have no such eyes will of course see nothingness, meaninglessness, the absurd; or at best the loving foolishness of a 'natural' – and space will be made for that reading, as always in Golding.

But before trying to analyse those most extraordinary places where Golding tries narratively, or more complexly through a character, for inclusive vision, containing all the paradoxes, and seeing the infinite *in* the grain of dust, it might be as well to reprise what 'inclusiveness' needs to be. Golding himself seems to have felt the same need, in setting out to make *Darkness Visible*, for at the beginning he clarifies the essential threefold process that he means by seeing. It must always be grounded in pure sense perception. For Golding the sceptic and modernist, that is indeed before all, and everything. But what comes through that seeing is another dimension in it, and another, each proving a lens for further and deeper focus, from seeing to insight, from insight to revelation. (And 'epiphany' is religious not Joycean, it has its full meaning of Apocalyptic showing forth, Revelation, coming through the act of seeing, but not the creation of the artist.) So the seeing of Holocaust must begin from the most delicate and precise visualization, entirely devoid of symbolism, done purely in terms of colours, shapes, the movements of light. 'Now the pink aura of it had spread. Saffron and ochre turned to blood-colour.' The last words have no metaphoric charge, the perception is of a shift in the spectrum of light and a precise discrimination of deepening tone and exact shade. Wilf Barclay will accuse language of being ninety-nine per cent metaphor and is none too sure about the one per cent. For Golding you can only be sure of truth by founding it there. But then, it is out of that terrible shivering glare that something moves and walks naked: a burnt child, recalling that most appalling of Vietnam photographs, whose survival is, again simply, miraculous. It should not be possible but 'they saw him plain' (14), the brightness all down one side, why he moves as he does, the burn. The child walks out of the fire. We 'see' as no more and no less a fact than the twentieth century inferno, the apparent miracle of survival. But it is as dark as it is bright, a horrible brightness, a scrap of humanity saved but terribly maimed, a glimpse of terror and of wonder. But then, thirdly, we must see a dimension more: the connection between the horror and the wonder, a hidden design. The captain of the fire-crew is forced to admit to himself the direct link between his own survival and the moment of cowardice and inhumanity before he could nerve himself to go to the child's rescue; he too is a maimed creature 'whose mind had touched for once on the nature of things' (16). So 'seeing' must focus dimension through dimension: first, and essentially, sense perception; then through sense perception to insight, both darkness and brightness, horror and miracle; and finally through insight to the revelation of a terrifying field of force and design in the universe, to which our normal experience is a concealing screen; through 'seeing' to 'skrying', though 'skrying' to 'revelation'. The truest seeing must be sight-with-insight, visual *and* visionary, ordinary and infinite, horrible and wonderful, objective and through tears, many and one. In the end it must develop in the spectator, the reader, in the space between the lines, wordlessly; with the risk that the space will not fill, that vision may fail, or be seen as delusion in the character, or the author.

It is no wonder that (if we take a section through Golding's work) his attempts to see whole have had to become much more imaginatively daring, complex and difficult, as they have sought to be more inclusive. Brilliant though they are – and I still take *The Inheritors* to be the most perfect of all – the first two books are relatively human sized compared with the next three. The field of vision (and weeping) is 'the darkness of man's heart', and only fleetingly do questionings arise that go beyond the human. In *Lord of the Flies* such moments come through Simon's eyes (though Ralph's tears at the end are for Piggy's kind of truth and wisdom), but to compare our last glimpse of Simon with the final focusing through Jocelin, is to see just what has happened to Golding's seeing.

After the horror of the series of 'seeings deeper' that began in game and have ended with the death of Simon, the language of the author confidently restores inclusiveness. Peace and beauty seem to follow violence as calm follows storm. As the Pacific tide comes in, Simon's body becomes part of the rhythms of the natural universe. The advancing line of phosphorescence 'bulged about the sand grains and little pebbles; it held them each in a dimple of tension, then suddenly accepted them with an inaudible syllable and moved on.' (189) Through its granular concreteness the seeing begins to reembody Simon's kind of vision, its 'acceptance' of what *is*, in a larger perspective, as we take in the fact of his disappearance, But what 'is' is neither horror nor beauty peace and order, because it is both. If the phosphorescence 'dressed Simon's coarse hair with brightness . . . and the turn of his shoulder became sculptured marble'; what it consists of is 'strange, moonbeam-bodied creatures with fiery eyes', the same transparencies that came in the daylight scavenging for food 'like myriads of tiny teeth in a saw'. The Pacific creates order, peace, as

> Somewhere over the darkened curve of the world the sun and moon were pulling; and the film of water on the earth planet was held, bulging slightly on one side while the solid core turned. The great wave of the tide moved further along the island and the water lifted. Softly . . . itself a silver shape beneath the steadfast constellations, Simon's dead body moved out towards the open sea. (190)

But though that stately procession puts the violence of man into perspective, the somewhat scientific language reminds one of the world's indifference to man. This is the same sea and tide that Ralph had seen on 'the other side', which 'travelled the length of the island with an air of disregarding it and being set on other business', and whose remoteness 'numbed his brain' (137). The vision is concrete and universal, has insight as well as sight, but its world is, scrupulously, only the physical universe and man (though Simon had had an inkling of something more than 'just us', both in horror and in hope). In *The Inheritors*, too, the vision is limited to the physical and human horizon – though the last line has a further resonance when Tuami 'could not see if the line of darkness had an ending'.

But with *Pincher Martin* the human and physical world eventually cracks open to reveal the metaphysical (including Tuami's question in its metaphysical form); and in *Free Fall* and *The Spire* the vision increasingly splits into such diverse and indeed opposite ways of looking, that bringing them together becomes as problematic as the books seem to have been difficult to finish. Moreover Golding ceases to write in his own voice; and begins to be more and more distrustful not only of pattern but of language itself. So complex and tentative is the final vision of *The Spire*, so much has to be got into it with such careful cross-reservation, that it is impossible to discuss it properly here[9] – but even brief comparison with the 'end' of Simon shows up major differences in the seeing. It has become immensely more complicated: patterns of insight multiply, but in doing so destroy pattern. Since each convinces, none can be exclusively true; and though we know more about Jocelin in more terms than any other character in Golding, it is only to exclaim when the oppositions exhaust themselves, 'Now – I know nothing at all!' (223). Secondly, the eye-clouding from egotism that began with Pincher has intensified so that we live not only behind one obsessed pair of eyes, but those of a visionary blindest of all. Yet again it seems that the road of excess may lead to the palace of wisdom, since the reaction also goes further than ever in grief and self-repudiation. Well before his death Jocelin's eyes have died to himself and become wholly objective, and his final focusing is caught at the instant of self-extinction. Thirdly, there is a new sense of the transience and obliquity of 'seeing whole'; the whole structured and patterned fiction is but a preparation for that single moment of perception, caught in a flash like the kingfisher from the corner of the eye against 'the panicshot darkness'. Seeing is indeed Conrad's 'everything' – for if it fails the whole work of creation fails and there is nothing but delusion. Yet for all its ambiguities, the ignorance that follows knowing, the need for self-extinction, the transience and obliquity, the fiction seems more convinced than ever that only the 'rock' of concrete seeing will hold everything – 'our very stones cry out'. Only focusing the spire *itself* can enable 'all things to come together'.

> The two eyes slid together. It was the window, bright and open. Something divided it. Round the division was the blue of the sky. The division was still and silent, but rushing upward to some point at the sky's end, and with a silent cry. It was slim as a girl, translucent. It had grown from some seed of rose-coloured substance that glittered like a waterfall, an upward waterfall. The substance was one thing, that broke all the way to infinity in cascades of exultation that nothing could trammel. (223)

All the opposites are there, the concrete and the infinite, the visual and the visionary, the divided and the one, the spiritual and the fleshly, the crooked beauty, the terror and astonishment, the falling and the soaring caught in the movments of the eye.

However, and this is the most important difference of all from the 'authority' of *Lord of the Flies*, one may say these things, but they are now very clearly only signs and sayings. The vision fails unless readers see for themselves; unless, when the words stop, something they can only point towards (though with such density and intensity) flashes across the 'inward eye' of which Wordsworth spoke. Even at the final one per cent one can only use 'likeness', but our image-ination must nevertheless pierce momentarily *through* the sign – for Golding is not in the end a modernist. Just as to have seen the apple tree gives Jocelin only a semblance of the power of darkness and blossoming abundance he glimpsed for one instant's wonder and terror in the spire, so our seeing of the spire through words must pierce beyond where words can go.

Which of course means that the fiction now plays for high stakes and risks losing everything. To the reader who must honestly say that he *doesn't* see,[10] there is only a partial reply. One may test whether all the preparation has been taken in, since all is necessary for the full ambivalence and inclusiveness to work – but if 'comprehension' does not issue in that flash which is beyond words and intellectual understanding, there is nothing more to be said. Indeed Golding has always allowed for the sceptical reading: for the possibility of delusion in Simon, or Pincher, or Jocelin (or Matty and

Pedigree); for an ending in nothing, or in ambiguity – though I think the imaginative pressure is otherwise.

And he clearly had to go further, to try to turn glimpsing into seeing-plain, in making darkness (and brightness) visible, and to try to see-to-the-end. Again there is no time to go into the extraordinary lenses, the careful structuring of preparation, the cross-cutting of Matty's book with Sophy's, the fracturing of points of view that follows, the testing to destruction of the unity that had momentarily been experienced by the lilywhite boys, the rivals, the gospel makers. It is clear, however, that Golding wanted the despair that precedes the final seeing to be even darker than in *The Spire*, because not confined to a single consciousness. It is not only to Sophy the nihilist that 'there is now nothing visible but darkness'. Sim Goodchild knows that all are guilty, that 'nobody will *ever* know what happened'; and the television screens everywhere turn his moment of deepest vision into mockery. Matty is dead, horribly on fire again, and there is no way of telling whether his death was accident or design. Or is there? For if in Golding's powerfully mythic view of 'reality' ordinary seeing is always a lens to something deeper, there can be no true seeing that does not try to 'tell' the ultimate nature of things, and dare to see (past death itself) whether, in those words from *The Inheritors*, the darkness has an ending. And *Darkness Visible* not only differs from *The Spire* in wanting to see where the spire ultimately points towards; it also reorchestrates *Pincher Martin* and *Free Fall* in its concern with whether, in the end, there can be *change*? Does what we are determine what we may be? In choosing to conceive the death of Mr Pedigree, Golding deliberately chooses the seamiest material to uncover 'where the connections are', and to imagine his answer to whether or not a man may cry out and be different . . . whether, in the end there is darkness, or light, or nothing at all.

Even though Pedigree is dying, what strikes one first about the seeing of 'last things' is its liveliness. This is sense-perception again: the sun on the skin, the sea of light, Matty. But there is now not only the familiar insight – that only with the extinction of himself can he see beyond the horrible appearance of Matty, into the love and forgiveness that were always there – there is also the newly sensed immediacy of the nature of the spirit that had moved 'in' him, 'the extraordinary lively nature of this gold, this wind, this wonderful light and warmth that kept Windrove moving, rhythmically'.

To him Pedigree can not only speak of the hell he knows and fears, but cry for help. Then in apocalyptic transformation, we see the Being Matty brought with him:

> For the golden immediacy of the wind altered at its heart and began first to drift upwards, then swirl upwards then rush upwards round Matty. The gold grew fierce and burned. Sebastian watched in terror as the man before him was consumed, melted, vanished like a guy in a bonfire; and the face was no longer two-tone but gold as the fire and stern and everywhere there was a sense of the peacock eyes of great feathers and the smile round the lips was loving and terrible. This being drew Sebastian towards him so that the terror of the golden lips jerked a cry out of him –
> 'Why? Why?'
> The face looming over him seemed to speak or sing but not in human speech.
> *Freedom.* (265)

But Pedigree who (like Sammy) cried out for help, cannot bear (like Pincher) to let go, and clutches closer to himself the many-coloured ball, his life, his heart, himself:

> But the hands came in through his. They took the ball as it beat and drew it away so that the strings that bound it to him tore as he screamed. Then it was gone. (265)

Do we 'see'? What Pedigree sees consumes all into itself. It costs everything, but if the power of the spirit does come into the world – as Matty saw (238) – *through* human deformity, then men can cry for help at the end and be transformed. Darkness is visible to the last in the two-toned face of reality, but then the last fire burns it away into brightness. And though it is intensely painful and destructive to the self, it is the music that frays and breaks the string.

Yet we cannot be 'told' this. Words can only bring us to the point where something either becomes 'visible' in the 'opening' between them, in the space beyond – or does not. And Golding scrupulously allows for those who cannot believe that 'the filthy old thing' that is our pedigree can ever be 'cured'. For both sets of readers there has to be a gap between 'book' and 'since'; between the telling and the final sense of cause and consequence. It is there on page 265 of *Darkness Visible*: an empty space that must fill with each reader's individual vision. Perhaps Golding has emerged from the underworld with a golden branch – *sit mihi fas audita loqui* – but some readers will see (and it is their right) only emptiness after the word 'gone'.

That gap, between the telling and the seeing whole, gets a sardonic underlining in *The Paper Men*. For all the mocking at the critic, it is the writer who makes and finally suffers the most cutting comments, on the media of vision. Any attempt at clarity in lucid prose is stigmatized, for (to the man who has seen the terror and the wonder) the hints of reality that matter, only come when words displace themselves into another dimension out of the hippety-hop of argot (126–7). Both the terror glimpsed in the cathedral, and the wonderful vision that transforms the seamy material of the Spanish Steps (160–1), require modes of perception beyond speech – and finally beyond eyesight too: those of light, and of movement; but then of music; and heart-stoppingly of silence. But not even a knowledge of the transforming power, not even tears and the desire for the destruction of the self, can finally open Barclay's eyes so that all things can come together. It is still paper, and words, and self that he is concerned with to the end. Only the last of the stigmata can strike home to where the lack is – more important than seeing in the end, and much more important than words.

NOTES

1 'The Marriage of Heaven and Hell', Geoffrey Keynes (ed.) *Poetry and Prose of William Blake*, Nonesuch Edition, London 1948, 183.
2 William Wordsworth, *The Prelude 1799, 1805, 1850*, Norton Critical Edition, New York 1979, 216.
3 Joseph Conrad, 'Preface' to *The Nigger of the Narcissus*.
4 *The Prelude*, op. cit., 424.
5 Mark Kinkead-Weekes and Ian Gregor, *William Golding: A Critical Study*, Revised Edition, London 1984, 16–21.
6 Page references given in brackets after each quotation refer to the Faber edition in each case.
7 The name seems a private joke, substituting for Simon the cynical bookseller of Golding's age, as 'seer'.
8 Blake's 'Auguries of Innocence', op. cit., 118.
9 Kinkead-Weekes and Gregor at least try in greater detail, op. cit., 229–235.

10 A good example, in an intelligent critic, is Laurence Lerner's 'Jocelin's Folly: or, Down with the Spire', *Critical Quarterly*, v. 24 No. 3 (Autumn 1984), 3–15. It seems to me that his strong response to the evil of the spire, together with his dislike of Golding's reliance on implication, cause him to miss or misinterpret a great deal that goes the other way. Given time, one would have to try to argue what is 'there' that is not destroyed by Jocelin's accusations (or Lerner's); and attempt to show that if implication is really artful, details do not exist in isolation, but are carried by a current of other details in a particular direction, and do add up in the end. But I can see the possibility (since response has become so much more important than interpretation) that even if one were to argue successfully, there might still be the answer: 'But I don't "*see*" what you do.' I think this is a risk that Golding, by pushing what he means by 'seeing' so far, has become increasingly willing to take.

'He Wondered': The religious imagination of William Golding

IAN GREGOR

I

Golding's work has often been described as religious. Whatever is intended by such a description can, of course, vary a good deal, but however varied the interpretation, we should continually remind ourselves we are discussing works of fiction with their own distinctive approach to truth. A remark made by Golding about *Pincher Martin*, arguably his most explicit religious novel, serves – if we neglect to remember this – as a salutary warning. 'It was written and rewritten before I knew what it was about at all. Indeed, if I am asked about that book I have to embark on a theological exposition that bores me as much as my questioner.' (*A Moving Target*, 163–4.)

Let me first widen the context of discussion by citing three positions which have been taken up in considering the relationship of religion to literature. The first is taken by the early twentieth-century writer, Arthur Machen, when he observes, 'Literature is the expression, through the aesthetic medium of words, of the dogmas of the Catholic Church, and that which is out of harmony with those dogmas, is not literature.'[1] This shows in a spectacularly forthright way what happens when credal formulations are made the criterion of judging imaginative truths. Not many definitions exhibit the confidence, or the extremity, of Machen's, but the essentials of his position are present whenever content in art usurps a life of its own.

My second test is more familiar, and immensely more sophisticated. It is Newman defining the role of literature in *The Idea of a University*. 'Literature', he remarks, 'is the life and remains of the natural man.'[2] And he goes on to clarify this. 'Man will never continue in a mere state of innocence; he is sure to sin, and his literature will be the expression of his sin . . . From the nature of the case, if literature is to be made the study of human nature, you

84

cannot have a Christian literature, it is a contradiction in terms to attempt a sinless literature of sinful man.'³ For Newman, the teaching of literature is prophylactic in intent. The university being 'a direct preparation for the world' it would be irresponsible to deny students access to 'the masters of human thought', who, because of 'an incidental corruption' were expert guides to the snares and delusions of the world. Of course, Newman had no doubt at all that literature had its positive benefits, but he found considerable difficulty in avoiding a defensive note because of his dualistic assumptions deriving from the radical division he entertained between world and spirit, body and soul, the natural and the supernatural. He relishes keenly the bracing climate of disjunctions: 'knowledge is one thing, virtue is another; good sense is not conscience; refinement is not humility, nor is largeness and justness of view, faith.'⁴ In the world of nineteenth-century liberalism which Newman set himself to anatomize, and to which, over a century later we are still heirs, these sharp distinctions still crackle and glow with life. But the distinctions which served him so well in the larger context seem reductive when applied to literature. Newman himself seems half consciously aware of this, when after a particularly rapturous paragraph describing the pleasure to be obtained from literature, from music, and from painting, pleasures which the Church has used, he was to remind himself that these are the pleasures of a fallen world. And he ruefully concedes that this creates 'a difficulty'. What we are seeing in his attitude to literature is an aspect of the unresolved tension which persists throughout *The Idea* between Newman the humanist and Newman the Christian Apologist. For us, it is precisely because the tension remains unresolved, allowing him an extraordinary empathy with intellectual positions and attitudes not his own, that gives *The Idea* its continuing vitality, because what we are encountering here is not, as Walter Pater described it, 'the perfect handling of a theory', but a mind in action tensely engaged in wrestling with difficulties.

My third text comes from Lawrence's essay on Hardy. It is precisely that element of tension that he makes central to the relationship between art and morality, morality in this context, having the form of metaphysical belief. 'Every work of art,' Lawrence writes, 'adheres to some system of morality. But if it be really a work of art, it must contain the essential criticism of that morality. Hence the antinomy, hence *the conflict necessary to every tragic conception.*'[5] Not disjunction, but creative tension, is what Lawrence is insisting upon. It is important to note that although Lawrence uses words such as 'system', and 'criticism', they are subsumed in the encompassing effort to define 'the reality of art'. Such 'reality' involves something much more than a counterpointing theme; it is inseparable from dramatic conflict, its existence is dependent upon performance, to be located within the writing itself.

It is with Lawrence's remark in mind that I would like to look at Golding's novels, because he, of all contemporary writers of fiction, reveals in the very grain of his imagination, his religious concern. That concern is quite different, in Golding's case, from the way we might use the term to describe the work of Graham Greene, or Mauriac, or Heinrich Böll, all of whom have shown themselves at one time or another to be interested in religious themes. Such an interest is tangential in Golding, if it is present at all; when we talk of Golding's exercising a religious imagination we feel that the primary effort has been to make us feel, within this world, the overwhelming importance of a world elsewhere, more precisely, a Creator elsewhere. Inquiries, however, which seek impatiently to extrapolate those religious concerns misrepresent the nature of his imaginative enterprise. A question like 'Is Golding's Theology Christian?' can only lead us away from the fiction, because of the usual perils of asking abstract questions about novels, so nostalgically reminiscent of those tests-for-orthodoxy that used to be applied by Catholics to the novels of Greene. To read a Golding novel is to be made to contemplate the grammar of fiction itself; that is to say, in its distinctive use of language we are made to realize anew the relationship between belief and creativity.

II

I would like to use as a starting point for a closer consideration of Golding's novels an essay called 'Fable', published in his collection *The Hot Gates*. It provides a clear and interesting statement of the intellectual background which lay behind *Lord of the Flies*. For someone whose novels are not short on ambiguity, the account is disarmingly explicit

Before the second world war I believed in the perfectability of social man: that a correct structure of society would produce good will; and that therefore you could remove all social ills by a reorganization of society. (86)

Experience of war, as well as of such totalitarian regimes as fascism and Stalinism, made him realize that 'man was sick – not exceptional man, but average man . . . the condition of man was to be a morally diseased creation.' (87). When he put this into theological terms this is how he expressed it in an interview:

Man is a fallen being. He is gripped by original sin. His nature is sinful and his state perilous . . . the proposition that man has free will because he was created in God's image . . . once you have free will and you are created, you have alternatives before you. You can either then turn towards or away from Him. And God can't stop you turning away from Him, without removing your free will, because that's what free will is.[6]

Behind this somewhat home-grown theology, we can see that Golding would seem to have subscribed to some of the fundamental articles of Christian faith – the creation of Man by God, man's free will, man's fall and original sin. About salvation and man's redemption he has been more reserved. It is hardly surprising that given such views he is able to describe himself as a religious man, though not at all surprising that he has no denominational allegiance.

Although from a Christian point of view there is a sense of incompleteness about Golding's theology, there remains an unwavering conviction that the nature and condition of man requires a metaphysical explanation. Golding writing about his novel *Free Fall* remarks:

. . . we do live in two worlds. There is this physical one, which is coherent, and there is a spiritual one. To the average man with his flashes of religious experience, if you like to call them that – that world is very incoherent. But nevertheless, as a matter of experience, for *me* and I suspect for millions of other people this experience of having two worlds to live in all the time . . . is a vital one and is what living is like.[7]

From one point of view this associates Golding's views with those of the great writers of Christian epic, with Dante and with Milton.

I was careful to say from 'one point of view' because, of course, from another he was radically different. Whereas for them the authorial presence was stable, for Golding it was the endless uncertainty of where such a presence is to be located, that makes him very much a novelist, and a novelist for our times. It is that factor that complicates the relatively straightforward account I gave of Golding's religious views as expressed in the essay 'Fable'. 'Never trust the artist. Trust the tale' is Lawrence's famous cautionary dictum. But we have to be particularly on our guard because Golding's consciousness of 'certain certainties' comes through so powerfully that we need to be constantly aware of the qualifications that lie in the margins. The reading of *Lord of the Flies* is noticeably different from that given by Golding in his account of the feelings that led to its creation.

To be fair to Golding, he is aware of this.

> I don't think the fable ever got right out of hand; but there are many places where the fable splits at the seams, and I would like to think if this is so, the splits do not arise from ineptitude or deficiency but from a plenitude of imagination . . . May it not be that at the very moments when I felt the fable to come to its own life before me, it may have become something more valuable, so that where I thought it was failing, it was really succeeding? (*The Hot Gates*, 99–100.)

'Splitting at the seams . . . plenitude of imagination . . . something more valuable', the direction of these phrases is fairly clear, so that although the point is a familiar one even in this early essay about the clearest of his novels, Golding is aware of a disturbing power in his imagination, which transfigures his intentions.

Even at the level of theme, the account which Golding gives of *Lord of the Flies* and the effect it makes upon the reader of the novel are different in emphasis, the checks and balances are already in operation. We can point out that Jack, the leader of the opposition, behaves resourcefully and sensibly, until disappointment and frustration set in when the early hopes of rescue fade; it is only when he begins to think of the immediacies of survival, that he falls victim to the pleasures of hunting. We can point out also that Simon, who is granted the central vision of the novel, is a withdrawn boy, prone to epileptic fits, and when he seeks to warn other boys that their fears about the Beast are groundless, his arrival coincides with the moment when their excitement and fear are at fever pitch, and in the dark they mistake the thing crawling out of the bushes for the Beast itself. We have little difficulty in recognizing why Piggy speaks as he does. 'It was an accident, that's what it was. An accident. Coming in the dark – he hadn't no business, crawling like that out of the dark.' (*Lord of the Flies* 173.) These are understandable human fears, even if they are too self-excusing about the possibility of a tragic outcome. We could point out, too, the importance of making at least a marginal gloss, that however violent the conflicts, however obtuse the naval officer may be in his realization of what has taken place, they are still a group of children, so that the novel is really about the *potentiality* of evil, rather than its full realization. We can gauge the force of this if we think how this novel would strike us if it had been set in a concentration camp instead of on a deserted island. Without wishing to modify in any way the tragic compulsion of Golding's narrative, the reader, even the relatively untutored reader, cannot fail to recognize that this is 'a story', and the ending, so deliberately contrived, is there to remind us of just that.

All these elements could be adduced to show how Golding subtilizes the account given in 'Fable', but it remains essentially a subtilization of 'the argument' of the novel, not its art. It is only when we look at the writing itself, that we catch the imagination at work, 'that synthetic and magical power', which Coleridge described, and which Lawrence pointed to as evidence of 'the reality of art'.

Let me take a passage from *Lord of the Flies* to show what I mean. It is a quiet moment in the novel, far removed from the formal conflicts, but I choose it precisely because I think it shows in a way that is unobtrusive and *pianissimo*, the tension rippling in the prose which builds up, incrementally, a sense of 'necessary conflict', gradually spreading to the entire novel. The passage occurs when Ralph is exploring the island:

Here, on the other side of the island, the view was utterly different.
The filmy enchantments of mirage could not endure the cold ocean water and the horizon was hard, clipped blue. Ralph

wandered down to the rocks. Down here, almost on a level with the sea, you could follow with your eye the ceaseless, bulging passage of the deep sea waves. They were miles wide, apparently not breakers or the banked ridges of shallow water. They travelled the length of the island with an air of disregarding it and being set on other business; they were less a progress than a momentous rise and fall of the whole ocean. Now the sea would suck down, making cascades and waterfalls of retreating water, would sink past the rocks and plaster down the seaweed like shining hair: then, pausing, gather and rise with a roar, irresistibly swelling over point and outcrop, climbing the little cliff, sending at last an arm of surf up a gully to end a yard or so from him in fingers of spray.

Wave after wave, Ralph followed the rise and fall until something of the remoteness of the sea numbed his brain. Then gradually the almost infinite size of this water forced itself on his attention. (*Lord of the Flies* 121–2.)

An extraordinary sense of space is created by the passage, of watery distance. The individual 'Ralph' becomes an all-registering eye. The reader too is implicated, so that Ralph's eye becomes the reader's. 'You could follow with your eye', as it negotiates repeatedly 'the near' and 'the far'. The insistences of the paragraph are clearly marked: 'Here'/'Down here'/'cascades and waterfalls of retreating water '/ 'seaweed like shining hair'/'arm of surf'. And, in contrast: 'the momentous rise and fall of the whole ocean'/'the remoteness of the sea'/'the almost infinite size of this water'.

This extraordinary ability to oscillate between conscious attention to detail and unconscious awareness, is the creative tension that runs throughout the entire novel. When the final sentence comes Golding has created the imaginative conditions which make us feel, instinctively, in the presence of an extraordinary mystery. 'Wave after wave, Ralph followed the rise and fall until something of the remoteness of the sea numbed his brain. Then gradually the almost infinite size of this water forced itself upon his attention.' The hypnotic rhythm of the first sentence balanced by the gradual self-consciousness of the second, located in 'followed/forced', captures in a tiny detail, the way the whole book is constantly on the move, as the reader is absorbed by the new, drawn on to contemplate the far. The theme, the sombre narrative whereby a group of schoolboys on a deserted island reveals 'the darkness of man's heart', is transformed by the imaginative awareness that creates at every point a resonance that resists formulation and makes us create for ourselves another, more subtle, story in the margins of the one that is explicitly told. 'Grief, grief, grief, sheer grief', is how Golding has described the theme, but if we say that there is nothing elegiac about the mood of the novel, then what we are responding to is not 'sheer grief' but 'sheer exhilaration' in the writing, so that we have little difficulty in seeing what the author meant by saying that at times he seemed to be merely tracing out words that already lay under the page. It is a transfiguring experience for the reader so that he is made to feel that even the most violent incident in the novel reveals a hint of cosmic benediction. 'Softly, surrounded by a fringe of inquisitive bright creatures, itself a silver shape beneath the steadfast constellations, Simon's dead body moved out towards the open sea.' It is a perspective that quietly accepts the contraries of experience, the 'dead body' of Simon, certainly, but also 'the *steadfast* constellations' which preside over it, indicating an order and a heroism within the human heart.

Nowhere is the phrase 'necessary conflict' more explicitly attended to than in *The Spire*: it rages within the protagonist. Dean Jocelin is a mass of pride and obstinacy with a belief, amounting to an obsession, that he has been divinely appointed to build a spire for his cathedral. He will brook no opposition, either by man or by nature, and the result is that he causes havoc wherever he goes. *The Spire* gets built – but at what cost? This is the question that would seem to be posed by the novel.

There is an explicitly Christian 'reading' – that is to say, in the end, Jocelyn is redeemed by the realization of his pride; broken in body and in will, he gazes up and sees the spire, a thing of beauty, 'the great dare' is justified. There is a sardonic 'reading' – that Jocelin remains, to the end, a victim of his delusions. There is also what, for want of a better word, I shall describe as a humanist 'reading', in which the process of suffering enables him to 'know himself' with clarity, or Golding presents his protagonist in such a way, that the reader feels this to be the case, even if Jocelin himself is no longer capable of realizing it. From all those multiple interpretations it will be gathered that, however the novel concludes, it ends with a vision rather than a view. There is no extractable proposition that can be taken from the novel. 'At every height we mine a new depth', Jocelin's remark can be made to refer equally to the building of the spire and to the writing of the novel. However we interpret Jocelin's gnomic, final remark, 'It's like the apple tree', one thing is clear, and that is that he has to undergo a radical revision of thought – the spire is not to be conceived, instrumentally, pointing towards something, a diagram of prayer, but as something supremely self-contained, a thing of beauty, in need of no justification. For Jocelin that is a matter for astonishment.

We come back to the act of writing itself as being the means, unique to the literary artist, of revealing 'the thing of beauty'. As with *Lord of the Flies* I would like to choose a passage from *The Spire*, the narrative drive of which is only obliquely related to the main concerns of the fiction. It is a moment far out in the novel, when Jocelin's master mason seeks to persuade him to stop building because the foundations are barely existent:

'Look down, Father – right over the parapet, all the way down, past the lights, the buttresses, all the way down to the cedar top in the cloister.'

'I see it'.

'Let your eye crawl down like an insect, foot by foot. You think these walls are strong because they're stone; but I know better. We've nothing but a skin of glass and stone stretched between four stone rods, one at each corner. D'you understand that? The stone is no stronger than the glass between the verticals because every inch of the way I have to save weight, bartering strength for weight or weight for strength, guessing how much, how far, how little, how near, until my very heart stops when I think of it. Look down, Father . . .' Jocelin's eyes were shut . . . For a moment, as he stood with gritted teeth, he felt the solid stone under him move – swinging sideways and out. The dunce's cap a hundred and fifty feet tall began to rip down and tear and burst, sliding with dust and smoke and thunder, faster and faster, breaking and sheering with spark and flame and explosion, crashing down to strike the nave so that the paving stones danced like wood chips till the ruin buried them. So 'clear was this that he fell with the south west column that swung out over the cloister bent in the middle like a leg and destroyed the library like the blow of a flail. He opened his eyes, sick with falling through the air. He was clutching the parapet and the cloisters were moving below him.

'What must we do?'

'Stop building.' (117–19.)

'Look down . . .', the sense of vertigo is made overwhelmingly present. As with the passage from *Lord of the Flies* it is the startling juxtaposition of space together with the intensely observed detail which creates the imaginative momentum; 'past the lights, the buttresses, all the way down to the cedar top in the cloister.'

'Nothing is but what is not', Macbeth's line catches at the feeling which pervades the passage – stone has the fragility of glass, 'he felt the solid stone under him move', 'stone snaps, crumbles, tears'. Appearances deceive, the echoes of that resound throughout the novel, all the way from 'the stone of the building' which has only rubble for foundations, to the motivations of the builders, where in Jocelin's case, spiritual aspiration masks a desperate egotism. The paradoxes and tension wrought within *The Spire* are so elaborate – every height means a new depth, whether into the cellarage of the heart or into the rubble of the foundation, 'like porridge coming to the boil' – that substance and form become fused. Golding, no less than Jocelin, is risking a great deal, in making 'the building' of the spire coterminous with 'the building' of the novel. It has a dangerous aptness about it; the novel itself is built on faith and tests out at every point his loyalty to his creation. 'Stop building' becomes a temptation not just for Jocelin, but for Golding too.

In many ways *Darkness Visible* is Golding's most ambitious novel. Conceived on a massive scale, it seeks to create a religious dimension, not for a group of schoolboys isolated on a deserted island, nor for a sailor drowning in mid-Atlantic, nor for a medieval ecclesiastic obsessed with adding glory to his church, but by asking what does it mean for a writer to have a religious imagination, in the violence of late twentieth-century life? What, in other words, would it mean to introduce 'a holy man', into a world of global crime and hijacking? Being a Golding character, the Holy Man turns out to be a very odd creature indeed, but it has to be said that odd or not, Golding succeeds in making him a compelling figure in a way that (for me) is only intermittently true of the other side of the novel, the world of the twins, of the hijackers. Of course, it raises fascinating questions about evil, imagined now with a new, and sometimes startling intensity, twentieth-century man has perpetrated 'darkness visible', in hells unimaginable to Milton – Auschwitz, Dresden, Hiroshima. Can the human imagination confront such horror? That is the challenge that is obliquely taken up by *Darkness Visible* and it is perhaps an indication of the gravity and troubling nature of the themes, that it is the only one of his novels he has made it his practice never to discuss. Here is the introduction of Matty (who is later to become the Holy Man) into the novel: he is emerging, literally, as a child from the flames:

The white fire, becoming pale pink, then blood-coloured then pink again where it caught smoke or clouds seemed the same as if it were the permanent nature of this place. The men continued to stare.

At the end of the street or where now, humanly speaking, the street was no longer part of the habitable world – at that point where the world had become an open stove – at a point where odd bits of brightness condensed to form a lamp-post still standing, a pillar box, some eccentrically shaped rubble – right there, where the flinty street was turned into light, something moved. The bookseller looked away, rubbed his eyes, then looked again. He knew most of the counterfeits, the objects that seem endowed with life in a fire: the boxes of papers stirred into movement by localized gusts of wind, the heat-induced contractions and expansions of material that can mimic muscular movement, the sack moved by rats or cats or dogs or half-burnt birds. At once and violently, he hoped for rats but would have settled for a dog. He turned round again to get his back between himself and what he was sure he had not seen.

It was a remarkable circumstance that their captain was the last to look. He had turned from the fire and was contemplating his wrecked machine with the kind of feeling that kept his chin still.

The other men drew his eyes to them by not meaning to. They turned away from the fire far too casually. Where there had been a whole set of eyes, a battery of them staring into the melted end of the world, that battery now contemplated the uninteresting ruins from a previous fire in the other direction and the failing jet of water in the crater. It was a sheer piece of heightened awareness, a sense sharpened by dread that made the captain look at once not where they were looking but where they were not . . .

What had seemed impossible and therefore unreal was now a fact and clear to them all. A figure had condensed out of the shuddering backdrop of the glare. It moved in the geometrical centre of the road which now appeared longer and wider than before. Because if it was the same size as before, then the figure was impossibly small – impossibly tiny, since children had been the first to be evacuated from that whole area; and in the mean and smashed streets there had been so much fire there was nowhere for a family to live. Nor do small children walk out of a fire that is melting lead and distorting iron.

'Well! What are you waiting for?'

No one said anything.

'You two! Get him!' (12–14.)

Water, air – now fire as a destructive force, Golding is always at his best writing about primal elements. The heat comes off the page, but it is the kind of attention that it gets from the fireman that gives it its peculiar force. It is the *fear* of seeing that runs throughout, 'heightened awareness, a sense sharpened by dread' – that is the phrase that lays bare the nerve of the passage. Consider how Golding makes us strain our eyes into the heart of the blaze. It is worth looking at the effects created by the first sentence of the second paragraph – with its repeated hesitations, in order to be scrupulously exact, in order to say nothing more than could be absolutely observed – 'something moved'. It is through the negatives, 'what he was sure he had *not* seen'/'drew his eyes by *not* meaning to'/'*not* where they were looking, but where they were *not*' that the acuteness of seeing is rendered. The unbelievable takes on incredible shape – so that the revelation, when it comes, is reported in a tone which is a mixture of amazement and acceptance: 'Nor do small children . . .'

And so Matty enters the novel – on fire and alive – a creature of the furnace, entering a world where men will avert their eyes from him. Darkness is made visible, mystery is made manifest, and the urgent flat instructions of the Captain 'You two. Get him', are to resound, in dramatically different tones, as the novel proceeds.

By now my argument is sufficiently plain not to need further labouring – that when we describe Golding as a writer whose imagination is haunted by and nourished by religious experience, we are not intending by that that he puts into fictional terms 'a theology', however subtle and complex, but that he returns again and again, to the primal act of seeing, of seeing *through* this world, to where 'something moved'. In *Lord of the Flies*, it was a perception of the inclusive movement of the cosmos; in *The Spire* it was a perception that he was building upon a vacancy.

Let me complete my collection of passages with a piece from *Free Fall* where that sense of seeing without understanding comes to the surface, and is made, unlike all the other passages I have considered so far, the explicit concern. It is a passage from *Free Fall* where Sammy Mountjoy is suddenly released from the darkness of his cell, and he sees the world about him, transfigured.

Therefore when the commandant let me out of the darkness he came late and as second string, giving me the liberty of the camp when perhaps I no longer needed it. I walked between the huts, a man resurrected but not by him. I saw the huts as one who had little to do with them, was indifferent to them and the temporal succession of days that they implied. So they shone with the innocent light of their own created nature. I understood them perfectly, boxes of thin wood as they were, and now transparent, letting be seen inside their quotas of sceptred kings. I lifted my arms, saw them too, and was overwhelmed by their unendurable richness as possessions, either arm ten thousand fortunes poured out for me. Huge tears were dropping from my face into dust; and this dust was a universe of brilliant and fantastic crystals, that miracles instantly supported in their being. I looked up beyond the huts and the wire, I raised my dead eyes, desiring nothing, accepting all things and giving all created things away. The paper wrappings of use and language dropped from me. Those crowded

5. Studio portrait by Howard Coster, 1955

6. Photograph by Carole Latimer

shapes extended up into the air and down into the rich earth, those deeds of far space and deep earth were aflame at the surface and daunting by right of their own natures though a day before I should have disguised them as trees. Beyond them the mountains were not only clear all through like purple glass, but living. They sang and were conjubilant. They were not all that sang. Everything is related to everything else and all relationship is either discord or harmony. The power of gravity, dimension and space, the movement of the earth and sun and unseen stars, these made what might be called music and I heard it. (186)

With the passages which preceded it in mind, we might be tempted into thinking that this passage belongs with them. There is the familiar opening, sight without seeing, 'I saw the huts as one who had little to do with them.' He sees *through* tears of joy, the dust, the trees, the mountains are transformed. He feels a profound harmony between himself and the world, a harmony expressed in terms of music that attends the primal creator. It is God's eye view of the world, given suddenly, gratuitously, to one of His creatures. Or is it? Sammy's view is too direct, too transparent, too 'visionary'. To be human is to see *in* the world, it is not to see *through* the world. This is not to say that Sammy's vision is false, it is premature. Man's vision has to be in a glass, darkly. Golding is a novelist writing in our times, he is not Dante or Milton, he is heir to all the possibilities of scepticism of contemporary writers of fiction, and nowhere does that scepticism express itself more fully than in the difficulty of locating the author and hearing his voice. It is not a Jamesian paper-chase which has forced the difficulty upon us; every distinguished writer of fiction in this century has used a variety of strategems to test out the authority of his vision, and invariably it is through indirections that directions have been found out.

III

Earlier in this paper I referred to an essay 'Fable' on the genesis of *Lord of the Flies*. I would like to conclude by referring to another essay, 'Belief and Creativity', which takes up precisely this issue of the writer and his writing. The difference between the two essays, written at a twenty year interval, is instructive. Where the concern of the first essay lies, as the title suggests, in describing the genesis of a fiction which illustrates a truth about the universe and the nature of man, the concern of the second is with the mystery of literary creation itself. Golding expresses it in this way:

> The writer watches the greatest mystery of all. It is the moment of most vital awareness, the moment of most passionate and *unsupported* conviction. It shines or cries. There is the writer, trying to grab it as it passes, as it emerges impossibly and heads to be gone. It is that twist of behaviour, that phrase, sentence, paragraph, that happening on which the writer would bet his whole fortune, stake his whole life as a *true* thing. Like God, he looks on his creation and knows what he has done. (*A Moving Target*, 197.)

It is the detail of writing – 'phrase, sentence, paragraph' – that summons the writer to become aware of the truth of what he is saying, it is by the quality of his utterance that he shall be known. It is in the moment when all things come together – a moment of truth, of grace, a moment when 'something moves' – that Golding is prompted to attest to the existence of God.

To appreciate the stress here it is useful to remind ourselves of some remarks made by Virginia Woolf in her essay 'A Sketch of the Past'. She is describing an experience which has much in common with Golding's, but her final emphasis is markedly different.

> It is the rapture I get when in writing I seem to be discovering what belongs to what; making a scene come right; making a character come together. From this I reach what I might call a philosophy . . . the whole world is a work of art; that we are parts of the work of art. *Hamlet* or a Beethoven quartet is the truth about the vast mass we call the world. But there is no Shakespeare, there is no Beethoven, certainly, and emphatically there is no God; we are the words; we are the music; we are the thing itself.[8]

However much the two passages have in common about the joy of literary creation, there is a striking contrast about the source of that joy. For Woolf it is creative absorption, '*we* are the words, *we* are the music', that constitutes the keenest pleasure; for Golding, it is contemplation of something completed, a design made visible, 'he *looks* on his creation and *knows* what he has done'. The distinction is a crucial one and Woolf and Golding are both conscious that their respective accounts must contain a religious implication, which she is as much concerned to reject as he is to invite. It is a crucial distinction and shapes the kind of fiction they write.

'Men do not write the novels they should, they write the novels they can.' Golding's self-deprecating remark implies that he assigns no exclusive rights to his vision, it is one way of looking among many. The hallmark of a Golding novel is its mythic nature; that is to say, it is an enterprise that remorselessly searches for the shape of a life beneath its surfaces, paring everything away to reveal the significant continuity. A simple illustration of what it is that drives Golding's imagination is a remark he once made about *Lord of the Flies*. He said he had two pictures in his mind: one of a small boy waggling his feet in the air on an empty beach in sheer exuberance; the other, of the same boy crawling bloodstained through the undergrowth, being hunted to death. How did one picture become the other? Everything is made subordinate to that overriding preoccupation; nothing is allowed to deflect the novelist's unswerving attention from the exigencies of following out the dramatic continuity that connects one with the other. Intense awareness of the physical world is accompanied at every point by an awareness, no less intense, of the metaphysical world. That Golding is aware of his duality within his imagination is suggested by his half humorous choice of epitaph – 'He wondered'. Wonder as contemplation of the natural world, wonder as speculation about its purposes, but above all, making one flow into the other, the wonder of the story teller, who sets out to discover where the connections are. Golding's imagination is always on the move, constantly seeing in a detail a hint of a larger design. The form and structure of his work are designed to concentrate the eye on that larger design, but paradoxically, it is through the concentration on the detail that we become most intimately aware of the whole. Ralph's vision of the vastness of the sea, Jocelin's of the falling spire, Matty walking out of the fire, Sammy's transfiguration of the camp – none of these scenes express 'the larger design' directly, but within them all we feel the imaginative drive that seeks to enlarge the horizon of discourse. Let Golding have a final word:

The novelist is God of his own interior world. Commonly men make God in their own image – he is a warrior, a lover, a mathematician, a father, son, mother, a remote universal and a small image in the corner of a room. Let us add our quota of inadequate description and say that he is of all things an artist who labours under no compulsion but that of his own creativity. Are we, in some sense, his novels? We are said to be made in his image, and if we could but understand our flashes of individual creativity we might glimpse the creativity of the Ultimate Creator. (*A Moving Target*, 200.)

The sense of a Creator constantly at work within His creation, a Creator whose presence is apprehended most surely in the detailed movement of the writing of the novel, but not circumscribed by it – these are the considerations, I suggest, we ought to have in mind, when we describe Golding's work as religious.

NOTES

1 A. Machen, quoted in W. K. Wimsatt *The Verbal Icon*, Univ. of Kentucky Press, 1964, 89.
2 J. H. Newman *The Idea of a University* (1959 edition) Doubleday, 232.
3 *Ibid.* 234.
4 *Ibid.* 144.
5 D. H. Lawrence 'Study of Thomas Hardy' in *Phoenix*, 1936, 476.
6 *Conversations with William Golding*, ed. Biles, Harcourt Brace, New York, 1970, 76.
7 *Ibid.* 79
8 Virginia Woolf, *Moments of Being*, Hogarth Press, London, 1978, 72.

Belly without Blemish: Golding's sources

CRAIG RAINE

Three axioms

1. Schoolboys on an island after an atomic war; Neanderthal man recreated, inside and outside, down to 'the little patch of hair over his big toe'; contemporary man prolonging his existence after death; a *Bildungsroman* whose settings range from a slum to a prisoner-of-war camp; the construction of a spire in the middle ages – despite thematic similarities, it is axiomatic that every Golding novel is different from its predecessors, each with a separate patent, each a new invention, as if Golding had decided to take the form at its word. No one's novels are more deliberately novel.

2. Set against this, though, another axiom – that all literary works have their sources, that all novels have navels, so to speak. Why has criticism hardly looked beyond Golding's own citations, *Coral Island* and Wells's *Outline of History*?

3. Then oppose to both a third axiom mischievously promulgated by Valéry in *Analects*: 'what has been believed by all, always and everywhere, has every likelihood of being untrue.' Which of the three axioms is true? Golding, whose *Lord of the Flies* systematically sets out to refute Ballantyne's sentimentality, would be drawn, I imagine, to Valéry's calculated provocation. But perhaps the axiom is trailing its coat so flamboyantly only because it doesn't have a leg to stand on.

What are Golding's sources? If he is father to a family of disturbingly different one-offs, who are the mothers? Is it possible to confront the pater familias with the odd maternity suit? I should like to propose a few plausible candidates. In *Free Fall*, for instance, there is a well known passage in which Sammy Mountjoy, after much intellectual circling, formulates a statement of polarities that seems central to Golding's fiction:

All day long the trains run on rails. Eclipses are predictable. Penicillin cures pneumonia and the atom splits to order. All day long, year in, year out, the daylight explanation drives back the mystery and reveals a reality usable, understandable and detached.

This is the world which is rational and operates according to scientific laws. But there is another world, quasi-mystical and anti-utilitarian:

> All day long action is weighed in the balance and found not opportune nor fortunate or ill-advised, but good or evil. For this mode which we must call the spirit breathes through the universe and does not touch it; touches only the dark things, held prisoner, incommunicado, touches, judges, sentences and passes on.

This dualism, with its Cartesian distinction between the world of extension and the world of the spirit, is one of which Sammy concludes: 'both worlds are real. There is no bridge.'

The crux is so characteristic, so individual, that one can almost run a finger over the hallmarks. It is odd, then, to encounter this twin in Aldous Huxley's *Antic Hay*:

> No, but seriously, Gumbril reminded himself, the problem was very troublesome indeed. God as a sense of warmth about the heart, God as exultation, God as tears in the eyes, God as a rush of power or thought – that was all right. But God as truth, God as $2+2=4$ – that wasn't so clearly all right. Was there any chance of their being the same? Were there bridges to join the two worlds?

Not an identical twin perhaps – Gumbril is less positive than Sammy, Golding more eloquent than Huxley – but the terms in which the problem is framed are strikingly similar. Yet will the bridge between Huxley and Golding take the weight of the source hunter? After all, in every other respect, *Antic Hay* (with its pneumatic trousers, femme fatale, and febrile farce) and *Free Fall* share no family resemblance and the metaphor of the bridge between different systems of thought isn't so rare. Does it help, if only tangentially, to note a similarity between *Pincher Martin*'s lust for Nat's girl and that of Anthony Beavis, in *Eyeless in Gaza*, for the girl of his awkward friend, Brian?

But what about *Crime and Punishment*, whose hero, Raskolnikov, begins as a free thinker determined to live in a world of 'daylight explanation', where a murder is neither good nor evil, simply 'opportune' or 'ill advised'? He ends, however, in the world of the spirit – touched, judged and sentenced by his own gagging conscience. To this one might add that Sammy and Raskolnikov share an interrogator – Halde and Porfiry, both of whom are a mixture of terror and compassionate understanding. Not that these general similarities would mean anything without the figure of Svidrigaylov, the man who commits suicide, unable to bear the knowledge that there are two worlds, both of them trivial. He unburdens himself to Raskolnikov:

> ghosts are, so they say, bits and pieces of other worlds, the beginning of them. There is no reason, of course, why a healthy man should see them, because a healthy man is, above all, a man of this earth, and he must, therefore, only live the life of this earth for the sake of order and completeness. But as soon as he falls ill, as soon as the normal earthly order of his organism is disturbed, the possibility of another world begins to become apparent, and the more ill he is, the more closely does he come into touch with the other world, so that when he dies, he goes straight to the other world.

Again, this is scarcely conclusive. However, Svidrigaylov immediately continues in a way that cannot help reminding the reader of Sammy Mountjoy's black vision in the broom cupboard:

> we're always thinking of eternity as an idea that cannot be understood, something immense. But why must it be? What if, instead of all this, you suddenly find just a little room there, something like a village bath-house, grimy, and spiders in every corner, and that's all eternity is. Sometimes, you know, I can't help feeling that that's probably what it is.

The plausibility of *Crime and Punishment* as a source is also increased by another reminiscence, this time of *Pincher Martin*, whose entire plot is encapsulated by the ruminating Raskolnikov:

> where was it I read about a man sentenced to death who, one hour before his execution, says or thinks that if he had to live on some high rock, on a cliff, and a ledge so narrow that there was only room enough for him to stand there, and if there were

bottomless chasms all round, the ocean, eternal darkness, eternal solitude, and eternal gales, and if he had to spend all his life on that square yard of space – a thousand years, an eternity – he'd rather live like that than die at once! Oh, only to live, live, live! Live under any circumstances – only to live!

On the other hand, to return to Sammy and the cupboard, there is the Henry James story, 'The Ghostly Rental', where the following passage occurs:

> 'Observe closely enough,' she once said, 'and it doesn't matter where you are. You may be in a pitch-dark closet. All you want is something to start with, one thing leads to another, and all things are mixed up. Shut me up in a dark closet and I will observe after a while, that some places in it are darker than others. After that (give me time), and I will tell you what the President of the United States is going to have for dinner.'

How far, if at all, does this parallel affect the status of *Crime and Punishment* as a source? On the face of it, Dostoevsky, a writer with more temperamental affinity to Golding, seems a likelier influence than Henry James. All the same, before we come out of the closet, we should emphasize that Svidrigaylov's version of eternity, even if it was Golding's starting point, doesn't go very far towards explaining what actually happens to Sammy. Sammy, in his strenuous efforts to explain the horror at the dark centre, never actually touches on the thing that bothers him about the darkness. What he has to confess is not what Halde wants him to confess, namely details of planned escapes. By ending *Free Fall* with the juxtaposition of the insane Beatrice and his release from the cupboard, Golding strongly implies the guilt in Sammy's heart of darkness, but earlier he has been much more explicit. It is, though, an ironic declaration which, at the time, is merely baffling: going off with Taffy, Sammy thinks to dismiss Beatrice with words that only attain their full meaning almost a hundred pages later: 'her only power now was that of the accuser, the skeleton in the cupboard; and in this bounded universe we can easily put paid to that.' This cliché, the skeleton in the cupboard, and all it might mean, is surely a source too? Perhaps, indeed, the primary source.

When Matty emerges from the fire at the beginning of *Darkness Visible*, does Golding intend us to recall Robert Southwell's poem, 'The Burning Babe'?

As I in hoary winter's night stood shivering in the snow,
Surprised I was with sudden heat which made my heart to glow;
And lifting up a fearful eye to view what fire was near,
A pretty babe all burning bright did in the air appear;
Who, scorched with excessive heat, such floods of tears did shed
As though his floods should quench the flames with which his tears
 were fed.
'Alas,' quoth he, 'but newly born in fiery heats I fry,
Yet none approach to warm their hearts or feel my fire but I!
My faultless breast the furnace is, the fuel wounding thorns,
Love is the fire, and sighs the smoke, and mercy blows the coals,
The metal in this furnace wrought are men's defiled souls,
For which, as now on fire I am to work them to their good,
So I will melt into a bath to wash them in my blood.'
With this he vanished out of sight and swiftly shrunk away,
And straight I called unto mind that it was Christmas day.

Clearly, it would be possible to argue that Matty was a more realistic, more sceptical and intelligent treatment of the concept of the incarnation than is usual among theologically-minded writers in the Christian tradition. Matty's struggle with the flesh, brilliantly and comically realized by Golding, may have been sparked off by Southwell's vivid and quirky poem.

Similarly, one might cite Kipling's 'The Knights of the Joyous Venture' as a possible source for *The Inheritors* – particularly since Kipling appears to anticipate Golding's mode of stylistic innocence which is one of the great joys of *The Inheritors*: 'he was yellow – not from sickness, but by nature – yellow as honey, and his eyes stood endwise in his head,' says Sir Richard Dalyngridge, describing a Chinaman seen for the first time, and sounding not a little like Lok. In 'The Knights of the Joyous Venture', Sir Richard and Hugh journey with Witta, the Norseman, to the coast of Africa, where, after a long sea voyage, they do battle with Devils 'covered with reddish hair'. The Devils are, of course, apes – though Sir Richard has to wait several hundred years to be enlightened by Dan, who has recently read 'The Gorilla Hunters – it's a continuation of Coral Island, sir'. The native population rewards the knights with vast quantities of gold, with the result that, on the homeward journey, they are afraid of almost everything:

> we were troubled for fear that the Wise Iron should fail us now that its Yellow Man had gone, and when we saw the Spirit still served us we grew afraid of too strong winds . . .'

Their fear of jeopardizing the cargo of gold makes the knights and the crew as paranoid as homo sapiens in The Inheritors, whom Lok describes as 'frightened of the air'.

It should be obvious already from this summary that Kipling's tale is remarkably like The Inheritors – if it was told entirely from the viewpoint, not of Neanderthal man, but of Tuami and Marlan. In each case, the unknown creature is perceived as a red devil. Golding, you could argue, has 'merely' shifted the viewpoint, just as, in his use of Wells's Outline of History, he has seized on Wells's supposition that Neanderthal man 'made no clear distinction between animate and inaminate things: if a stick hurt him, he kicked it'. In each case, however, you wonder if it actually matters – when you consider the example given by Wells and compare Golding's imaginative depth and reach, which transforms stagnant water to water which is 'not awake like the river or the fall but asleep'. More, Wells would have been incapable of Golding's astonishing negative capability (in the vulgar sense) which endows Neanderthal man with a fear of water – a fear whose cause Golding requires his reader to work out unassisted, so confident is he of his overall portrait. Given the importance of smell to the Neander-thaler, immersion in water and the subsequent loss of scent amounts to a kind of death, as Golding hints when Lok loses all trace of Fa and assumes she is dead.

Still, there are ideas in Wells which Golding builds on. Wells modifies the expert picture himself:

> for the little tribe Mr Worthington Smith described, there has been substituted, therefore, a family group under the leadership of one Old Man, and the suggestions of Mr Atkinson as to the behaviour of the Old Man have been worked into the sketch. Mr

Worthington Smith describes a squatting-place near a stream, because primitive man, having no pots or other vessels, must needs have kept close to a water supply, and with some chalk cliffs adjacent from which flints could be got to work. The air was bleak, and the fire was of great importance, because fires once out were not easily relit in those days. When not required to blaze it was probably banked down with ashes . . .

Golding rejects Wells's supposition that the Old Man was a tyrant who drove out the young men when they approached maturity, so that 'the fear of the Father passed by imperceptible degrees into the fear of the Tribal God'. On the other hand, he appears to accept Wells's version of Neanderthal woman:

the woman goddesses were kindlier and more subtle. They helped, they protected, they gratified and consoled. Yet at the same time there was something about them less comprehensible than the direct brutality of the Old Man, a greater mystery. So that the Woman also had her vestiture of fear for primitive man. Goddesses were feared. They had to do with secret things.

From Wells, too, perhaps, comes the idea of chopping off Pine-tree's finger:

a queer development of the later Palaeolithic and Neolithic Ages was self-mutilation. Men began to cut themselves about, to excise noses, ears, fingers, teeth and the like, and to attach all sorts of superstitious ideas to these acts.

In this one case, Golding tells us very little more. Elsewhere, his imagination floods Wells's sketch with colour and life: take, for instance, Chapter XII of Wells's *A Short History of the World*, 'Primitive Thought', which Golding also probably read. 'Primitive man probably thought very much as a child thinks, that is to say, in a series of imaginative pictures.' Who but a genius could transform this idea until it is possible for Fa to rebuke Lok with the crushing remark, 'You have fewer pictures than the new one'?

This consideration of Wells puts the whole idea of sources into proper perspective. They account for very little of any great work of art, however interesting they may be. Suppose, for example, that we knew for a certainty that 'The Knights of the Joyous Venture' lay behind *The Inheritors*: would it make the slightest difference to our appreciation of Golding's novel? H. G. Wells, whom we know Golding read, is only of importance because Golding read him and disagreed.

For myself, I believe that the real sources of Golding's novels are not Dostoevsky, Huxley, Henry James or Kipling. They are the books themselves, despite their manifest heterogeneity. This is Ralph running: 'once more Ralph dreamed, letting his skilful feet deal with the difficulties of the path.' In *The Inheritors* this becomes 'Lok's feet were clever.' But if their feet are clever, their brains are less so: both find consecutive ratiocination difficult. Ralph: 'A strange thing happened in his head. Something flittered there in front of his mind like a bat's wing, obscuring his idea.' Lok: 'there came a confusion in his head, a darkness; and then he was Lok again, wandering aimlessly by the marshes . . .' As Lok is to Mal, so Ralph is to Piggy. Ralph thinks in pictures too:

> By now, Ralph had no self-consciousness in public thinking but would treat the day's decisions as though he were playing chess. The only trouble was that he would never be a very good chess player. He thought of the littluns and Piggy. Vividly he imagined Piggy by himself, huddled in a shelter that was silent except for the sounds of nightmare.

In *Ulysses*, Stephen meditates on Eve: 'she had no navel. Gaze. Belly without blemish, bulging big, a buckler of taut vellum.' In my view, this is a good image of Golding as a novelist. In *Lord of the Flies*, he takes a group of civilized children and shows us that they are savages. In *The Inheritors*, he takes a family of savages and shows us that they are more truly civilized than homo sapiens. In *Pincher Martin*, he again inverts his previous idea: from a being, Lok, who can scarcely think, he presents us with a man who can only think, whose existence is predicated on thought. Pincher is completely self-centred, a living example of Descartes's *cogito* – 'I think therefore I am.' In *Free Fall*, he examines not so much the self-centred and selfish human being as the dark centre of the self. *The Spire* continues this debate from a different standpoint. Jocelin, inspired, loses his self in the larger purpose, which is the diagram of prayer – even if Golding finally insists on the necessary imperfection of such transcendence. This, as an account of how writers work, seems to me to be truer than the indebted modes wished on literature by critical procedures. Perhaps Valéry was right after all.

Golding's Pity

BARBARA EVERETT

Golding has called his most recent novel *The Paper Men*, and it is perhaps a paper book. Its theme and its effect are one. The first-person narrative, which describes a writer's attempts to evade his academic would-be biographer, in the process reveals both men as they are: literature and learning are to each really nothing but paper; and the forms of love and hatred that come to bind them together, isolating them from other people, are paper too (when the writer is at last apparently shot dead by the biographer the novel ends on the unfinished word *gu*). This diagnosis of egoism among superficially civilized men as emptiness or 'paperiness' has one notable side effect. It can be rather hard to remember if one has actually read the book, which is eerily forgettable – it dissipates in the mind like smoke. It is in short a paper book.

The self-reflectiveness of *The Paper Men* suggests usefully why Golding's work can be hard to talk about critically. The novels dissolve, on the one hand, into their own critique, which the interested can only re-echo; and on the other they take the form of theory's opposite, an undiscussable whole world peculiarly substantial in itself, thingy and definite. Even *The Paper Men*, if not Golding's most successful work, has this quality – one wouldn't discuss every novel's thinness in terms of its 'paperiness'; and the most memorable thing in it, a horribly striding solid silver Christ in an island church, has all Golding's distinctiveness of concept. The novels are strewn with highly memorable objects – a sprig of mistletoe (*The Spire*), a 'vintage two-seater', (*The Pyramid*), a love letter in a dustbin (*The Paper Men*); the stories themselves, in their contained limits, come to resemble these material properties, like a desert island, known as well as the back of a hand, or a recollected house-surrounded village green, or a prehistoric firelit cave, or a Regency ship in full sail for Australia. If Golding's novels are 'paper', they are paper boxes, with things inside – corners, secrets, ideas, allusions and perspectives; and the things stay in the mind, with their own glowing solidity.

Because of this love of the material or created, a Golding novel can give a pleasure close to that of a beautifully crafted handmade toy. This is a likeness Golding has himself used. When the narrator of *Pincher Martin* drowns on its second page, the transition is marked by a conscious image, perhaps itself an image of consciousness: a toy which consists of a glass jar, brightly lit as a stage set and of uncertain size, and holding a small figure that can be made to drown or to survive, just like Pincher himself; and the toy calls up in the narrator only a moral blankness suggestive of mean ruthlessness:

> By varying the pressure on the membrane you could do anything you liked with the glass figure which was wholly in your power.

Most of Golding's heroes, or villains, have an aspect from which they may be characterized as surrogates for the writer and reader in their full consciousness. There is always a double possibility: a book, like a life, may create or destroy – may liberate or may merely exercise power. It is this burden of deliberation in the novels which has led many critics to call them 'fables', the writer himself having adopted this term in discussing *Lord of the Flies*. The peculiarly 'thingy' or substantial nature of the novels has also made the word 'myth' popular more recently.

'Myth' and 'fable' are respectable concepts, but both can get in the way of seeing what a given book is actually doing. Almost all modern novels are, after all, marked by critical awareness. And the Novel's involvement with a world of real experience would make us look for some presentation of life as lived among things. There is room within the Novel for considerable questioning of its own means without its needing to be categorized as myth or fable. Mary McCarthy has neatly defined one extreme limit of the Novel form by locating its origins in the social circumstances that saw the rise of the newspaper: moreover, through the assumed etymology of its genre name, she relates the true novel to the world of 'news' itself. *The Paper Men* happens to be the most newspapery, the most socially realistic of all Golding's fictions, set (uncharacteristically) in the immediate present and taking the form of direct reportage by a novelist some of whose data – the beard, the fame – appear to belong to Golding himself. Yet this effect of near-journalistic world-touring jet-setting surface is intrinsic to the book's illusory quality. There is more and deeper human reality in *The Inheritors*, a book which is as near as makes no matter to being about animals. This does not prove that *The Paper Men* is a myth or fable; only that it is a novel capable of questioning the nature of that 'social reality' which novels are about. For there may be very different ideas, not only about what constitutes a novel, but about what constitutes social reality.

It can at least be agreed that Golding's fictions, the earlier in particular, enjoy the specifically novelistic diurnality and mundanity: that the daily hunt for food plays as important a part in *Lord of the Flies*, *The Inheritors* and *Pincher Martin*, just possibly with a certain irony, as it does in *Robinson Crusoe*, one of the first and most pseudo-literal novels that we have. Golding can moreover achieve a degree of mimetic reality, of fidelity to sense-experience, not surpassed in recent fiction. Most readers finish *The Spire* feeling that they can now go out and build one (an impression that can lead the critic to assume abnormal expertises in the novelist, or access to books of other men's expertises). What gets overlooked here is the fact that the sense of reality is not in itself identical with reality; that a medieval mason would be as bewildered by *The Spire* as would its readers by the actual necessity to build Salisbury Cathedral. All that needs to be imputed to the novelist is an unusual degree of the sense of reality, and an unusual capacity for creating it in the reader.

The sense of reality which we meet in Golding's fictions is more substantial (and not less, as we might expect of myth or fable) than is ordinary existence: only a certain permeability in the real makes existence possible for us at all. Golding's worlds are by contrast intense and coherent. Both these qualities are obtained by virtue of a characteristic distance—the novels take place as much 'long ago and far away' as is compatible with their also being not romance. The occasional weakened moments at which romance does take over (Simon confronting the Head, Goody Pangall's over-sweet charms) show how rarely theological fiction or historical romance is allowed to invade the novels – how severe and steady a control the writer maintains. In general Golding treats his times and places with assurance and authority: an assurance and authority deriving from the fact that he is using them as something near to metaphor. What is at issue is not the social data as such, but the human experiences which they manifest; and the distancing is the measure of the detachment from which the *merely* 'social' is viewed. The true social life may be lived on a rock, in a cupboard, up a spire; as a Neanderthal, as the twin of a female terrorist, even as a successful writer; in Pincher Martin's solitary greed, or Lok's defeated animal suffering. It begins with the lonely act of the writer writing, and finishes with the lonely act of the reader reading.

To say this is to say that the novelist's gift, as much as that of any other writer, is to find true images of feeling – a 'truth' definable here in terms of a life in which other human beings have unassailable reality. In this way the Novel shares a middle ground with the poem. Golding himself (like another excellent novelist, Kingsley Amis) might have chosen rather to distinguish himself in verse; just as even a poet as fine as Philip Larkin has made it plain that he might have preferred to excel as a novelist. What gets called, and to some degree rightly, an effect of fable or myth in Golding's novels may be merely the result of a structuring of feeling presented at extremity as in a poem: an extremity, that is, still compatible with the sense of the social existence of other human beings.

Golding's extraordinary power to convince, as a novelist, is indissociable from his ability to communicate feeling directly, as in a poem. His first novel, *Lord of the Flies*, enjoyed a success which none of the others has ever quite equalled (though there is richer and subtler writing in the work that followed it), perhaps simply because the book is Golding's most 'popular' poem – its public widened by its use of the Fall story and by its choice of children as protagonists. The children are a subject I want to return to later. Here it is enough to say that Golding as a schoolmaster evidently 'knew' children, and he invested the diagrammatic lines of his fable-story with a solidity and substance abstractions are rarely given. When the kneesocked, spectacled and doomed fat Piggy clambers backwards on to Golding's first page, the Home Counties and the jungle fused in his scenery, Just William is (to use Piggy's own phrase) 'caught up' between Eden and Apocalypse. Blake said that Eternity is in love with the productions of Time; in the case of Golding's small boys, the sense of the extreme embraces the solidly familiar. A response almost personal, almost affectionate, is evoked from the reader by the use of a complex of conventions at once social and literary; every likely reader of the novel has read 'children's stories', or romances, or has had children, or has at least been a child himself.

I am proposing that if one is defining the characteristic sense of substance in a Golding novel, that sense in fact derives from the burden of feeling which images come to communicate. The immediate *now* of the social will in Golding's fictions crystallize into the behaviours of a small prehistoric family community, or a group of medieval ecclesiastics and artisans joined in being destroyed by the cathedral spire they proudly erect, or the actors and musicians who put together an operetta in a small country town in England in the 1930s; and in all these cases, however vivid the social mimesis, what we remember is what we feel. To bring this about, Golding will take remarkable risks. It could be argued, for instance, that the true substance of *Pincher Martin* consists mainly in its last brief apparent coda, the few pages in which two tired human beings do what they can for the dead body, 'this poor officer . . . that poor derelict': a passage of feeling, extraordinarily solid in the rendering, to which the whole saga of Martin's spectral egoism has acted as hardly more than prologue by contrast. Conversely, a reader's difficulty in feeling anything for *The Paper Men* may derive from the writer's bold confinement of its two main characters to two men culpably unable to feel.

Golding's novels are perhaps fruitfully and refreshingly uneven. No other fiction written now seems so hard to judge; no other novels have so individual an amassment of successes and failures, of brilliancies and uncertainties, of solidities and 'paper men'. But the writing has its simplicities too. In his first and probably still most admired novel, Golding's sense of reality required a group of children unaccompanied by any adult, for whose efforts to live together we come to feel a peculiarly direct and intense emotion. I want to suggest that the books that follow are similarly charged with and able to illuminate feeling, and that the most generative of these feelings is the experience of *pity*.

The most tenderly 'pitiful' of Golding's novels in practice is *The Inheritors* – which starts, one might say, from the moment at which it begins to end, Lok's silent tears:

Suddenly, noiselessly, the lights became thin crescents, went out, and streaks glistened on each cheek. The lights appeared again, caught among the silvered curls of the beard. They hung, elongated, dropped from curl to curl and gathered at the lowest tip.

'The People', represented here by Lok's little family-community, have been hunted down by the arriving New Men; Lok himself, at last inheriting the role of leading male, has contributed to their destruction by ignoring the advice of his far wiser mate, and insisting on trying to recapture a child she knows to be lost. Loneliness and grief kill Lok, the last survivor, in his turn.

The 'noiselessly' in Golding's description has its importance. As a writer, Golding has many brilliant talents, but perhaps lacks a marked personal style: it is not precisely by 'the words' (as with many literary artists) that the novels most hold us. What is remarkable is how much the writer achieves in terms of intensity and authenticity without this personal style. The lack sometimes bears fruit in the assumption of other men's styles (Golding is an actor, a master of pastiche: *Rites of Passage* in particular is a rhetorical tour-de-force in the elegance with which Talbot and Colley, two men socially far apart, are finally through the private shame of their journals 'brought together'). But it can also issue in another kind of effect, an art of luminous silence.

The story of the People has as its central consciousness Lok, who is their clown and their least intelligent member; his very lack of cleverness wholly unfits him for that part of leading male which he is called on to play. Of them all, he is (one might say) furthest from speech. The People's intelligence is sensitive and telepathic, and though utterances are given to them, the words read almost like glosses of glance and touch and intimation. Lok and the others lack that defined delimited ego which – the novel suggests – develops its own advanced system of verbal communication; they cannot therefore hope to defend themselves against the New Men, who possess both nervous aggression and the language to serve it. *The Inheritors* is, as a result, essentially a 'silent' book, which articulates what we equally tacitly recognize as (in Auden's phrase) 'the sadness of the creatures'. What speaks through Lok and the others is our pity, our capacity to register in detachment the suffering of the creaturely estate, which men and animals have in common. Lok, crying, weeps for the small family and tribe he loved, and for himself as its lonely survivor. But the movement of the prose here, for the first time withdrawn from Lok's consciousness to observe his tears and find them 'beautiful', suggests a larger theme: his grief is also a lament for people as human *things*, naked to observation as animals are in zoos. Lok and his family lack that covering garment of secretiveness and deceit which is the chief shield and two-edged weapon of the New Men (since words permit lying): like the ambiguous knife, able at once to make and to wound, which is being carved at the end by the New Men's Tuami, the artist in love.

The 'pity' of *The Inheritors* is not in Lok's tears alone; it is in our witness and understanding of what causes them. The book requires the participation of the observer, the visitor to the Zoo – the reading self which, at first wholly absorbed in the People, at last comes to recognize itself in the New Men, our direct and destructive ancestors. The story itself explains our double ancestry in terms of two children of the People, one eaten by the New Men and the other likely when full grown to interbreed with them. But the whole book explains it too in the way that it involves the affection, the complicity, and then the shame of the reader. As a result of this double inheritance *The Inheritors* is 'pitiful'; but it betrays at the same time that moral ambiguity of pity which by its conflicts generates much of the charge of Golding's writing.

Pity is in itself now a somewhat dated concept – it has been displaced by *compassion*. Though a more attractive, even democratic quality, *compassion* helps to show that words profit by staying definite and limited; for the larger resonance of the more modern *compassion* not only entails a faint pretentiousness, it has lost the earlier term's sharp-edged morality. Not merely sharp-edged but (like Tuami's knife) double-edged; for *pity* has in fact a moral ambiguity which no doubt led to the adoption of a vaguer, kinder term. The derivation of *pity* had originally united it with *piety* (the shared tenderness of the People is more religious than the cruel ceremonies of the New Men). But by the time Blake, in the later eighteenth century, is advising his reader in his *Songs of Innocence* to 'cherish pity, lest you drive an angel from your door', the word had come to hold an irony or reserve made plainer in 'The Human Abstract' of *Experience* ('Pity would be no more/If we did not make somebody Poor'). Blake's first image of the angel may recall Shakespeare's great vision of pity, two centuries earlier, 'like a naked new-born babe,/Striding the blast': a vision which the dramatist chose to give to his king-murdering pitiless Macbeth. Throughout the modern period, pity has been a moral concept true to the world of experience that nourishes it, a world of power, hierarchy and status; and for this reason it is ambiguous. Insofar as it makes us identify ourselves with those sufferingly below us, it is generous and humble; but insofar as it encourages us to believe that some creatures *are* 'below us', it is arrogant and capable of savagery. Pity is therefore both naked babe and angry angel, an image of the heart's revenges dreamed and feared by the murderer of a king.

When Lok weeps, something as much ape as man suffers – and we suffer with him that pain of the animals so hard to endure because inarticulate, out of reach or inconsolable. But at the same time the light-reflecting water 'caught among the silvered curls of the beard' shows him for a moment like the sable-silver-bearded ghost of Hamlet's murdered father, crying by night for vengeance. Lok is after all a King, who has failed his People. This double image of the Neanderthal, this questioning of pity by an ironic ranging from 'low' to 'high', holds much of the intensity and intellectual activity of Golding's novels. It is the very fact of the range of levels that involves the irony. If these fictions manage almost always to balance their pathos with a vivid humour (even *The Inheritors*, the most painful, can be touchingly funny) the reason for this tragi-comic poise is that pity moves Golding's stories towards the forms of mock- heroic: a serious game in which scales and stances continually reverse, and the pitiable and the pitiful change roles in a moment.

This might be restated by saying that Golding's fictions care a good deal for human dignity. Pity is a private and inward experience; if translated into a fully public and social context it tends to involve a situation of *shame*. Shame (which is perhaps conceived of as a kind of 'fallen' pity, just as pity may become a 'fallen' love) – shame and the closely-related dignity are criteria near to the bone of Golding's novels. Only innocence prevents Lok from dying of shame, as – most notably – Colley does after him, in *Rites of Passage*.

This, possibly Golding's best-written novel, gets its coolly glittering surface from the sense of equal withdrawal from both its protagonists: Talbot and Colley, two young men of very different social class and background who in the end are joined, not in friendship but in exchange of shame; Talbot at least learns to feel a little shame for his pleasures, Colley has at least been given a little joy by his shame. But Colley's abasement finds many echoes in Golding's other novels. A good many readers of *Lord of the Flies* have probably come to think of Piggy as its hero, and are led to do so, one suspects, because among all the more theoretically glamorous prep-school children Piggy alone has the definitively human physical shortcomings that focus sympathy on him: fat, pale, wheezy, slow, and finally nearly blind. He is so abjectly 'shameful'.

It is from the resonances of pity and shame that stories by Golding in themselves not much more than modestly anecdotal can acquire such odd and ironic depths. *The Pyramid* is of course lighter than *The Inheritors*, but it has something of the earlier book's affection and holding power. These depend on the way the story's feeling seems to centre on the two Evelyns, the book's essential achievement (though the narrator's mother is wonderfully evoked); and the two Evelyns are characters who have – for all their social context – something in common with Lok and the People in their peculiar haunting physicality of presentation. It's hard to forget the gliding ball-bearinged erotic walk of Evie, at once ludicrous and impressive; or the flexing trembling knees of the ageing 'artist' Evelyn, kindest and most intelligent of well-bred clowns. The two Evelyns are far apart in social class. The adolescent narrator, Oliver, looks down on young Evie Babbacombe, who comes from the village slum and seems well on the way to developing into an amateur whore; just as he looks up to Evelyn de Tracy, who comes down from London to produce, as best he can, the terrible snobbish small-town operetta pointedly called *The King of Hearts*. But the two Evelyns, though unequal in status, are equal in reacting to Oliver with feeling of a truthfulness well beyond his casual pitying social use of them. Evie, who gives him her body, revenges his hard-heartedness with a mocking and public contempt; Evelyn, who falls in love with him, wearily yet generously frees him from the conventional 'passion' that is making him miserable. Both Evelyns are pitiable by virtue of their intense, their in fact humiliating existence in their own bodies. When Oliver roars with laughter at Evelyn photographed in a tutu his laughter is ignorant but in a way innocent; Evelyn is after all a comic character. Yet acceptance of themselves gives the two Evelyns an honesty and truth of feeling more genuinely 'pitiful' than anything the student Oliver has yet learned. Each goes off into the darkness with an odd dignity the narrator as yet knows nothing about.

These reversals often give Golding's novels their moral kick. I've already mentioned the startling effect of following Pincher Martin's unremitting egoism (which heroically digests even the clinging foot of the limpet alive) with the quiet talk of Campbell and Davidson, doing what they can for 'all these poor people'. The story's hero is a nonentity, the two bit-part players are entire men. Jocelin, the heroic ego of *The Spire*, is a far richer character than Pincher, with more to him both as a person and as a narrator. But he too shows what he is in the first pages of the book, sending his overpowering 'arrows of love' after all and sundry and steadfastly overlooking Father Adam at his elbow, to Jocelin's consciousness merely 'the little man':

> he has no face at all. He is the same all round like the top of a clothespeg. [Jocelin] spoke, laughing down at the baldness with its fringe of nondescript hair.
> 'I ask your pardon, Father Adam. One forgets you are there so easily!' And then laughing aloud in joy and love – 'I shall call you Father Anonymous!'
> The chaplain still said nothing.

There is a kind of pity, clearly, in that 'laughing down', just as there is in the asking of pardon; and it must be these that earn him at last the right to the pity of Father Anonymous, who alone stays to nurse Jocelin when he is dying.

The ironies, and more than ironies, with which these two novels conclude are a feature of all Golding's earlier endings. The naval officer of *Lord of the Flies* thinks himself adult because he can 'distance' himself (it is the last word of the novel) from the grief of the children, by which he is 'moved and a little embarrassed'; the children, who have experienced in their own being 'the end of innocence', know more than he does, and know it crucially.

Something of the naval officer's false poise attends the New Men who at the end of *The Inheritors* look back, as the reader too is ironically invited to do, and see the defeated gentle People as dangerous animals. These vertigos of perspective brought about by pity and shame always include a balancing dimension of tough comedy. The 'King of Hearts' section of *The Pyramid* is flawlessly funny; and a touching and pungent short story like 'Clonk Clonk' converts a dark situation into comic romance: somewhere early in human history in a little community living under a volcano, the weak but artistic boy named Chimp by the other men (as it might be, the rugger toughs) suffers painfully from social shame before the wisdom of the Head Woman makes a happy male Cinderella out of him. However sharp the pathos, this amused anecdotal quality always has a place in Golding's writing; the fusion of pain and humour constitutes a part of its essential character.

Golding's gift may be said to be the construction of worlds that hold at their centre, rightly and justly, characters that are the essential creations of pity: Piggy, Lok, the two Evelyns, even the daemonic but forgivable Jocelin. Where these conditions don't obtain an interesting idea can go wrong. *Free Fall* is in design the writer's most ambitious study of pity and shame, yet it seems to communicate its intentions to curiously few readers; for all its rich detail, the novel is lifeless. Its striking idea is therefore perhaps worth mentioning here. An artist seeks for meaning in his life's experience, recalled fragmentarily and achronologically in the narrative. Three incidents haunt him, all private and distressing in a life of much public success and some happiness. While telling of his poor and illegitimate but often vividly happy childhood, he mentions a sad small incident in it: the backward child who shared his desk at infant school was one day so overcome by attention shown her by a distinguished visitor to the school that she wetted on the floor in her misery. Much later in the story the artist recalls a second incident of pain and squalor, this time not trivial to him. In middle life, married and 'distinguished' himself and now returned from the war, the artist returns to his old village and visits, in the asylum that was once the Great House there, the woman whom he had (so he tells us earlier in the narrative) loved, idealized and betrayed: and in her horror at his presence poor wretched Beatrice behaves precisely as did Minnie years before. The great pain of this encounter, only intensified by its association with the first, is confronted and resolved by a third memory of shame. During the war the narrator, imprisoned in a German camp, was frightened to the point of hysteria by a threat of torture which proved in practice no more than imprisonment in a dark cupboard. It is the memory of this experience which brings liberation to the narrator.

When first set free from his cupboard, the artist Mountjoy had stumbled out into the camp and set about creating what would become the greatest of all his works, the portraits of his fellow prisoners as 'Kings of Egypt' – after the iconic cigarette-card images of worldly glory the artist had in childhood so craved for. Mountjoy cannot, that is, stand clear of that involvement with the world which enriches his art even as it unclarifies his spiritual progress; conventional religion remains a world apart to him. He must find his illumination in experience itself. This illumination takes the form of the enigmatic sentence allowed to end the narrative, words first spoken in apology by a camp guard concerning the Inquisitor (a man as much admired as feared by Mountjoy): 'The Herr Doctor does not know about peoples.' Mountjoy's love for his Beatrice had always expressed itself, like the Inquisitor's interest in *him*, as an intense desire to 'know' her. But perhaps what the Doctor does not know about people is that they cannot be known. They may only – it is the design of the novel to suggest – be other things than known. They may, for instance, be understood: by something like that feeling power of imagination which helps us to read books about other human beings. By suffering an extremity of shame in the camp Mountjoy has become one with Beatrice in her experience of the abject. Their reconciling also brings together the 'distinguished artist' Mountjoy with the pathetic almost forgotten backward child Minnie, and so puts an end to that lifelong flight from poverty and its squalors by which we may interpret the artist's restless ambition, enabling him at last perhaps to forgive even himself. This reconciliation works in *Free Fall* by virtue of that exchange of vulnerabilities which is essentially what I have called the process of *pity* in these fictions.

If this impressive concept never quite comes alive, it is for reasons the writer himself hardly needs instructing on. In the course of the narrative Mountjoy voices a moral dilemma: he cannot imagine a

Beatrice *both* innocent enough to be able to forgive him, *and* experienced enough to know what there is to be forgiven. His dilemma reflects the ancient (in fact Augustinian) difficulty of reconciling the goodness of God with his omniscience. The problem could be restated a third time at the level of a practising novelist's technical difficulty. For the artist in pity there seem to be only two kinds of protagonist: the innocent and the knowing. The trouble with the knowing is that they act fictionally as they do morally: they absorb everything into their ego. As a result, in *Free Fall* we see only Mountjoy's world, which has a tendency to seem unreal; for all its distressing events, everything in it is 'beautiful', like a hand-crafted toy. Though the last encounter of Mountjoy and Beatrice is imagined with harsh truth, she remains in herself all the same a toy woman. But innocent characters have their problems too. Like Father Anonymous in *The Spire*, they may tend towards nonentity, even their names, like Matty's surname in *Darkness Visible*, becoming unclear; or they may induce, like the People of *The Inheritors*, a certain calm plotlessness because like poetry (to quote Auden again) they 'make nothing happen'.

For the novelist of pity there is one perfect protagonist, the child on the brink of adolescence. Because he is by then well equipped in human knowledge (it is experience he lacks) he is therefore guilty: the inventive orthodoxy of Golding's first published novel, *Lord of the Flies*, is to make its plot out of precisely that sequence. But because the child *is* still a child, our natural protective or pitying relation keeps him 'unaccountable'. Knowledge and innocence exist in him in an exquisite poise; Ralph experiences, as well as a child can, the 'fall through the air', yet this ruthless story never loses a kind of tenderness, even a kind of lightness. Therefore this first brilliant fiction hit a centre, and held a balance, that earned the great popularity it has enjoyed, and made it justly a modern classic (though the writer has perhaps done subtler and more interesting work since); and one can't overestimate the importance, in this success, of Golding's choice of boys of twelve years old for his protagonists.

The 'childishness' of Ralph and Piggy, Simon and Jack gives their history a dimension of mock-heroic or grave burlesque. The horror of the political side of the action, which needs no stress here, is both sharpened and lightened, made personal and strange, by being played out by little boys. The power-politics which have their place in a study of pity, and the reign of terror they bring with them, retain their ugliness but at the same time (as, ironically, the naval officer sees; wrong about many things, he is right about this) they are reduced to a kids' game, to nightmarish child's play. The fact that the children are children has something of the moral effect crystallized by the moment in the next novel, *The Inheritors*, when Lok, watching with bright interest an arrow move towards him, thinks it an offering. The children's innocence diminishes the 'adulthood' their corruption is helplessly in love with.

But *Lord of the Flies* does not work only at this public and political level. Ralph weeps at the end for 'the fall through the air of the true, wise friend called Piggy', a fall which focuses all their wretchedness. It may be that now Ralph has in fact grown up, its sign being that he is able to deceive himself sentimentally. For the book makes us feel that he is weeping not for Piggy, but for the loss of a dream or an illusion: the belief that he and Piggy *were* 'true' or 'wise', that they could have lived up to some romantic ideal of friendship. The novel is also a story of feelings and loyalties, and Ralph carries for a moment a mocking pathetic shadow of full-grown heroes like Othello and his 'the pity of it'; the children discover horrifyingly the limits of the life of feeling, and in the end Jack hunts Ralph with a stick 'sharpened at both ends', love converted into hatred in his hands. Golding sketches in the boys' relationships with fine economy and delicacy. Briefly, Simon is the only one capable of solitude and impersonality; and within the essentially social bearings the boys impose on their situation, even this virtue takes on an aspect of weakness: he 'faints'. Of the other three leading characters, Ralph, the central personage or 'boy with fair hair' – the romance version of the ordinary decent soul – is at once attracted to his equal and opposite, the dark and helplessly power-loving Jack. The struggle which Ralph and Jack engage in over the opposed claims of house building and hunting quietly and ironically echoes the terms of many marital battles and male-female confrontations. The only role left for the intelligent, sympathetic and wholly undesirable Piggy is that of the unrequited lover, trailing along after Ralph (' "Wait a minute . . . I got caught up" '). And his undoubted if unimaginative shrewdness works not, as it should, to reconcile Ralph morally with Jack, but to keep them separate: Piggy is jealous of Jack as well as frightened of him, and indeed Jack is dangerous in every way. In the first pages of the story, Piggy 'takes to' Ralph, the boy with fair hair – the archetypal English romance hero, the friendly, charming, attractive and above all *average* boy; and Ralph responds by casually performing his first significant action in the book. He betrays to the large jeering social group of boys, Jack chief among them, the secret name confided to him by Piggy, the would-be chum. From that moment the boys on the island are finished.

Golding's children act out the childish pitifulness of the grown man. We don't, I think, necessarily 'pity' Adam and Eve, nor the modern states as they discover their own powers of barbarism. But the novel's children we do pity, in their advance into adulthood and history as across a minefield. This is because the book always balances the extremity of its action with a humanity or tenderness, a quality of pity in the writing. There is even at one point of *Lord of the Flies* a long descriptive passage which in its dual movement comes curiously close to that double working of pity which I have tried to outline here. At the end of the ninth chapter, Simon, the only one of the children capable of true altriusm, has climbed the mountain and released from its bonds the dead body of the parachutist which, lodged among the rocks at the top and seeming to exact a horrible obeisance to itself, has frightened the children away from their signal fire; but when he comes down to tell the others they have nothing to fear, they drag him into their mad hunting dance and kill him. An extended descriptive passage begins here. The wind, rising by night, dislodges the parachutist:

> On the mountain-top the parachute filled and moved; the figure slid, rose to its feet, spun, swayed down through the vastness of wet air and trod with ungainly feet the tops of the high trees; falling, still falling, it sank towards the beach and the boys rushed screaming into the darkness.

But this wind-carried downward descent that creates terror in the children is completed by a further tenderer movement of natural powers. Gradually, as the night wears on, the tide turns, and the withdrawing water catches and lifts the other body, that of the child on the beach: bearing it, under the 'constellations', out to sea, 'gently', 'softly, surrounded by a fringe of inquisitive bright creatures'.

The Impersonality of William Golding: Some implications and comparisons

JOHN BAYLEY

The novel as an art form is designed, in a very particular way, to give satisfaction. The concept of satisfaction, merging with that of self-satisfaction, could indeed be said to be the hallmark of the form, its badge of office. Not for nothing did Tolstoy in *War and Peace* use the word *samodovolnost* – not often but with an unmistakable resonance. Nor is it surprising that we take farewell of Nikolai Rostov, in a memorable passage at the end of the novel, as he grows more and more into the pleasant, and pleasantly self-satisfying, habit of sitting by himself in his library and reading his books for a certain number of hours every day.

Satisfaction arises, and appears to be shared both by novelist and reader, from the peculiar nature of the intimacy between them. It is this which William Golding forgoes in his novels. The consequences, in terms of the power and originality of his art, seem to me so unobtrusively remarkable that I should wish to approach that art in the light of the much more frequent transaction that takes place between novelist and reader – a transaction so usual that neither party is necessarily conscious of it. Golding's novels admit no intimacy between himself and his reader. And this is a singular circumstance, for the opposite situation occurs so easily and naturally that novelist and reader are, as it were, accustomed to accept it without question.

It would not be too much to say that the 'reality' of most fiction depends on such an intimacy. The feel of Scott in this respect is inimitable. His sense of achievement in getting the past down on paper, at so many sheets per day, is reciprocated by the reader's steadily augmented complacency in the operation of the process. The past comes alive, with a life that is of course wholly *sui generis*, but which depends on the relationship – equally close as smooth – between the writer who is creating and the reader who is accepting it. In living, we could say, things only appear to happen, whereas in fictions such as this they really do.

If this sense of things really happening, people really existing, depends on our close rapport with the novelist, it must also be the reason for the unexampled subjectivity of our response to the novel form. We 'don't like him' or 'can't get on with him', meaning the novelist himself, is a sentiment that leaves open and to one side a judgement of the novel he has actually written. Subjectivity is a condition of that conviction and acceptance which mutually complacent intimacy between ourselves and the author can bring. Our favourable subjectivity of response brings into being our sense of objective truth in the writer's creation; or, in other words, we cannot believe the man without feeling at home with him. And to enjoy a novelist is by extension to enjoy oneself, as the writer appears very well to know.

In *War and Peace* Tolstoy goes so far as to make self-satisfaction the key not only to the reader's enjoyment but to the proper discharge of living in general. In Conrad (*Lord Jim*, *The Shadow Line*, even *The Heart of Darkness*), in Trollope or Dickens, in Balzac and Zola and George Eliot and Henry James, all things are in their own ways made perfect by personality working on and through art and language. In the powers of creating and conveying satisfaction Scott at one end of the century and James Joyce at the other are blood brothers – *Old Mortality* and *Ulysses* superb and similar creations. In either case the language of personality cannot help but create a world, a solid world of mysterious perfection, in which art cannot conceal, cannot indeed but enhance, the pleasure taken by the author in his creation. That pleasure is not only compulsive in itself but creates the author for us parallel to his own creation, and by what seems the same art and the same means.

And that is unique to the novel. Poetry shows us nothing like it. Can we imagine Shakespeare, or Shakespeare's pleasure, from the story of Hamlet, or of Benedick and Beatrice, or from some such felicity as the Prince's 'This is the English not the Turkish court; not Amurath an Amurath succeeds, but Harry, Harry?' But it is Jane Austen herself who is revealed in the state of mind of Anne Elliott or the discomfiture of Miss Bates, no less than Charlotte Brontë in the situations of Jane Eyre or Lucy Snowe. This is bound to occur where the novel is – as it usually is – a weapon and a refuge for its creator, a justification and a reward. To put the matter at its crudest, the alcoholism of a Raymond Chandler or a Malcolm Lowry is transformed in their art into a species of higher gratification, the rich attribute of a self-portrait all the more accomplished for being largely involuntary.

Judgement of the novel becomes difficult, if not impossible, in cases where the reader is unable to tolerate or cooperate with the writer's satisfaction. The element of 'can't get on with him' may be nobody's fault, but a novelist who is pleased with himself (or herself), and a reader who is not, produces an impasse hardly to be found in any other form of art. Sensing the importance of this, D. H. Lawrence tried to get round it by urging us to trust the tale and not the teller: futile advice where most novels – including his own – are concerned, for it is the teller who is revealed by the manner and purpose for which he creates the tale. The post-Lawrentian novelist, like Doris Lessing or Margaret Drabble, whose self-affirmation fails to carry the reader along, has no tale to fall back on.

What sort of novels are outside this process? Golding's are, it seems to me, and further comparison may help to show why. He shares with Dostoevsky the power to disappear from any situation as he creates it. Form in his work itself eliminates not only the artist who fashions it but the self which the novelist normally gives to things, and with which he becomes inescapably identified. Dostoevsky ('*Form, Form*', he keeps exhorting himself in his notebooks) has many ways of eliminating himself. As a youthful author he promised himself and the critics that his own 'ugly mug' would be nowhere visible in what he wrote. One of the ways he achieved this was by an extension to the dimension of form of the idea of the 'double', which always obsessed him. As a man who lives in different worlds ceases to have his own personality, so an author who uses an existing literary form, but in the process dissolves and disintegrates it, ceases to exhibit any of those complex satisfactions which make up the reader's image of the novelist's world and the novelist's being. Dostoevsky referred to his method as 'the deeper realism', in contrast with such self-conscious realists as Balzac and his successors, who inhabit the worlds they have constructed with such solid artifice.

7. Ann and William Golding in Stockholm, 1983

8. Receiving the Nobel Prize from King Gustaf.
(Photo Leif R. Jannson, Svenskt Pressfoto)

This deeper realism could be described in terms of the properties physicists now associate with matter itself, that matter whose solidity in classic fictions is a paradigm of their readers' sense of it in fact. The intensity of the relative mode causes matter to slip, slide, collapse, and reform. 'Reality strives towards fragmentation' says one of Dostoevsky's narrators. In terms of the deeper realism men, like matter, have to be somewhere but have nowhere to go, whereas in the classic novel all persons have their appointed place in their proper historic and geographical environment. We live in Dostoevsky's world under the floorboards of a non-existent house, and *shatost* – radical insecurity and instability – is his equivalent of Tolstoyan *samodovolnost* – self-assurance and self-satisfaction. Dostoevsky's method – to infiltrate and undermine some conventional literary reality, so that it ceases to operate in its solid and previously reassuring guidelines of artifice is, as I shall try to show, parallel to Golding's own more inconspicuous practice.

Dostoevsky's early novel *Poor People* is in this way a kind of parody of Gogol's *The Overcoat*. (We have all come from under that garment, Dostoevsky is supposed to have said: if true, a typically ambiguous statement.) His poor clerk has a continuous and unending, what Russian critics call an 'imperfective', existence, while Gogol's poor clerk is a proper creation, to be introduced, *seen*, and taken away. The ultimately satisfying thing about Gogol's Akaky Akakyevich is that he could only exist in a novel, in which his peculiarities are fixed in an immortal rapport with those of his creator. The planning and making of his overcoat are like the manufacture of the arms of Achilles: its loss is as final as the fall of Troy. Dostoevsky's power of removing the achievement of the personal from his characters and their stories appears in an even more striking way in a quasi-documentary novel, *The House of the Dead*. All other accounts of the life of a Russian prison camp, for example Solzhenitsyn's, or Varlaam Shalamov's *Kolyma Tales*, depend upon the presence of the author-narrator at the centre of the conditions he describes and makes live for us. But grim as are these records, which their talented authors have raised to the level of great art, they cannot hold a candle to Dostoevsky's masterpiece in its capacity both to inflict sheer overwhelming oppression on the reader, and to free him into unexpected moments of redemption or joy. We stand outside the other stories, while Dostoevsky has the secret of involving us totally in *The House of the Dead*. Like a novelist revealed by the work of which he is owner and inhabitant, Solzhenitsyn and Shalamov earn, as it were, the right to own their camps by undergoing with their fellows all that was there, while at the same time becoming their own man by writing about it. Dostoevsky's hero, on the other hand, remains a disembodied voice under the prison floor. Although the author himself knew and felt all he describes, his secret is *not* to say, not even to imply: 'I am the man, I suffered, I was there.' The more disembodied Dostoevsky's stories are the more disquietingly they involve us.

And something comparable seems to be happening in Golding's novels. Their secret is in their lack of build-up of a world with a complete inner coherence of its own based on the world view, and thus on the personality, of the author – Graham Greene, Evelyn Waugh, George Orwell, whoever it may be. Such complete and satisfying situations – enigmas and salvations, degradations and nightmares (like that at the end of *A Handful of Dust*) take a shadowy form in the background of a Golding novel, but then vanish in the common light of daily muddle and daily necessity. The process un-fixes, too, any idea we might get of the author's special individuality. It dissolves in the same light. Dostoevsky's grand effects of radical instability and contradiction, extending to his historic personality as a great writer, are, naturally enough, not present here. In Golding's *The Paper Men* we glimpse, among other things, the irony of a situation in which the critic biographer seeks to possess the writer by identifying him *as* a writer.

Other novelists can be readily identified or recognized in Golding's work. The use he makes of them is highly original, but the common factor in each case is the completely unobtrusive dissolution of the predecessor's particular sort of literary reality. Towards the end of *Free Fall* Sammy Mountjoy, talking at the asylum to his alienist friend Kenneth, says: 'People don't seem to be able to move without killing each other.' On the face of it a sufficiently banal remark, yet it acts as a sudden revelatory pointer to the novel's form and mechanism. In the world of artificial made-up tragedy it is literally true that people cannot move without killing each other. Hamlet stabs Polonius through the arras, meaning to kill the King,

and drives Ophelia into madness and drowning. Claudius
accidentally poisons the one being he loves. In the context of tragedy
we take these things for granted, 'enjoying' them in a literary way
which is abruptly made strange by the creepy appositeness of
Sammy's definition. In a POW camp he has himself suffered the
process in a nightmarish and farcical way, shut up by his interroga-
tors in a broom cupboard, about which he has to feel his way in total
darkness.

That scene is of course one frequently repeated in Golding's work,
a scene in which movement, and its accompanying gestures and
explorations is depersonalized and distorted, so that our image of the
individual forming himself out of his environment as a dancer forms
himself out of the steps and rhythm of the dance, is blanked off.
Stylized in art, movement becomes the essential ingredient of
personality. But in *Lord of the Flies* a corpse drops from the
stratosphere on its parachute, and, tangled in the growth of a desert
island, mimics the movements of life. Pincher Martin gropes his
place in consciousness by blind suction, like a limpet on a stone. The
Pharaoh on his sacred run to bless the fields in *The Scorpion God*, his
portliness swaying and puffing about him, insults our preconception
of what a Pharaoh's movements should be like. Rituals of being are
thrown into reverse.

An elegant variation inspires *Rites of Passage*, whose title itself
draws attention to the process. Talbot's verbal style seems his own,
and is so in his own view, but it embodies the same conventional
outlook as do the stage gestures and speech of Miss Brocklebank
during the seduction. 'We were all borne along upon a tide of
melodrama' in which the madly uncoordinated movements of lust
inside the tiny 'hutch' loom magnified by the jocular attempts of
Talbot's diction to get them under control. The ship (not named, no
personality) is both a stage on which parts are played, and a setting
for blind unpredictable killing movements. In *The Paper Men* a
graphic scene of movement on what the narrator thinks to be a
precipice is imploded by the realization that no precipice was there.
The narrator, the talented writer, creates such things, which are
reduced to the movement of his fingers on the typewriter, and the
murderous silent damage he does to himself and others outside his
genius and his books.

Some comparisons will show how intensive and original is Golding's vision here and how other novels contrast with his, while at the same time giving to his own world a kind of background of stability and a scale of difference. In Robert Louis Stevenson's *Treasure Island*, young Jim Hawkins both sees others and behaves in terms of literary action, which Stevenson's skill renders with peculiar vividness. In his fight on board the schooner with Israel Hands, Jim fires his pistol involuntarily as the coxswain's knife, thrown from below, pins his skin and sleeve to the mast. His enemy falls overboard and presently appears through the clear water of the bay, shot and drowned on the sandy bottom, with a fish or two whipping past. For many young readers it must be their first experience of the power of words to convey visual reality. In *Lord of the Flies* there is nothing like it, for the narrative tension of that novel holds the appalling nature of visual commitment just below the level of the reader's awareness. It is, for Golding, something too serious to be invented; and the consequence is a power of impersonal dispassion which broods over the events of his novel and makes their nature abundantly clear. Stevenson, on the other hand, reveals his own hand by self-indulgence, for he cannot let well alone. The coxswain's previous victim, thrown overboard by Jim, presently appears on the bottom too, with his bald head across the legs of the man who had killed him. Stevenson's interest in violence is revealed as a *personal* matter.

The contrast is between the reader's readiness to see action through the writer's description, and thus be in close touch with the writer's own 'readerliness' – his imagination and personality at work in a book world – and the refusal of a writer like Golding to satisfy the reader's expectation of a novel's choreography of action into spectacle. It is the difference between 'reality', which is a created matter, and 'actuality', which is not. Evil, for example, can be accommodated by reality as an accepted part of the total creation the writer offers: in Golding it remains unassimilated; unassimilable by, and as, art. The unspeakable Sophy, in *Darkness Visible*, has a private vision of her small kidnap victim, and what she will do to him, which is so real to her that the reader recoils from it utterly, and from the fact that she thinks it is taking place, as in her head. Both author and reader seem wholly outside this scene, as in several of Golding's, with no way of cooperating, visually or actively, with what this third – external – person is doing. Actuality is like that.

Although *Treasure Island* is no more 'a boy's book' than *Lord of the Flies*, Stevenson's limitations, in any genre, are apparent in his imagination of action as literature. His strongest suit is his own relation to it, which is his sense of Jim Hawkins's relation to Silver, or David Balfour's to Alan Breck in *Kidnapped*. As Henry James perceived, he both sees through and admires his ruthless men of action, who escape as it were, from literature through the intensity of the personal bond he feels with them. Without it, and the reader's ensuing sense of Stevenson the man, his achievement would be much slighter, for he has no way of impersonalizing and analysing the matter that excites him to creation.

It is arguable that Golding forgoes literary reality for the sake of the actual, for a process in which impersonality is not so much a premise as a by-product. Modern critics tell us that genre is inescapable, and that in commenting on fiction's relation to life we are merely choosing between different sorts of 'literariness'. The point is not worth arguing, for what matters is the impression the reader receives; and although any novelist almost by instinct presents his picture of life as more authentic than that of others, the reader is still entitled to judge between his sense of the novel's reality, on its own terms, and the sense of actual and nonfictional experience which it appears to transmit. The fictional reality of *Lord of the Flies* is deliberately meagre, its island borrowed almost perfunctorily from the truly created one of Crusoe, or of Jim Hawkins. What matters is the actuality of the mass of boys, their movements, their emotions, and these are not seen from a personal angle but emerge as they inevitably are, irrespective of time and place. Impersonality in *Lord of the Flies* is in fact secured by a very inconspicuous device: placing wholly actual and authentic children in an uncreated and unimagined background. In this way there is nothing to frame them and no one to *see* them, a point finally driven home by the arrival of the naval officer on the beach, who is in fact the schoolmaster coming into the playground.

In *Free Fall* and *Darkness Visible* Golding uses in more subtle ways this contrast between psychological truth and disembodied background, and again the effect is to prevent us from 'enjoying' the story and the situation in a fictional way, and to compel our concentration on the impersonal intensity of the theme. The effect is the opposite of the normal dualism inherent in the novel: that between our sense of the writer as actor, self-creator, magician, and our simultaneous awareness of his more involuntary life in the background of what he creates. Such a dualism produces, for instance, our sense of Jane Austen, in the novels she writes: her spirit and humour creating in the foreground, while in the background is the boredom, the fear and the frustration of actuality, the conditions of life implicit in a letter to her sister mentioning the lady who became the model for Miss Bates. 'Poor Mrs Stent! It has been her lot to be always in the way. But . . . perhaps in time we may come to be Mrs Stents ourselves, unequal to anything and unwelcome to everybody.' In the awareness that the writer who enchants us could live in fear of being 'unequal to anything and unwelcome to everybody' – an awareness that is clearly if darkly present when we read her novels – is our full personal sense of her as a writer. Golding's power of disappearing from the situation he creates means that he avoids giving us this picture and forces us instead to concentrate wholly on what has been made actual.

Intensity, in his context, removes intimacy. Keeping out his 'ugly mug' is one of the most difficult and demanding tasks a novelist can perform, and Golding's unobtrusive mastery of it in *The Spire*, *Pincher Martin*, and the stories of *The Pyramid*, comes clearest in the narrators of *Free Fall* and *The Paper Men*, who are as near to disembodied intensities, and as distant from their author, as is Dostoevsky's Underground Man. These narrators, with their lack of the careful cocoon of human reality which most novelists would instinctively spin round them, are too abstract for normal fictional pleasure. Conrad's Marlowe, though designed to stand between us and the author, also brings Conrad closer to us, being, as it were, Conrad himself in fictional form. To create himself, in a form suited to the particular kind of reality his novel deals in, is natural to the novelist and one of the ways we get to know him. Jane Austen is both Elizabeth Bennet and a letter writer who fears she may end up 'unequal to anything and unwelcome to everybody'. But Golding's narrators seem to take us further away from Golding himself, while not achieving that other identity of 'novelist as character'.

The implications of this feat – for that is what it is, whether it comes about naturally or by careful calculation – are most evident in what is to my mind Golding's most subtle masterpiece, *Rites of Passage*. The style and personality of Talbot, the well-connected young narrator who is keeping a diary of the voyage for his godfather, are a deft pastiche of a style and outlook of 1812 or thereabouts, so deft that it seems to float free of history and the novel by imitating them as it does. The enjoyments of this pastiche, as the reader comes gradually to realize, are quite separate and different from the actuality that emerges from Talbot's diary of the voyage. The narrator does not enclose or have any true contact with his narrative, and the almost unbearable sense of what has occurred – its pathos and its helplessness – seems to reach us without any contact with the shaping personality of the author or his narrator.

Other novels are made use of in the same way as is the style of the period in which the voyage takes place. Most notably in the background are Melville's *Billy Budd* and Conrad's *Heart of Darkness*. In Melville's story the sexual element, the unspoken relationship between 'the handsome sailor' and the odious master-at-arms, is elevated to a literary plane of the mystical and heroic. The evil Claggart has been 'struck dead by an angel of God, but the angel must hang'. And when Billy 'ascends, and ascending took the full rose of dawn', the figure at the yardarm remains motionless, except for the movement produced by the ponderous roll 'of a great ship, heavy-cannoned'. War, heroism, the past ('the starry Vere') meet evil and sacrificial good on literary terms to form Melville's masterpiece. *Heart of Darkness* conveys in the words of its title Conrad's need to exorcize what he had found on his Congo voyage which, as his most recent biographer testifies, had left him with feelings of inadequacy and mere degradation, by raising those experiences to the level of elaborate art, embodied in the quietly heroic Marlowe and the suitably satanic figure of Kurtz.

What Melville and Conrad have in common is their ability, as artists, to escape from the embarrassments inherent in being their personal selves, while at the same time it remains clear to what extent those selves have contributed – in the unvoiced privacy of their own troubles and difficulties – to the success of the work of art. Those two stories earn their reality, as it were and their removal from the local world of actualities, by the way in which their authors have mortgaged their personalities to us in the process. Their art escapes but they do not. In *Rites of Passage* the opposite is true. The art of the tale remains imprisoned in its examination of what has actually occurred, an occurrence which affects Talbot, the narrator, as much as it does ourselves, but comes nowhere near the writer.

In *Heart of Darkness* Marlowe gets in touch with Kurtz's 'intended' and tells her, among other proper things, that the last word he spoke was her name. What he had in fact spoken – 'the horror, the horror!' – was equally improbable in actuality but proper to the reality of the tale. After Colley's death in *Rites of Passage* young Talbot foresees the letter he must write to his sister. But the misery and upset involved has nowhere to go, no conclusion in irony or in dramatic mystery. For days Colley lay like dead in his cabin, his hand clasping a ringbolt, motionless as the ascended Billy Budd, but motionless because there is nothing to be done or uttered. Billy Budd, foretopman, become another handsome sailor, 'of a build that might one day be over-corpulent', a foretopman whose name is Billy Rogers, a name which, like much else in *Rites of Passage*, suggests actualities which art can make nothing of.

The triumph of *Rites of Passage* is that its own kind of art leaves us in possession of a situation about which there is literally no more to say. In touching our hearts the author does not reveal his own, and in this context that makes the impact more powerful and its kind of truth more unexpected. So far from being, in Melville's mysteriously beautiful poetic phrase, 'a great ship heavy-cannoned', the huge old nameless vessel, ballasted with stinking gravel, has for years been 'laid up in ordinary' and is now impressed with an indeterminate complement and cargo. (Even her predecessor, which disappeared on passage, had a name, the *Guardian*.) In terms of art this ship never reaches harbour either, for all that, as the parson Colley touchingly writes his sister, she is 'a universe in little in which we must pass our lives and receive our reward or punishment'. Brocklebank, the marine artist bound for Australia with his two ambiguous ladies, launches when in his cups a disquisition on the need for a painter to consult his public and not to 'confuse art with actuality'. Golding's art here is to set up its own kind of actuality in the lee of other marine stories; not to discredit them – for how could

Melville and Conrad be discredited? – but to suggest that actuality can lie beside art in a relation that reveals what each is and each can be. Brocklebank feels that the introduction of portraiture among the aborigines of Australia 'will lead to complacency among them which . . . is next door to civilization'.

Rites of Passage respects those qualities. In *Lord of the Flies* the literary background was deliberately perfunctory, in order to reveal what was true about the human situation. *Rites of Passage* takes the opposite course. By exaggerating and accentuating the way art strives to make sense of things the novel contrives to give us not only all its artificial pleasures but also indicates the nature of their relationship to what is actually going on. Melville and Conrad compel art and actuality to become one in the reality they create, a reality that is personal to them and cannot, as it were, exist without them. In making an art radically different in intention and scope Golding forgoes this kind of literary reality.

Of course many of the pleasures are similar, nonetheless. The detail and humour in the novel are masterly, richer than in any other of Golding's books. The way things are, and the way they are described, are sometimes stood on their heads to admirable comic effect. It is from Colley's letter, composed in a style of quaint affection and evangelical platitude, that we learn the robust fact – never before vouchsafed in a naval yarn from Mr Midshipman Easy to Captain Hornblower – that the wheel and compass binnacle of a ship of the line are at 'the front end' of the quarter deck, 'and rather below it'. We also learn that sailors enjoy making literature out of their lives, and that their tales of carving snuffboxes out of salt beef and using cheeses for mastcappings are strictly to amaze and amuse the layman: their food in fact is usually prosaically more than adequate, in quantity and quality. And yet it is true that they are, as the warrant officer observes, 'here today and gone today'. The comment might serve as a gloss on Golding's methods. The lives lived in his art (witness *Pincher Martin* and the end of *The Paper Men*) are not extended enough, or complete enough, to become a personal matter.

Intimations of Mystery

ANTHONY STORR

In his lecture 'Belief and Creativity' Golding writes: 'I have always felt that a writer's books should be as different from each other as possible.' (*A Moving Target*, 198.) He doesn't tell us why, and professes to envy those authors who write the same book over and over again. I suspect that he is a man who feels compelled to challenge himself; always to set himself new tasks, to solve new problems. I have just reread all his published novels, and they are indeed so different from one another that it is hard to delineate connecting threads. The studied pastiche of *Rites of Passage* is remote from the visionary passion of *The Spire*. The ostensibly autobiographical *Free Fall* has next to nothing in common with *The Inheritors*. Yet, because this series of very different books is the work of one man, however many-sided, it must be possible to find some linking factors, some vision of man's nature which runs through all his work.

Bertrand Russell wrote of Joseph Conrad: 'He thought of civilized and morally tolerable human life as a dangerous walk on a thin crust of barely cooled lava which at any moment might break and let the unwary sink into fiery depths.'[1] I think these words apply equally to William Golding. Although Golding calls himself an optimist, there is little evidence in his novels to support that claim. The madness of violence, of lust, and of fanaticism seem always just below the surface. Like Koestler, Golding sees man as a species which is irredeemably flawed, and which is only too likely to bring about its own destruction. This is, of course, particularly obvious in what is still his most popular book, *Lord of the Flies*. Has Golding ever read accounts of those American experiments in which boys were taken to a holiday camp, divided into two groups, and set against each other? The experiments had to be brought to an end lest murder be committed. Golding doesn't need to read such mundane stuff. He knows it all already, both from his experience as a schoolmaster, and from searching his own heart. 'Kill the pig. Cut her throat. Spill her blood' (86). A savage chant and the putting-on of war-paint are enough to make Jack and his hunters lose their inhibitions against violence. The signal fire forgotten, it isn't long before the sand is stained with human blood as well as with that of pigs.

Sex, also, is more a matter of violent compulsion than of loving tenderness. Golding hates Freud, along with Marx and Darwin. He calls them 'the three most crashing bores of the Western world'. (*A Moving Target*, 186–7.) Yet, when Lok and Fa observe two of 'the new people' having sexual intercourse, it looks to them like a fight.

> The two people beneath the tree were making noises fiercely as though they were quarrelling. In particular the woman had begun to hoot like an owl and Lok could hear Tuami gasping like a man who fights with an animal and does not think he will win. He looked down at them and saw that Tuami was not only lying with the fat woman but eating her as well for there was black blood running from the lobe of her ear. (*The Inheritors*, 175.)

Golding may dislike Freud, but this is precisely Freud's picture of the child's interpretation of the 'primal scene'.

> If children at this early age witness sexual intercourse between adults . . . they inevitably regard the sexual act as a sort of ill-treatment or act of subjugation: they view it, that is, in a sadistic sense.[2]

Sadism crops up in other places in Golding's work. Evie, the tarty girl in *The Pyramid*, cries: 'Hurt me, Olly! *Hurt* me –' But, at eighteen, he doesn't know how to hurt her, nor how to adapt to the sexual rhythm she requires (79). Evie allows Captain Wilmot to beat her, and shocks the adolescent Oliver when her weals are displayed (90). In *Pincher Martin*, Mary so maddens Chris by her poised inaccessibility that he fantasizes:

> Those nights of imagined copulation, when one thought not of love nor sensation nor comfort nor triumph, but of torture rather, the very rhythm of the body reinforced by hissed ejaculations – take that and that! That for your pursed mouth and that for your pink patches, your closed knees, your impregnable balance on the high, female shoes – and that if it kills you for your magic and your isled virtue! (149)

She agrees to go out with him, refuses to comply. Driving dangerously enough to scare her, he brings the car to a screaming stop and
attempts to rape her on the verge of the road (152). In *Free Fall*,
Sammy is frustrated by the utter passivity of Beatrice, the girl he
adores but whom he cannot get to respond to him.

> What had been love on my part, passionate and reverent, what
> was to be a triumphant sharing, a fusion, the penetration of a
> secret, raising of my life to the enigmatic and holy level of hers
> became a desperately shoddy and cruel attempt to force a response
> from her somehow. Step by step we descended the path of sexual
> exploitation until the projected sharing had become an infliction.
> (122–3)

The relationship doesn't last. Sammy finds himself another girl, and
the passive Beatrice ends up in a mental hospital, with Sammy
wondering whether he is responsible for her total retreat into chronic
mental illness. In *The Paper Men* Wilfred Barclay behaves with the
utmost cruelty to Rick, the American academic who is pursuing
him; the sadism of power rather than of sex, but sadism nonetheless.

Golding dislikes homosexuality, but he is expert at describing its
compulsions. The inhibited, paranoid Father Watts-Watt in *Free
Fall*, the drunken, effeminate Mr de Tracy in *The Pyramid*; the
egregious, paedophilic Mr Pedigree in *Darkness Visible*; the appalling
Mr Colley in *Rites of Passage*, are all memorable figures whose sexual
preferences are even more central to their personalities than those of
Golding's heterosexual characters. But, whatever the nature of the
sexual impulse, in whatever direction it is pointed, it seems, in
Golding's work, to be as much pain as it is pleasure. Moreover, sex
never seems to be integrated as part of the whole man or woman. It
remains something which takes over, subdues the will, and forces
the subject, often against his own intention, to comply with a
compulsion over which he has no control.

Sex is not the only emotion which takes over the individual.
Golding has a pre-Freudian vision of man in which the notion of
repression plays little part. He thinks much more in terms of
dissociation and even of possession. Actual loss of consciousness is
surprisingly common in the novels. Simon, the Christ figure in *Lord
of the Flies*, is an epileptic. He loses consciousness, not only on his

first appearance in the book, but also after the pig's head delivers its
sermon to him. It is worth recalling that epilepsy was called the
'sacred' malady until Hippocrates affirmed that it had natural causes.
In *Darkness Visible*, Sophy suddenly loses consciousness at a party
when presented with a Rorschach ink blot which everyone else sees
as part of a game. She does so again after her terrifying fantasy of
murdering the kidnapped boy. Earlier in the same book, Matty loses
consciousness twice after his agonizing encounter with the abor-
igine. De Tracy passes out from alcohol in *The Pyramid*. Confronted
with an image of Christ, Wilfred Barclay, the alcoholic, pursued
author in *The Paper Men*, loses consciousness and wakes up in
hospital. 'Surrounded, swamped, confounded, all but destroyed,
adrift in the universal intolerance, mouth open, screaming, bepissed
and beshitten, I knew my maker and I fell down.' (123). Sammy
nearly faints after his encounter with the psychotic Beatrice in *Free
Fall*. Jocelin, in *The Spire*, loses consciousness more than once, and,
when dying, has an 'out-of-body' experience of the kind often
described by those who have been close to death.

Nor are faints, fits, and drink the only things to obliterate normal
consciousness. Madness is never far away. It takes over Miss Bounce
in *The Pyramid* as well as Beatrice in *Free Fall*. It hovers round the
heads of both Jocelin and Roger Mason in *The Spire*. It is an essential
ingredient in *Pincher Martin*.

> 'There is always madness, a refuge like a crevice in the rock. A
> man who has no more defence can always creep into madness like
> one of those armoured things that scuttle among weed down
> where the mussels are.' (186)

Golding acknowledges his belief in God, but his vision is not that of a
Christian. It is closer to that of the ancient Greeks, in whose language
and literature he is so profoundly steeped. The Greeks believed that
the onslaughts of passion which assail human beings were the work
of the gods rather than the responsibility of men themselves. Lust,
aggression, ecstasy, inspiration, and prophecy possess men unpre-
dictably and are not within human control. Emotions appear from
nowhere, and have to be examined and evaluated before they can be
understood. In *The Inheritors*, when Liku has been captured by 'the
new people', Lok 'examined the feeling of heaviness in his head and

body. There was no doubt at all. The feeling was connected with Liku.' (130). Later, when Fa's tracks and scent have disappeared,

> Lok began to bend. His knees touched the ground, his hands reached down and took his weight slowly, and with all his strength he clutched himself into the earth. He writhed himself against the dead leaves and twigs, his head came up, turned, and his eyes swept round, astonished eyes over a mouth that was strained open. The sound of mourning burst out of his mouth, prolonged, harsh, pain-sound, man-sound. (190)

'He clutched at the bushes as the tides of feeling swirled through him and howled at the top of his voice.' (191). Lok is not *homo sapiens*, but, in Golding's vision, although *homo sapiens* has developed language to a greater extent than Lok, he has not gained much more control over his emotions, nor integrated them as part of the totality of his being.

It is partly for this reason that human identity is more fluid, more easily lost or dissolved than in the work of other writers. The sense of continuing identity is, for most people, rooted in the body. There are passages in Golding's novels in which dissociation from the body is as complete as it often is in Kafka. In *Pincher Martin*, the drowning man's 'mind inside the dark skull made swimming movements long after the body lay motionless in the water' (16). Later, when the sea has deposited him on the rock,

> The hardnesses under his cheek began to insist. They passed through pressure to a burning without heat, to a localized pain. They became vicious in their insistence like the nag of an aching tooth. They began to pull him back into himself and organize him again as a single being. (24)

This experience of dissociation from the body is like that experienced in high fever or other serious illness. Virginia Woolf describes something similar in *The Voyage Out*. Has Golding ever been seriously ill? The description of Sammy Mountjoy's mastoid in *Free Fall* (67–72), as well as Jocelin's 'out-of-body' experience referred to above suggests the possibility.

However this may be, Christopher Hadley Martin, alone on his rock in mid-Atlantic, asks himself:

'How can I have a complete identity without a mirror? That is
what has changed me. Once I was a man with twenty photographs
of myself – myself as this and that with the signature scrawled
across the bottom right-hand corner as a stamp and seal. Even
when I was in the Navy there was that photograph in my identity
card so that every now and then I could look and see who I was.'
(*Pincher Martin*, 132.)

One might argue that Martin was an actor, a role player with less
than average sense of being continuously the same person, but
the theme of uncertain identity recurs too often for this to be a
convincing explanation. '"What is it like to be you?"' asks the
adolescent Sammy in *Free Fall* of his girl friend Beatrice.

What is it like in the bath and the lavatory and walking the
pavement with shorter steps and high heels; what is it like to know
your body breathes this faint perfume which makes my heart
burst and my senses swim? (103–4)

A natural enough enquiry for an adolescent who is still in the
business of self-discovery, but this quest for identity is persistent in
other contexts. In *Darkness Visible* Mattie recurrently confronts
those dreaded questions, 'What am I for? What am I?' In *Free Fall* the
Nazi interrogator, Dr Halde, says:

'There is no health in you, Mr Mountjoy. You do not believe in
anything enough to suffer for it or be glad. There is no point at
which something has knocked on your door and taken possession
of you. You possess yourself. Intellectual ideas, even the idea of
loyalty to your own country sit on you loosely. You wait in a
dusty waiting-room on no particular line for no particular train.
And between the poles of belief, I mean the belief in material
things and the belief in a world made and supported by a supreme
being, you oscillate jerkily from day to day, from hour to hour.'
(144)

A novelist who wants to write a series of books as different from one
another as possible is better without too rigid a set of beliefs or too
fixed a sense of his own identity. One recalls Keats's famous letter to
Richard Woodhouse in which he affirms: 'A Poet is the most
unpoetical of anything in existence, because he has no Identity; he is

continually [informing] and filling some other body . . .'³ One way of looking at Golding's novels is to see them as a voyage through all the contradictory possibilities he finds within himself; a quest for some sort of coherence and consistency. 'Yet I am a burning amateur, torn by the irrational and incoherent, violently searching and self- condemned.' (*Free Fall*, 5.)

> I have hung all systems on the wall like a row of useless hats. They do not fit. They come in from outside, they are suggested patterns, some dull and some of great beauty. But I have lived enough of my life to require a pattern that fits over everything I know; and where shall I find that? (*Free Fall*, 6.)

Has Golding found such a pattern? One should not assume that he shares the requirements of a character he invents, and, as we have already seen, he is profoundly intolerant of those great reductionist pattern makers Darwin, Marx and Freud. We know from his most revealing lecture 'Belief and Creativity' that he believes in God, and in both the truth and the mystery of the imagination. Golding has one of the most powerful imaginations of any living writer, which is why he convinces even at his most obscure. It seems to me that he believes that imagination can sometimes penetrate what, in *Darkness Visible*, the captain who rescues the child Matty calls 'the screen that conceals the working of things.' (16). This is what gives the poet and the novelist absolute conviction, the 'voice of authority, power' to which Golding refers in his lecture (*A Moving Target*, 193). It is a profoundly irrational, anti–intellectual view of reality; and so it is not surprising that, in the novels, it often seems to be the primitive or the simple who come closest to it. *The Inheritors* used to be, and may still be, Golding's own favourite amongst his novels. The 'pictures' which Lok and his fellow creatures share are both precursors of thought and intimations of a reality which thought cannot penetrate. In *Darkness Visible* poor, ugly, burned Matty may perform inexplicable rituals and have psychotic visions, but he finally 'knows' what he is far more clearly than do any of the more conventional characters. Golding believes that the violence of our century is, at bottom, a revolt against reductionism. Perhaps this is what he is getting at when, in *Darkness Visible*, a truth appears in the mind of Sophy. '*The way towards simplicity is through outrage.*' (167)

I count myself fortunate in having known William Golding for over twenty years. He, and some of his best work are still mysterious to me. He would not want this any other way, and nor would I. Intimations of mystery are what the twentieth century needs.

NOTES

1 Bertrand Russell, *Portraits From Memory*, Allen & Unwin, London 1956, 82.
2 Sigmund Freud, Standard Edition, Vol. VII, Hogarth Press, London 1953, 196.
3 *The Letters of John Keats*, ed. M. B. Forman, Oxford University Press, London 1935, 228.

Golding and 'Golding'

JOHN FOWLES

John Fowles

I have met William Golding only once, at a pleasant small private occasion in the autumn of 1983, just three weeks before the announcement that he had won the Nobel Prize; a coming honour he must have known, but breathed not a word of at our lunch. We were both outshone by David Cecil, who was also there. It is rather difficult to be anything else before someone with amusing memories of being snubbed by Virginia Woolf in her own drawing room, and the like; but I think our being outshone by a skilled conversationalist and raconteur is fairly typical of most novelists in such situations. Our talent seldom lies in the spoken, or in the leaving, after such informal encounters, an indelible impression. I hasten to add I was not disappointed in my famous fellow author; much more, slightly dislocated. Somehow Golding the man, the presence that day, did not quite fit how I had supposed he might be either from his books or from what small gossip I had heard of him – did not fit what I need really to put in inverted commas, an entity made purely of words, 'Golding'.

This must seem naive and foolish in me, since I have long had to realize that I share my own life with just such an entity as 'Golding'. In an extremely unfair kind of way something called 'Fowles' has become my representative in the public world, a kind of vulgar waxwork figure with (it seems to me) only a crude caricature resemblance to the original. I believe the Japanese set up stuffed hate figures in their factory gymnasiums, for the workers to take out their resentments on; that is 'Fowles'. Occasionally this monstrously insufficient surrogate provokes something rather different, a kind of foolish idolatry, like some sort of obscure local saint in Catholic countries . . . but in both simulacra remains equally remote from recognizable life.

The real Golding: an affable, gentle man in all outward respects, though not without the bluff asperity or disagreement now and then. Had I not known who he was, I might have guessed a spry retired admiral, as indeed he appears (with clearly comic intention) in one of the crew photographs in the very recent *An Egyptian Journal*. In the flesh he shows a mixture of authority and reserve, with a distinct dry humour, a tiny hint of buried demon; a man still with a touch of the ancient schoolmaster, and also of what years ago in the Marines we used to call the matlows . . . as anyone who has read the potted biography on one of the backs of his books could foresee. He looked older than I expected. I had always thought of him as of my own age; not of his being a decade and a half my senior, white-bearded, as he is in reality.

For some reason he reminded me that day – it must seem absurdly – on the one hand of an Elizabethan bishop-scholar of the more tolerant, humanist kind, a sort of quietist Sarum that never was; on the other, of a Slocum, someone who had done long voyages single-handed, metaphorically at least, but preferred now not to talk of them. We managed one or two compliments, when attention was elsewhere. He told me his new novel (*The Paper Men*, not then published) was to be about a novelist being persecuted by a literary researcher, and we discussed briefly that aspect of both our lives; the letters, the academic visitors, the thesis writers. We chatted about his interest in small boats and sailing (which I understood) and a lesser one for horses and riding (which I did not, my dislike for the animal being exceeded only by suspicion of its human admirers). It would have been a very flat occasion for anyone present that had swallowed the old myth, that novelist must equal brilliant talker . . . wit, outrageous gossip, profound intellectual discourse, all the rest of it. I am (temperamentally, and now upon something like principle) a complete failure in that line, and I sensed that Golding felt no need to excel in it, either. But what really that meeting most brought to me was how little I knew of Golding, this agreeable elderly man beside me; and how much more of 'Golding', that is, a semi-mythical, semi-fictional figure. In plain English, not of him as he is, but as I imagined him.

I know the friends who hospitably brought us and our wives, and Lord David, together did so with the kindest intentions. But I must confess that I have a long distaste for literary meetings of any kind, however congenial and well meant in other ways, and fascinating to spectators. In my admittedly very limited experience there is an essential precondition if they are to succeed. It is that the two writers are alone . . . no wives or husbands, no third parties, above all no other literary person, no bookish audience. Perhaps some writers do meet each other for the first time with pleasure and enjoyment, something beyond idle or cautious curiosity; but I must beg leave to doubt it.

Both parties know too much, for a start, of the very special nature of their joint pursuit. They may know very little of each other's private triumphs and disasters, of their dark nights and sunlit days, their fair winds and foul, of their experience on the voyage; but at least they know they are with someone who has also been at sea. They know what havoc their solitary profession performs on the private psyche; of its guilts and anxieties, its vices and egocentricities, its secret pleasures, its sloughs of despond, its often appalling personal costs; of what they are in reality, and what they have become, in quotes. I remember meeting a young American writer years ago (a would-be Hemingway, needless to say) who demanded to know how many times a day I pulled myself off. He meant, how many hours I spent writing. His metaphor, as every writer knows, has a certain truth, whatever it lacks elsewhere. One can no more think of making fiction without onanism, or selfishness (ask our wives), than of the sea without waves.

Nor usually can we writers ever meet each other without a sense, however subdued, of rivalry. The absurd model of the beauty contest or the athletics race haunts such occasions; or perhaps I should liken the ghost to that of a sinister and irrational football league, where the place, even the division, of one's own club is never fixed, the standards of judgement never clear, and in any case always fluctuating in themselves. Most older writers are, I think, wise enough not to lose sleep over this; they know they will be asleep for ever, well out of the stadium, by the time the final match is decided. It is only face to face with each other that the question of comparative status threatens to raise its ugly head.

Both Golding and I have, in our different ways, been through an experience denied the majority of writers – that is, a degree of both critical and financial, and international, success. We have both been best sellers in America – and seen our status in Britain suffer for it. We have both seen our work endlessly discussed, analysed, dissected, have been over praised and over faulted, victims of that characteristic twentieth-century mania for treating living artists as if they were dead – a process that may please teacher and student on campus, but which (speaking at least for myself) does something rather different to the still-breathing subject on the anatomy table, especially when he is expected gratefully to welcome the dissection and happily play corpse. I think Golding himself once described how absurd he found it when he realized that more books had been written about him than he had actually written himself. The contempt in *The Paper Men* for both persecuted and persecutor speaks for itself.

I have till now been speaking objectively about 'Golding', but that is misleading. Despite the ordinariness of our meeting, it is not how I feel about him. That is much more subjectively, and in ways that I suspect neither ordinary readers nor academics generally suppose writers feel about other writers. I am quite often asked that question beloved of interviewers: which other living writers in English have most influenced me. To that I usually, and wickedly, answer Defoe; but driven from my quibbling over what 'dead' or 'living' really means in the context of literature, and forced to answer the question, I have for many years named William Golding, with the paradoxical (for the interviewer) proviso that 'influence' is not the word; that I should have to use something like 'exemplar' or 'tutelar' to come near it, but even they are not accurate.

It is simply that I have always had a warm feeling, a quasi-fraternal, quasi-nepotal affection for 'Golding'. I was delighted, in almost a family sense, when he won the Booker Prize, and even more so when he was awarded the Nobel; not, I am afraid, a very frequent reaction on my part to the winners of either honour. Far more usually it is nine parts sheer indifference. I was appalled, when the Nobel was announced, to hear from one well known Fleet Street literary editor, who telephoned for my reaction, that he was having difficulty getting anything suitably warm (Doris Lessing was an exception) from various other English novelists he had approached. Again, I felt it almost as a personal slight. Such lack of generosity mystified me (and the editor) then, and mystifies me still.

A cynic will say it is childish, or disingenuous, to be surprised by lack of generosity in other writers. Perhaps; but I could interpret it only as a sort of parochial blindness, an incomprehensible inability to see the role Golding has played in the contemporary novel by remaining (I put it very simply) so conspicuously *sui generis*, his own writer, his own school of one. I could take this coldness only as one more proof of the English fixation on schools and traditions, so close, beneath the surface, to our wretchedly enduring love of social class; and of suspecting anyone not immediately placeable within that system. So close also, with the tone of so much reviewing and even in how we usually talk about books in ordinary conversation, to the literal middle-class school, in which the writer is cast as an eternally backward pupil and the critic, amateur or professional, only too often as sarcastically reporting or sadistically caning prep-school master. In my experience even the most hostile and damning reviews in non-English cultures are at least from adult to adult, not from schoolmaster (or mistress), in the implicit context of the classroom, with the whole weight and power of a supposedly unquestionable senior institution behind them, *de haut en bas* upon the head of some contemptible and irritating young dunce. *De gustibus* . . . of course one may dislike, even hate a book. It is the gratuitous invocation of a disapproving establishment beyond such personal judgement that is the national malady.

I can see 'Golding' has faults and weaknesses as a writer, beside his outstanding virtues. (So does any writer read any other, I would not let the greatest – among my greatest, at any rate – off blameless there: not Defoe, not Austen, not Austen-drowned Peacock, not Hardy, not even Flaubert). I suspect I don't share some of his views of life, or the priority he puts among those I do have sympathy with; and as I explained above, I can't claim to have paid him the traditional greatest compliment; that is, I don't feel influenced in any textual sense. Yet all this is, for me, next to nothing. I do not write like him; yet he remains generically, if not specifically, the kind of writer I most try to be. We shook hands when we met, like conventional middle-class Englishmen, as part of both of us is; but something in me wished that I could have found, or circumstances allowed, something a little more Latin and demonstrative; a *cher maître*, a Gallic embrace, I don't know. In England, alas, one must play such cards close, or be counted peculiar.

Another of my *bêtes noires* is the confusion of writers with pop

stars, sporting 'personalities', film actors . . . all that presumes the
very act of writing for a public must be synonymous with craving
constant limelight, always more publicity. That we write to be read,
no novelist, no writer of any kind, would deny; it is the assumption
of our thirst for *any* sort of glory that I would like sent to China (like
the too clever Greek inventor Phanocles in that dry little fable, *Envoy
Extraordinary*).

Of course there are novelists who do encourage this popular
delusion; whose belief in themselves, in their talent, their 'genius' (or
their sales and size of advances), in the face of the icy wind of reality,
deserves immediate entry into any *sottisier* of literary folly. I suspect
this is why some do indeed become actors in a sense, half aware
schizophrenics; expert at projecting whatever public persona they
have elected, or let themselves be forced, to wear. In advanced stages
of the disease they can grow much closer to the mask than they are to
their real minds and selves. Little discourages this process of self-
inflation; certainly not publishers or agents or the literary world in
general, for whom the writer and his public ego, his robbinsisms and
rowseries, are always the choicest fodder, not his texts.

This refusal to be a personality in the above sense, to allow
Golding and 'Golding' to drift apart, is one of the first reasons I have
always liked Golding's work: the feeling that here, by some miracle,
was a writer content to be himself, to rest his case simply on what he
wrote, not on how grandiosely, or bizarrely, or publicity consciously, his persona made him behave. In that he is for me the
quintessential amateur writer, not the professional.

Expectability is both the great defect and the great virtue of the
English novel. Defect in its sometimes too eager and complaisant
willingness to obey the conventions of the genre (as in life, those of
society); and even to obey those self-established by an author in his
own earlier work, whereby he sometimes founders on his own forte
(self-parody is every well known writer's dreaded reef); virtue in the
richness it can derive from an outwardly narrow range and restricted
palette. If the novel must be written on a few inches of ivory, we are
not to be beaten in England. This palladium still lies in a sacred
triangle, among hatred of excess, respect for the past and good taste.
Its devotees run, from the time when the waters began to divide,
from Richardson, reached a silvery climax in Jane Austen, and have

continued today in such gifted women novelists as Elizabeth Taylor and Barbara Pym. The other side first declared itself in Defoe and Sterne and reached an apotheosis in this century with Joyce and D. H. Lawrence.

All these latter writers have been dissenters from the received traditions of their various times. Some gently, some as bulls in a china shop, they have always in some way *broken*, whether it be in language, character portrayal, narrative technique, emotional or sexual frankness, or a thousand other things. This distinction between breakers and conformers is very rough, and provides singularly little guide to quality, since a good conformer will always beat a bad breaker, and *vice versa*. Nevertheless, another thing I have always liked about 'Golding' is the lack of expectability (so closely allied to respectability) I have always found in his themes, indeed even in his line-by-line style. At heart it derives, I am sure, from an honesty and an independence, a will to follow his own imagination, wherever it may lead. Publishers' readers may groan here, and certainly the one who once described to me, as the ubiquitous fault of the many typescripts she had in her time rejected, 'too much imagination, not enough technique'. This too-much imagination, or refusal to write what is safe and expected, may sometimes have led Golding astray. But I think this not a fault of tyros. It is endemic in the novel, even at the highest level; and almost its main source of energy. Imagination is always ahead of the technique to express it; and one of the greatest pleasures of writing is trying to make the laggard catch up . . . just as how well or how variously the novelist attempts this is certainly one of the greatest pleasures of reading. This also I like particularly in 'Golding': how he seems to attack the problems afresh in each book, and by no means always on the lines of past successes. No one disputes that he has been a master fabulist, and a brilliantly creative interpreter of remote history (*The Inheritors*) when he wants; but he has never rested on one given approach, one given power.

Being possessed of one's own imagination, having the courage to let it dictate to technique, rather than the reverse, is to my mind one of the most enviable gifts or states a novelist can have or be in, for all its obvious dangers and penalties. It must, in the nature of things, attract enemies. One battalion must come from the publishing trade itself, who dote on repetition in the extreme form on the so-called recipe novel, written as much by the commissioning editor as by the writer. To all that sick tendency in modern publishing to let carefully calculated commercial considerations rule over any natural artistic ones, 'Golding' remains a peremptory denial; and equally to those other enemies, the unreasoning worshippers of received tradition, whose fixed ideal of the novel is held rather as an orthodox churchman holds his faith, and who tend to regard any infringement of that ideal, any lapse of observance towards it, as the equivalent (at any rate in the venom with which it is commonly prosecuted against the offender) of blasphemy. This is why I think of 'Golding' as tutelary and exemplary. Look, he has come through; it can be done, and on one's own.

I don't suppose that my own idiosyncratic view of other writers, both dead and alive, which thinks of them primarily in a natural history way (that is, far less morally and evaluatively than on the principle that all species are equal – or at any rate, to misapply Orwell, more equal than we usually like to think), makes much sense to anyone else; but nor, I think, does an unhappily prevalent opposite view, one I associate with a question I have here in Dorset had asked of me on more than one occasion: Why can't you modern people write like Thomas Hardy? I did once, goaded beyond bearing, answer that I was profoundly glad I couldn't write like Hardy – and was promptly damned beyond redemption for unspeakable vanity and *lèse-majesté*. Readers, alas, the world over, ignore the etymology of 'novel'; for them it was always better in the past. There also 'Golding' has always stood for me like some ancient menhir or monolith, enduring proof that there are other beliefs, other religions.

Perhaps neither Golding nor 'Golding' will like this presenting of him as something of an iconoclast in the Holy Chapel of Eng. Lit.; yet part of the unspoken meaning of that lunch did lie for me in David Cecil's presence. A Martian present would, I think, have assumed Lord David the well-known novelist, and the rest of us his votaries, which I must confess I am not – or once was not. When I was an undergraduate (in French) at New College in the 1940s, we were fiercely divided over him, and far beyond the English Faculty. To some (the puritans) he was an intolerable lightweight, a dancing damsel-fly on the river of life; to others the very personification of the literary life, knowing everyone, knowing everything; above all, in the drab austerity of that immediately post-war Oxford, he was *different*. One might see him, leaning gracefully and aesthetically in the evening against a wall beneath a wisteria overlooking the College Gardens, reading some slim volume, and seemingly oblivious to us noisy undergraduates playing bowls on the lawn; or hear him, at the right angle in New College Lane, a weirdly disembodied voice, as he recited Tennyson aloud to himself before walking into sight. Apocryphal anecdotes about him, in that easily parodiable, pouncing-gabbling voice, were legion, as they were of another don, Sir Isaiah Berlin, also by chance my 'moral' tutor. ('Don't for goodness' sake come to me with any problems, my dear fellow. I know positively nothing about young men's morals.')

I remember seeing one of them, I forget which, entering the front quad with an exotically dressed Dame Edith Sitwell on his arm, a far more impressive (I nearly wrote empressive) sight than that of the present Queen, who had visited us shortly before. This was Literature herself; and her companion infinitely more honoured by her presence than by any rank or title – or indeed scholarly reputation – given by society at large. That vision was symbolic of the image I had of living literature at Oxford – it was a profession for immensely exalted beings alone, almost as remote from ordinary life as that terrible café society crew on Olympus. All lay in 'famous' names, and knowing them, being seen with them. I did not really reject that fame-besotted view of literature until I became a writer myself, and learnt at first hand what an illusion the popular notion of a 'successful' literary life is; its pleasures very seldom those the public supposes and most of its pains to be found in what they imagine we must welcome with open arms. To be sure, one may pick up a certain *savoir faire*, or *savoir écrire*, at Oxbridge (though even those can be mixed blessings, elegant bracelets that can – in terms of the novel – grow into iron manacles). But university is, I think, no guide to the realities of the writing life.

Now I am afraid this meretricious and dream-inducing side of a past literary Oxford had become rather linked in my mind with the figure, no, the aura of Lord David (as also with the most envied undergraduate of my vintage, Ken Tynan). That aura had been resurrected only a few years ago, when I was sternly threatened with a libel action by the secretary of the Thomas Hardy Society. A magazine had published a remark in which I compared some of the more idolatrous members of the Society to pop groupies. The secretary had taken it upon himself to inform me that the comparison was outrageous and would give grave offence to 'members like Lord David Cecil'. Such pomposity was not in the least Lord David's fault, of course; I am sure his opinion had not been asked, nor had I in the least meant his sort of scholarly member. Any irrational resentment I might still have felt against what I had chosen to make him stand for at Oxford very soon disappeared before the reality again at our lunch, nearly forty years later. And yet . . .

The source of what I felt was, I think, no more than that Golding and I chanced to be seated together in an inglenook bench on one side of the table, and Lord David was opposite us, on the other. Clearly he and Golding held each other in friendship and respect. Yet there drifted into my mind, as we all sat there, the presentiment of an ancient polarity, that between distinguished literary establishment figures and self-made (all novelists are self-made) writers; just the very faintest whisper of a confrontation, purely symbolical, between the discriminating professor, with all the memory of his celebrated family hovering imperceptibly behind him, and the fallible living novelist, that heretic humanist I mentioned at the beginning. All this was purely in my mind, not theirs; I describe something in no way present in anything that was said. Such a polarity was, of course, between what I alone had made of them both, two figments of my imagination, a 'Golding' and a 'Lord David Cecil'; between someone who has a knowledge of literature from reading, teaching, thinking and writing about it, and someone who is willy-nilly literature, because he makes and constitutes it. Perhaps I should more decently say that for a moment I felt the unbridgeable abyss that lies between even the most sensitive and knowledgeable critic and exegetist and the creator. Their lives may seem intertwined, in many ways they are. Only in their essence are they eternally separate.

I neither can nor propose to speak of Golding's books in the manner perhaps expected on such occasions as this present book, to celebrate or analyse, to list those I particularly like, and why. In that I would guess I am like most novelists in regard to each other's work; that is, we have normally only a very approximate *Gestalt*-like picture of our contemporaries, the very opposite of the serious student's precise and detailed one. We cannot really deal with them, academically. They are far more presences, vaguely hostile or vaguely sympathetic, vaguely admired or vaguely envied, in a shared house. One's relation to them is particularly difficult to put in words, not least because language here is so dominated by the vocabulary of professional study and criticism. We cannot judge family; we have too much an interest, either for or against, in their cases.

I wish now to say only that in that self-made confrontation, I felt myself, metaphorically as literally, very firmly at Golding's side. There are a number of other living English novelists I admire for various reasons, but none that, like him, I feel almost emotionally, certainly imaginatively and empathetically, attached to; inalienably, of his party. Perhaps, who knows, if we knew each other properly as ordinary beings, we should not get on at all. Golding might turn out a much more difficult proposition than 'Golding'. We both have formidable quirks. He should never get me into jodhpurs, or into anything less than a 'floating Hilton', on the Nile. But after all, I don't think it matters that I do not know him, outside those quotes. Golding will die (though I hope not for many years yet); 'Golding' will not. I know him as the future must.

The spry admiral, the Joshua Slocum . . . I fancy he may not like all this nautical imagery, and I dare not add the privateer. Yet he has done his own free voyage, which makes him a precursor; has by his example helped carry me, and I am sure other writers, through many of our own storms and doldrums; has shown us the vital importance of trusting our own noses (or imaginations), of letting them steer, even into error; and of remaining oneself, in the face of convention, fashion, critical ups and downs, commercial 'wisdom', all the rest. Such is my debt, at any rate. And now to hell with embarrassment, either his or mine . . . once he called me in print 'young Fowles', which mortally offended me. In revenge I call him *cher maître*, and most warmly embrace him.

Schoolboys

IAN McEWAN

I read *Lord of the Flies* at boarding school when I was thirteen in an edition specially strengthened, without irony or, probably, much success, against the quotidian savagery of schoolboys. The mint new copies were distributed in class one summer's afternoon. The double thickness cardboard covers were bright gold, the colour, it came to seem, of desert island sands and the author's name. It was the kind of book that crackled when first opened, and the binding glue gave off something faintly faecal, the smell, it was soon established, of little boys gorging on tropical fruit and 'caught short' on the beach. The text was enticingly clear, at one with the limpid waters of the lagoon. The novel's reputation must have reached me for I already knew that this was a serious book, written by a grown-up for the careful attention of other grown-ups. At that time I was eager to be involved in the ways of real books. I started on the first page hungrily and read too quickly for I formed the impression of a boy with an enormous scar and a bird that could talk. I began again, more slowly this time, and was initiated, though I could not know it at the time, into the process whereby writers teach you how to read. Not all scars are on people; this one was in the fabric of the jungle. And the cry of a bird could be echoed by, and therefore resemble, the cry of a boy.

Two related discoveries gave me immediate pleasure. The first was that in this, an adult book, adults and all their grey, impenetrable concerns were not prominent. Here was the very stuff of my fantasy life and of my favourite childhood reading. For years I had day-dreamed of grown-ups conveniently and painlessly dissolved (I didn't want them to suffer in any way) leaving me and a handful of competent friends to surmount dangers without ever being called into tea. I had read *Treasure Island* and *Coral Island* of course, and I knew all about the less respectable end of the tradition, Enid Blyton's Adventure series in which four chums and a dog broke up international crime rings in their summer holidays. What was so attractively subversive and feasible about Golding was his apparent assumption that in a child-dominated world things went wrong in a most horrible and interesting way. For – and this was the second discovery – I *knew* these boys. I knew what they were capable of. I had seen us at it. As far as I was concerned, Golding's island was a thinly disguised boarding school.

As a contemporary of Ralph, Piggy and Jack, I felt intimately acquainted with their problems, the most pressing of which – since I didn't want the boys rescued – seemed to be the difficulty of talking something through in a group to a useful resolution. I read the accounts of the meetings round the conch, the inevitable drift and confusion, with anguished recognition. At the age of twelve or thirteen it was just possible, given a little privacy and necessity, to develop a line of thought alone, to reach some kind of hazy conclusion. To do this with a group of friends was near impossible. We were at an age when we craved secret societies, codes, invented rituals and hierarchies; these all needed talking through before the fun could begin and countless elements conspired to subvert us: pure excitement, competitiveness, aggression, horseplay, power play, boasting, the need to find a joke at every turn, wild, associative thinking and everyone talking at once. We could not organize a thing among ourselves. One's own thoughts melted away. ('Ralph was puzzled by the shutter that flickered in his brain. There was something he wanted to say; then the shutter had come down.') Golding knew all about us. In *Lord of the Flies* I saw the messiness and insufficiencies of my little society spread out before me. For the first time in my life I was reading a book which did not depend on unlikeable characters or villains for a source of tension or evil. What I had known, without ever giving the matter much thought, from my crowded, dormitory existence, was confirmed and clarified; life could be unhappily divisive, even go fabulously wrong, without anyone having to be extravagantly nasty. No one was to blame – it was how it was when we were together.

I was uneasy when I came to the last chapters and read of the death of Piggy and the boys hunting Ralph down in a mindless pack. Only that year we had turned on two of our number in a vaguely similar way. A collective and unconscious decision was made, the victims were singled out and as their lives became more miserable by the day, so the exhilarating, righteous urge to punish grew in the rest of us. Neither of the boys was an obvious candidate for victimization, neither was ugly, stupid or weak. One combed his hair with a parting we found rather too precise. The other had an intimate, confiding manner and was sometimes over-generous with his sweets. Together we convinced ourselves the two of them were intolerable. Alone, none of us could have contemplated the daily humiliations, the little tortures we, the invincible, unknowing pack, inflicted on these two boys. Their parents had no choice but to take them away. When the uncomprehending father of the boy with the neat hair came in his car to collect his son, no one dared defy the group by going out at the last moment to say goodbye.

It did not take me many years to discover that schoolboys have no monopoly on unreason and cruelty and that they are not the only ones incapable of settling differences with calm discussion. This, of course, is Golding's whole point. The boys set fire to their island paradise while their elders and betters have all but destroyed the planet. When yet another assembly breaks down and the boys scatter across the beach, Ralph, Piggy and Simon are left behind and begin to catalogue with yearning the many competent ways the grown-ups would have managed things better. Golding interjects: 'The three boys stood in the darkness, striving unsuccessfully to convey the majesty of adult life.' At thirteen I too had sufficient faith in adult life to be immune to Golding's irony. *Lord of the Flies* thrilled me with all the power a fiction can have because I felt indicted by it. All my friends were implicated too. It made me feel ashamed in a rather luxurious way. The novel brought realism to my fantasy life (the glowing, liberated world without grown-ups) and years later, when I came to write a novel myself, I could not resist the momentum of my childhood fantasies nor the power of Golding's model, for I found myself wanting to describe a closed world of children removed from the constraints of authority. I had no doubt that my children too would suffer from, rather than exult in, their freedom. Without realizing it at the time, I named my main character after one of Golding's.

I cannot break completely from the memory of my first reading of *Lord of the Flies*. Whatever else it might be, and it is clearly many things, it remains for me a finely observed novel about schoolboys, the way they talk and fall out and turn into imitation aeroplanes mid-sentence. The din of the lower school common room at the Bishop Wordsworth School was not wasted on Golding. After all, the satanic authority of the Lord of the Flies himself is conveyed in words that Golding might have used in the classroom. 'The Lord of the Flies spoke in the voice of a schoolmaster. "This has gone quite far enough. My poor misguided child, do you think you know better than I do?"' At the age of thirteen I was not to know that Golding was interested in far more than observing schoolboys and was making exemplary use of a limited experience for enormously ambitious and successful ends. I felt that odd elation induced by artistically achieved pessimism; as far as I was concerned, the novel's blaming finger was pointed at schoolboys like Jack, Piggy, Ralph and me. We were manifestly inadequate. We couldn't think straight, and in sufficiently large groups we were capable of atrocities. In that I took it all so personally, I like to think that I was, in some sense, an ideal reader.

Baboons and Neanderthals:
A Rereading of The Inheritors

TED HUGHES

As a fiction, about an episode in the Prehistory of man, *The Inheritors* carries no more of the flint and bone record than it needs. Any doubts we might have are soon allayed by Golding's good creative conscience. After taking his hint from the museum scenario, where Cro-Magnon man appears, about thirty thousand years ago, and exterminates the Neanderthals, he goes his own way, and makes a fable. The pedantry of archaeological fact, one supposes, or even the fantasy of archaeological speculation, would be the least likely tools for opening new levels in a work of this sort.

His fable takes our accepted belief in man's evolutionary progress, and turns it upside down. He establishes his ironic inversion, quite carefully, even before the book starts, in that prefatory paragraph. When the eminent 'new man' H. G. Wells describes the 'Neanderthal' as a 'possibly cannibalistic, gorilla-like monster', he speaks for the enlightened opinion of the earlier part of this century – an opinion which still prevailed when *The Inheritors* was written. He also speaks, as we become aware later, for Golding's 'new men', those clever, homicidal, definitely cannibalistic Cro-Magnons of his, who occasionally put one in mind of the Yahoo (and of modern man simultaneously).

It may be, we hear other echoes of *A Voyage to the Houyhnhnms* in Golding's treatment of Lok and Fa. These are fairly unorthodox types. According to the plentiful evidence, Neanderthal Man could just as easily have been regarded as a rather sophisticated creature. He made exquisitely dainty flints. He used funeral ritual and so presumably held religious beliefs. And in spite of his apish, prognathous countenance, his brain was about the same size as ours. But Golding ignores these clues. He finds more affecting material for his case. Above Lok's massive eyebrow ridges there is – shockingly, when we first see it by reflection through Lok's own eyes – nothing.

Fa bounds along – again, a startling glimpse – as an odd sort of beast, covered, like a Yeti, with a thick pelt of red hair. In other words, Golding pushes his primitives back beyond Neanderthal. He slips quietly past skull-cracking King Kong Pithecanthropus. And he brings his vision to rest on a round-eyed, pongoid, innocent dawn creature of no particular name (Australopithecus Afarensis, maybe – if, in the 1940s those forebears hadn't still been sunk in their three or four million year sleep). The displacement is artfully adjusted. Golding tunes the evolutionary gap between his two groups till it resonates at the most anguished pitch – the wavelength on which his 'Neanderthal's' fascination with the 'new men' is most richly confused and vulnerable, and his 'new men's' alienation from the 'Neanderthals' is most understandably hysterical and pitiless.

Our final impression is of a comfortless judgement for the Cro-Magnon but for the 'Neanderthals' – authentic tragedy. The total effect is beautiful, powerful, objective. But its real impact derives from the story's vitality as a symbol – a visionary dream projected from a calamity which is happening at this moment, in the inner life of the reader, before and during and after his reading. One can hardly imagine how this private trauma could be touched more directly.

Nevertheless, Golding's effects can be enhanced a little, by two items from the Paleo-Anthropological file. One concerns a well known fact about the ape's foetus, the other a quite recently identified peculiarity of the Neanderthal female's pubic bone. The light these cast into the book is admittedly oblique, and travels via a more or less murky prism of speculation, but it has slightly changed my own sense of the outcome.

As a literary property, the basic theme of *The Inheritors* is old – so old, and so central, that it is tempting to regard this mismatch between 'intelligence' and 'instinct' (putting it in its simplest, broadest terms) as the result of some genetic accident, with an explanation, maybe, somewhere in Prehistory. Rather like that other genetic accident – which also ought to have made our lineage less successful – which deprived man of the ability to generate his own Vitamin C. If it *was* an accident, and if it has an explanation, then all the cultural rearrangements and re-interpretations of its projections, from the myth of Marduk and Tiamat onwards, become glosses on that mystery point X – the point in our evolutionary line where we changed from a mere Homo Erectus to the problematic Homo Sapiens Sapiens, and almost doubled our investment in brain, from 800 or so grammes weight to around 1360 (Swift's was 2000).

Perhaps that estrangement between 'instinct' and 'intelligence', as a prototype of the human tragedy, is what Graves meant by 'There is one story and one story only' – but here in a prehistoric cloud of Anthropological dust. Homo Erectus sniffed into it, following the spoor of an animal. Homo Sapiens rises and falls confusedly within it. Homo Sapiens Sapiens wanders out of it, trying to separate his street map from the legal conditions for divorce. *The Tempest* makes the best of it, in terms of the redeeming triumph of civilized human values. *A Voyage to the Houyhnhnms* reveals the worst of it, in terms of the breakdown of the same. But Golding's book comes close, maybe, to formulating this agon in its own terms.

The South African zoologist Eugene Marais, who lived for several years with (more or less) a colony of baboons in the Transvaal, just after the Boer War, made an intriguing observation about the difference between intelligent and not-so-intelligent baboons. It struck him so forcibly, that he developed it into a whole theory of the 'subconscious', which he proposed seriously as a corrective to Freud's.

He noticed that the more intelligent his baboons were, the less access they seemed to have to the gifts of instinct – and vice versa. The intelligent ones, that is, didn't know what food to avoid (till they had learned by experience), were more liable to accidents, walked more blindly into trouble of every kind. In general, though they were more experimental and ingenious and could learn much more than the others, they had less idea how to behave as baboons – less idea how to live. In a very practical sense, the 'intelligent' ones were burdened with what looked like a special 'stupidity'.

Marais wondered whether this apparent lack of instinctive know-how, in the 'intelligent' baboons, was a real lack, a biological defect, or was rather a psychological condition. He suspected the latter. It seemed likely to him that the instinctive information was not so much lacking, in these individuals, as simply suppressed – by that extra function, the hyperactivity of a free intelligence.

And he proved this was so – or at least he proved it to his own satisfaction. In a curious series of experiments, he hypnotized human subjects, and was able to demonstrate how, when their interfering 'intelligent' consciousness was suspended, the old animal brilliance of the senses emerged, still intact, as bright as any baboon's, performing nearly incredible feats of perception, in an aura of full-blown intuitions of the kind commonly regarded as sixth sense or extrasensory. These abilities closed down again the moment the conscious intelligence was allowed to wake up.

By asking what happened to all that awareness, during ordinary dull wakefulness, he got the answer that it lived on 'subconsciously', in a state of suppression.

The implications of this obviously are – or were then – revolutionary. In Marais' definition, the 'subconscious' became the contained but for the most part inaccessible world not only of the 'brute' components of instinct but of instinct's positive attributes as well – those superior senses, superior intuitions, and that superior grasp of reality. The conscious mind found itself correspondingly deprived. That is, 'Intelligence' found itself cut off from 'Intelligence'.

Marais let this paradox speak for itself. Though he did not put it in such words, he had really defined the subconscious as the lost, natural Paradise, where the lack of intellectual enquiry and adaptive ingenuity coincided with a perfect awareness of being alive in the moment, and in reality, (an awareness approaching, maybe, a state of blessedness), and an inborn understanding of 'how to live'. He had explained, in a sense, man's perplexed feeling of being everywhere an exile, everywhere separated from his true being. And without saying that his smarter baboons had suffered something like The Fall, he had brought zoological evidence to the argument that the free intelligence is man's original enemy.

Whatever one may think of it, since Marais' day this theory, in one form or another, has come to influence almost every modern therapy, just as it can now be recognized behind most old religious/ mystical disciplines and behind the 'one story' that has preoccupied myth and literature.

Marais' criteria were impressionistic. Within his single, inter-breeding group of baboons, the only physical difference between the two types was the noticeably 'more intelligent look' of the intelligent ones – those who made up for their instinctual amnesia by a greater display of experiment and ability to learn. Speculation about the genetic event, in Prehistory, which so hugely amplified the tendency in Homo Sapiens Sapiens and at the same time produced a new and physically unique primate, has for a long time, on and off, revolved around a peculiarity of the ape's foetus.

Quite late in its term, the ape's foetus passes through a stage where the face and head arrive at an uncanny resemblance to the human being. The neck is long and comes in more from beneath than from behind the skull, the jaw is small, the face vertical, the brow smooth and vertical, the skull globed, smooth and high. Conversely, one of the most curious things about modern (Cro-Magnon) man is that his distinguishing physical features – smooth, high, globed skull, smooth, vertical brow, vertical face, small jaw, long, erect neck, body covered with downy lanugo – are all, considering him as an anthropoid, foetal characteristics. This neotany has long been recognized for what it is, and the idea of man as a premature ape has had a lively history.

Like everything that touches a base truth, the idea has its comic side. Yet it is very possible, if not certain, that whatever stock man sprang from somewhere along the line his period of gestation suffered an abrupt foreshortening. This is supported by calculations based on brain weights and gestation periods in other animals, which suggest that man's proper gestation period should be very much longer than it is. His persistent neotany, the fact that after birth he grows towards maturity so much more slowly, and goes on growing for so much longer, than any other primate, never indeed maturing at all as an ape, could be less complicated than it looks. A small genetic change, inducing that premature birth, might well be enough to entail all those other interrelated consequences.

More specific supporting evidence for this is supplied by the Neanderthal female's pubic bone. The shape of this bone shows that the birth canal of the Neanderthal female was 20 per cent larger than in the Cro-Magnon. This in turn suggests that the little Neanderthal foetus sat tight through a much longer gestation than the Cro-Magnon, to emerge much more developed at birth. The calculated gestation period for a Neanderthal is upward of twelve months.

The debate about Cro-Magnon's takeover from Neanderthal is unsettled, but there is at least a strong likelihood that the one did evolve from the other. Since the time span of the replacement is so short (they overlapped), the big physical difference between them has always made this seem unlikely, while gradualism held sway in evolutionary theory. But gradual change via Natural Selection does not account for everything. In fact, it has to be accepted that most species appear full formed, and last with comparatively modest local variations for an average of ten million years, before they become extinct ('the skeletons in the cupboard of evolutionary theory'). Given the large, inclusive effects of crucial, slight mutations, such sudden entrances seem to be normal. And so for Homo Sapiens Sapiens the whole thing might have been quite simple.

In some isolated group, a Neanderthal mother sported a gene that ejected her foetus at nine months, carrying the same gene. In conditions which evidently nursed him, the miscarriage got a hold. Now one imagines him fixed in that immaturity, the clock of his biological unfolding slowed right down, all his internal, instinctual wiring three months short of completion, the high domed skull still dangerously frail, his skin too thin and covered only with a downy lanugo – a jittery Ariel among the Calibans. He found others like himself – a few sisters carrying the same gene. It would be enough if the new gene were dominant. So he bred true and multiplied.

This is all it needed. And what may be thought to be a big problem – the evolutionary leap from the Neanderthal – can just as easily be seen as quite a small problem. Cro-Magnon did not have to evolve by slow degrees, in some forcing house of the Os Frontalis. He was there all the time. He had come along with Neanderthal the whole way, evolving within the same womb, a fellow-traveller in Amnios, phasing himself out three months before each Neanderthal birth – a perpetually superseded doppelgänger – till this accident gave him the chance.

One can imagine what the subjective results might be, if the inner ontogeny of this little monster corresponded to the outer. What Marais glimpsed in his baboons, was here wrenched beyond all natural limit – wrenched right out of the order of natural adaptation. And the penalty, for this provisional Adam, is that only three-quarters gestated means three months short of completion, it means never properly born, still equipped only for the mysteries of the womb, still only three-quarters attuned to the world as it really is. It means, in other words, a totally new kind of creature: born outside the laws, detached from them and with no direct means of learning them: the first animal to be out of phase with life on earth. The Neanderthals had their metaphysics, but in this new being that divorce from the body of adapted instinct is violently fortified and confirmed: the liberation of the 'intelligence', from the animal unit, is potentially complete.

One wonders what became of that frustrated, only three-quarters completed gestatory programme of the Neanderthal foetus. Suppressed – or out of gear – or suspended – it can only have become a convulsive drama, in the subconscious. Maybe, among other things, a vision of all-redeeming and yet unattainable bliss – unattainable, that is, on earth, and in life. A tantalizing vision that can never be realized because it is, at bottom, in the glandular fuel supply of its cravings and expectations, nothing more nor less than that last, lost three months, the disappointed final ripening, in the Neanderthal womb, for birth at full term, perfectly adapted as all primates before him, into the real world. Just as if a dragonfly larva were arrested in the subwater stage, and afflicted thereafter by inexplicable dreams of flight and copulation in the sunlight and air, as some higher activity for which it was created.

So Cro-Magnon man came to, from his fallen birth, burdened with a vision of a more real second birth, into a more real reality – which would simultaneously be bliss and perfect life. But this vision, as the impossible thing, had to make its home in his subconscious. And there it combined with what belonged to it anyway, the disconnected world of sensation, feeling, intuition, and that full apprehension of reality, in which the Neanderthal had lived. The sources of art and culture, in other words, were supercharged. The inner world of symbols was intensified, gigantified, and almost supernaturalized by the deprivation of his having been miscarried, only three-quarters finished, instead of born.

Thirty thousand years before Christ, he has a modern look in this too. Brain freed and in overdrive, converting his physical and instinctual inadequacies into an arsenal of overcompensations, tossing and turning in the pains of withdrawal (from his natural self), he lives in a fevered lust to find substitutes for what cannot possibly be found after the shortfall of his untimely birth, or to complete mentally the process that has been foreclosed physically:

> Ravening, raging and uprooting that he may come
> Into the desolation of reality.

It would explain a lot, if it were true.

The point is, there could well be truth in it. In Golding's dream, Lok and Fa peer out of that lost Primate Paradise. It is both a buried land and a blazing source, supplying the radiance that squeezes into even the details of syntax. In spite of their brutish fate, Lok and Fa live – like saintly defectives – in that other kingdom of our duality. Even their suffering is a kind of awful joy, as Golding takes pains to show. As if this 'joy' were merely the 'feeling-tone' of the fully operational body of instinct and the senses, of a perfect fittedness to the world's and the self's reality. By comparison, the 'rejoicing' of the Cro-Magnons seems debased, ugly, meaningless, artificial, desperate, pitiable.

In this perspective, the 'Neanderthals' appear mesmerized and appalled by their own *enfants terribles*. Those clues in the foetus and the bone enter the substance of the story. And they bring it closer to the actual genetic mishap, the decisive accident, which implanted the biological deadlock – the riddle which has sprouted, in equal measure, our peculiar mentality and our peculiar unhappiness. And closer, too, to the terms in which each of us feels this. As a result, *The Inheritors* becomes less Swiftian, more Shakespearean. The Cro-Magnons begin to look less like demons of original depravity, more like helplessly possessed and forlorn castaways, who are full of plans and plots and enterprise, but do not know 'how to live'. Figures who are, by their very nature, tragic. Subjects, maybe, for Golding's later books.

NOTE: According to an interesting piece of recent biological research (published since this essay was written), the Mytochondria inside the cells of all modern human groups share an identical genetic structure. Since we inherit our Mytochondria only from our mothers, this means that all living human beings descend from one mother, some unique female in Prehistory, and from her daughters. If this is true, then my hypothetical first neotanous mutant, my Ariel, should not be 'he' but 'she'.

Parable Island
for William Golding

SEAMUS HEANEY

I

Although they are an occupied nation
and their only border is an inland one
they yield to nobody in their belief
that the country is an island.

Somewhere in the far north, in a region
every native thinks of as 'the coast',
there lies the mountain of the shifting names.

The occupiers call it Cape Basalt.
The Sun's Headstone, say farmers in the east.
Drunken westerners call it The Orphan's Tit.

To find out where he stands the traveller
has to keep listening – since there is no map
which draws the line he knows he must have crossed.

Meanwhile, the forked-tongued natives keep repeating
prophecies they pretend not to believe
about a point where all the names converge
underneath the mountain and where (some day)
they are going to start to mine the ore of truth.

II

In the beginning there was one bell-tower
which struck its single note each day at noon
in honour of the one-eyed all-creator.

At least, this was the original idea
missionary scribes record they found
in autochthonous tradition. But even there

you can't be sure that parable is not
at work already retrospectively,
since all their early manuscripts are full

of stylized eye-shapes and recurrent glosses
in which those old revisionists derive
the word *island* from roots in *eye* and *land*.

III

Now archaeologists begin to gloss the glosses.
To one school, the stone circles are pure symbol;
to another, assembly spots or hut foundations.

One school thinks a post-hole in an ancient floor
stands first of all for a pupil in an iris.
The other thinks a post-hole is a post-hole. And so on –

like the subversives and collaborators
always vying with a fierce possessiveness
for the right to set 'the island story' straight.

IV

The elders dream of boat-journeys and havens
and have their stories too, like the one about the man
who took to his bed, it seems, and died convinced

that the cutting of the Panama Canal
would mean the ocean would all drain away
and the island disappear by aggrandizement.

William Golding talks to John Carey
10–11 July 1985

JC. You don't like being interviewed, I know. Is it because you want to be private? Or is it because you feel that a writer writes, and that is his medium, and talking is something entirely different?

WG. I think it's mostly, if not all, a writer writes. There is nothing to a writer but his books. After all – this Egypt I've just been to – there's nothing of a scribe but his hieroglyphics. That's his signature, his moira, his fate.

JC. So it's almost like saying, Why should a painter be asked to expound his philosophy? He paints.

WG. Yes, that's right.

JC. Could we, though, talk a little about your life? You have written about your father, who was obviously a remarkable man. Did you ever feel in his shadow?

WG. Yes. I did: unconsciously, I think, for a long time. But later, when one starts looking back over one's life, I did see that I'd been in his shadow, particularly, I suppose, philosophically, in that he had made of himself a Wellsian rationalist – should I call it – and because he was who he was, I took this; and for a long time I suppose I half convinced myself I was a rationalist, atheist, and so on. Whereas I don't think I was instinctively any of these things at all. This is a condemnation, I suppose, of a human relationship. Because I should have freed myself from him early, or he should have pushed me off, or something. But there it was.

JC. Might that not provide, though, a very rich conflict within you – the rationalism, and the reaction against it? It might seem, for a creative writer, almost a desirable kind of split.

WG. Well, that may be so. But of course I wasn't thinking of myself

171

in terms of creative writer: I was thinking in terms of myself as a free and unencumbered being.

JC. In *Free Fall* you show the science master, Nick, as a rational, kindly, atheistic scholar. I've often wondered whether that was, in any sense, a portrait of your father.

WG. I think so. I think it was inescapably based on him. But how accurate it was is not for me to say.

JC. I'm not sure when your father died?

WG. My father died in – I think it was 1957.

JC. I wondered whether he had lived long enough to see your success; and he had.

WG. Oh, yes, he did – just.

JC. Was he very pleased?

WG. Oh yes. Very pleased. He was pleased when – I remember saying to him what a curious life he'd had. It was a parallel in many ways with Wells, except that my father hadn't been a writer. And I said I'd like to write about him one day; and this pleased him very much. He was tickled pink by it. But he died soon after that. I was curious about his early life, and about the society he'd lived in, you see; and I said, 'I'd like to ask you a lot of questions, that maybe wouldn't have come suitably from a boy to his father – but we could perhaps talk about them now, because I'd like to write about you.' He liked the idea of that, but he died before we could do any talking.

JC. You write about him a little in *The Ladder and the Tree*.

WG. Yes. In a sense that does point up the confusion – well, any relationships are confused, aren't they – and the closer they are, the more confused they get – the more emotional the confusions must be. Father and child . . .

JC. Do you think fatherhood changed you? Why I ask is because some people say you take rather a harsh view of the choirboys in *Lord of the Flies*, but I've always been impressed by the tenderness to children in your books. There's a beautiful bit in *The Inheritors*, where you see the firelight reflected in the child's eyes: and Sammy Mountjoy, too – the way he sees the teachers as trees. Do you think that tenderness is attributable to fatherhood?

WG. Not entirely. To some extent. Not entirely. I think it predates fatherhood.

JC. You felt – you've always felt for them as victims?

WG. I suppose so. I've always felt for them, I think really, in the sense – I didn't know it, but I was thinking of them in the sixteenth or seventeenth century sense that childhood is a disease – you know; it's a sickness that you grow out of. It seemed to me that this is what they were, perhaps – they were born to sorrow as the sparks fly upward, and born to sorrow because they were children, and only as adults would they stand any chance of avoiding it. But then, of course, we know that even that's untrue.

JC. Yes. At the end of *The Pyramid* Miss Dawlish says that she'd rather save a budgie than a child from a fire. You seem to use that as a moment of great wickedness, or madness.

WG. It's meant to be a summation of what life had done to her. She'd really been robbed of her life. Humanity had done this to her, and her humanity was gone. But I do think of it, yes, as about the ultimate.

JC. You know you just now said, 'Born to sorrow as the sparks fly upward'. I've noticed that the combination of child and fire does tend to turn up in your books: Matty, a child with a mark on his face, coming out of the fire; and in *Lord of the Flies* the child with a mark on its face disappears into the forest fire. Is that something you're aware of, that connection?

WG. Do you know, when you said about boy and fire, child and fire: this is the first time that has occurred to me. It really is. That there are two specific situations there, which are children being burnt . . . Yes, well, your guess is probably a great deal better than mine – because I certainly hadn't thought of it. You know, the thing I find difficult to explain to people is that I can only just write my books. Do you see what I mean? – that I'm very grateful for anything that occurs. You see, it isn't as though I had immense wealth there that can be drawn on at any moment. It's that at any moment it may disappear, between this page and the next. And that's why I write so fast – because if I don't get it on there, it will be gone for good.

JC. Another thing about childhood: you make Sammy in *Free Fall* say that he wants to find the connection between the little boy, clear as spring water, and the man like a stagnant pool. I know you have said you believe in Original Sin, but it looks there as if you don't – as if the child is not tainted, is innocent, and that the fall comes later, as we grow up. Or is that too theological – to ask you about that?

WG. Original sin – I've been really rather lumbered with original sin . . . I suppose that . . . both by intellect and emotion – intellectually after emotionally – I'm convinced of original sin. That is, I'm convinced of it in the Augustinian way. It is Augustine, isn't it, who was born a twin, and his earliest memory was pushing his twin from his mother's breast? I think that because children are helpless and vulnerable, the most terrible things can be done by children to children. The fact that they are vulnerable, and ignorant of their own nature – can push the twin away from the breast without knowing that they are injuring themselves, without knowing that it's an antisocial action – that is ignorance. And we confuse it with innocence. I do myself. But I still think that the root of our sin is there, in the child. As soon as it has any capacity for acting on the world outside, it will be selfish; and, of course, original sin and selfishness – the words could be interchangeable . . . You can only learn unselfishness by liking and by loving. And it seems to me that children – their love can be absolute passionate, profound love. And this is where their unselfishness comes, through their own need of love; so that anything they can do for this . . . demigod, is something they are happy to do. That is, they learn unselfishness through this extraordinary nexus between people – maybe between parents and children, nurses and children. But this doesn't add up, I don't think: I'm not doing it very well. And the answer to that is that you are really asking me the question – you are saying, Golding, explain sin.

JC. Yes, that's why I was worried about the question, it is rather theological . . .

WG. Well, it's a theological question which no one has really been able to settle – that they're still arguing about.

JC. Augustine would believe, wouldn't he, that a child who died unbaptized would be damned – because of original sin – that's not part of your belief, is it?

WG. I haven't got time for fringe religion, you see, which is what it seems to me so much theology turns into. It starts from a perfectly – to me, I'm afraid – reasonable position, not of 'I've got rid of my doubt of the existence of God', but 'can't I for God's sake for a moment get rid of my belief in God?', you know, 'why am I lumbered with this?' – when you have that, then, moving out from this centre you get theology; and of course theology contradicts itself, and must contradict itself, because it's dealing with questions that cannot be answered, to which it must find an answer or be useless. Well, it is useless. So I don't concern myself with fringe theology.

JC. To get back to your own parents. You write about your father and mother campaigning for votes for women on the steps of the town hall. Was your mother also a strong influence on you? She was Cornish, wasn't she?

WG. She was Cornish, yes. What can one say about one's mother? Yes, of course she was a strong influence on me, and it was an extraordinary relationship really because she and I were very like each other. We even looked like each other – poor woman – even facially we resembled each other, you see. I gave her a hell of a time, because I had a certain crude wit which I was not beyond using, I'm ashamed to say, on my own parents; and she was a woman of very strong emotions, interests . . . and I define her situation as being fond of me, but not able to stand me. I think this is quite understandable, because I think as a boy I must have been – I can't think how anybody could stand me. I certainly couldn't have stood myself. I remember my father's diary . . . his last sentence in the diary – and it must have been written certainly before 1920 and I think actually in 1918 – was his only mention of me. He says, 'Billy is the artistic member of the family. He is a little rascal.' That's the only time I figure in my father's diary. My mother – she was fond of me, I'm sure she was fond of me, because if I appealed to her she always helped me. But there was something – we were so much like each other that . . . she was fond of me but she really couldn't do with me.

JC. Don't you think a lot of mothers find the maleness of young sons very trying?

WG. It may be that. And I never have had a large component of the female in me. I've always been pretty masculine – I don't mean in the bold sense, I think I mean in automatic assumptions.

JC. And you never had a sister?

WG. Well, no. I never had a natural sister, would one call it, from my mother. But her sister had two children; and the father, that's my uncle, and my mother's sister, they both died of TB. The eldest child died of TB – well, as a young man – and the girl, who was much younger, was adopted by my father and mother. And so, in a sense, she – I treated her always as a sister, and in normal conversation I would introduce her as my sister . . .

JC. So that gave your mother a female in the house.

WG. Yes. There was a tiny little sort of female caucus formed.

JC. One extraordinary childhood experience you have written about was a sort of waking dream you had, in which you were present – or so you imagined – at the unwrapping of a mummy in a museum – it was Bristol museum, wasn't it? – and you were about ten at the time. Was that a unique experience? Or did you pass easily, as a child, between illusion and reality?

WG. I don't think so. I saw things, once or twice – I imagined things so strongly that I thought I saw them. I had a vivid imagination, and made no distinction between what was true and what wasn't. To me the main thing about something was whether it was interesting or not: if it was interesting, well, it was true. In fact I was – I suppose I am – a congenital liar – you see – is what it comes to.

JC. Children are, aren't they? They have to be taught truth.

WG. Well, yes, one comes through to a sort of semi-moral position of being able on the whole to recognize that telling a sort of factual dull truth sometimes is useful. But it's a learnt habit, I'm afraid . . . By the way, about that mummy in Bristol museum: the joke is, it's all come true. That was the one they unwrapped.

JC. But you describe it in great detail, don't you: that's to say, there are amulets under the bandages . . .

WG. Yes, there are, too.

JC. That's uncanny, isn't it?

WG. I hope not. I'm scared stiff of the uncanny – always have been. This is the Cornish coming out. My mother used to tell me – I don't quite know why she did it – it seemed almost at times as though she couldn't stop herself – and in that sense, you see, again, I'm like her, or she's like me – she'd tell me some of the ghost stories – not the ones that get into books, but the local ones, the Cornish ones, the ones she knew because she lived there . . .

JC. And you were terrified?

WG. I was terrified, yes. Because she – she was good. I remember one phrase that made my hair stand on end, practically literally, you know? I felt myself freeze. She was telling about a girl who committed suicide – and this was back in what my mother called 'the old days', and that to her meant the distance which, to Cornish people, was really quite close in one sense, but vastly distant in another. It was a kind of almost Arthurian thing, but was close up, you know, it was just behind your grandparents . . . And in this time she was talking about suicides were buried at night, in ground near the churchyard, but not in the churchyard. And they went at night and buried this girl, and she had come from a farm, d'you see? And my mother said, 'And as they turned away, they looked across the valley, and they saw lights moving in the farmhouse. She got back before they did.' Woosh! Hair straight up! I can still remember that 'She got back before they did' – that's pretty terrifying.

JC. How old were you – tennish – that sort of age?

WG. This has gone, the actual age. That is so much a part of my past that it stands there, like a menhir.

JC. After you finished at school you went up to BNC to read science, didn't you? What sort of scientist were you going to be?

WG. Some sort of botanist – a microscopist, I think is the word.

JC. I was talking to Professor Lovelock, who said that you gave him the name for his Gaia hypothesis. That idea is one that attracts you – the idea of the earth as a self-regulating system?

WG. Well, I've always thought that Jim assumed an awful lot when he thought that my view of Gaia was the same as his view of Gaia. However, he certainly picked up the name from me, and did use it to mean what he would call a closed system, I think; what I would call a personality. But then a personality is a closed system. We're probably just chopping words about.

JC. In *The Inheritors* you have the goddess Oa, who produces all life from her belly – that's the same sort of thing, isn't it?

WG. Yes.

JC. Then you changed to English at Oxford. Do you remember any of the tutors or lecturers?

WG. No, I don't in fact . . . C. L. Wrenn, was he . . .?

JC. An Anglo-Saxonist, wasn't he?

WG. Yes (*gloomily*) he was an immense scholar . . .

JC. Tolkien was not there then?

WG. I think he may have been, but I don't remember him . . . I don't remember any of them.

JC. After BNC you were a professional actor for a time, and you acted at – was it? – Hampstead?

WG. Yes. The Little Theatre at Hampstead, and there was a Citizens' Theatre at Bath. But it was very much fringe, and I was a sort of occasional hanger-on. I probably, at some point in my life, said, when asked by people – 'Oh, I was doing acting', because I didn't know what to say about it – but it was very, very trivial sort of spear-carrying.

JC. Then you became a schoolteacher.

WG. Yes. I wasn't teaching because I wanted to teach, I was teaching because it was a way of earning enough money to keep myself alive while I moved towards other things.

JC. I remember talking to one of your ex-colleagues at Bishop Wordsworth's School in Salisbury, who said that he thought you had found schoolmastering a chore. That would be right, wouldn't it?

WG. That would very much be right.

JC. You did teach, early on, at a Rudolf Steiner school, didn't you? Is that because Steiner's ideas attracted you at all?

WG. No. It was because I happened to know some people who were Steinerites – and I thought, well, this is as good as anything, you know.

JC. It's a belief in rhythmic movement, isn't it? And astrology . . . ?

WG. God knows. Belief in practically everything, yes . . .

JC. And I think you taught for a time at the local jail.

WG. This was because I taught for a time in Maidstone Grammar School, and there were evening classes at Maidstone jail – trying to keep the place alive, I suppose. And I was there very briefly, because then the headmaster of the school in Salisbury wrote asking whether I'd like to come there. So I moved from Maidstone to Salisbury, I think, in less than a year. But during that time I was in Maidstone I did occasionally – once a week – teach English – but it was more or less the three R's, because most of the prisoners were illiterate. I suppose I must have had some vague idea of doing good. But, thank God, it didn't last!

JC. Could I ask you a bit about music? You play the piano well. And the oboe. And your friends have tended to be musicians – there was Tony Brown, who was Director of Music at Canford, and John Milne, the Salisbury music master. Did you find the escape from words into music important?

WG. Both my parents were very musical, and I played the cello, badly, in an elementary way, when I was so small I had to use it as a double bass and stand up with it. And music has always been natural to me, only I have no capacity for inventing it . . . I wonder whether I could . . . well, if one didn't, one couldn't, I think one has to say this. But certainly music has played an immense part in my life. It's always been there, and for a long time my ambition was to be a concert pianist, but I would never have made the grade, partly, basically, because I'm left-handed. But also because I don't think I had the talent that a soloist really needs.

JC. Perhaps, at Salisbury, music was an escape from the school?

WG. To some extent, yes. To me it never seemed more or less than the natural thing to do, over against this entirely unnatural educational system which was going on round it. Why aren't we doing this all the time? – that was really it. Only the world's not like that, one never has the luck for the world to be of such a sort that one is doing music all the time.

JC. You're said to be a ferocious chess player. Does that relate to liking solving problems?

WG. I don't know: it's mildly aggressive, and I said I was masculine; I don't like being beaten. But I'm not very good – an amateur, and not a very good amateur. But I've always liked chess, and always known more about what was happening in the chess world than the man in the street does.

JC. Did your father teach you?

WG. Yes, he did. But only because I nagged him. He didn't like it. He liked draughts. He said chess was too complicated. I learnt quite quickly to beat him at chess.

JC. Let me ask you about your time in the navy. You've written, in that essay 'The English Channel', about the D–Day operation, when you get separated from the fleet.

WG. My first lieutenant lost the whole bloody invasion!

JC. Someone said that you were involved in the sinking of the *Bismarck*. Is that right?

WG. Well . . . I was one of the sailors in that operation. There were thousands. We were rushing all over the Atlantic trying to find the damn thing.

JC. Were you near to it when it was sunk?

WG. No, I wasn't, thank God. The nearest I got to the *Bismarck*, I blush to say, was forty miles away. I used to say that I was the sailor in the crow's nest of *Galatea* when we failed to sight *Bismarck*. But . . . it is true I was in the crow's nest, but I couldn't have sighted her because she was too far away. In any case, we had radar, even in those days. So we knew were she was – at that time. She got away later on.

JC. Going into the forces is for a lot of young men an experience which makes them very aware of traditions of service and loyalty. A lot of people find it very influential and seductive. Is that something you found?

WG. Yes. Very much so. I came to admire the navy as a structure, very much indeed. And of course there's no doubt that, if you want tradition, as long as there's been any sort of English life there's been a navy: and the traditions do date back. Yes: I was probably uncritical of it, for a time, I think. And you see I was quite old – I was 28 or 29 when I went into the navy. But it was very impressive. I think also that is perhaps natural to man, you know, because of this group activity thing. I think the hunting group comes out very much in that.

JC. When you came out of the navy you were a keen small-boat sailor. Had you sailed before?

WG. A bit. But only in hired boats. I'd always wanted to, but could never afford to.

JC. It struck me that there might be an analogy between sailing and writing: in that they're both lonely things, and you never quite know what's going to turn up in either of them.

WG. (laughing) 'All I ask is a tall ship, and a star to steer her by.'

JC. That's all false, isn't it – Masefield hated the sea, didn't he?

WG. Anybody who knows the sea enough hates it. It's really incredibly hateful and loathsome: beautiful, grand, tremendous – God, it's hateful. You see it's really the cruellest bit of nature. Its cruelty is past believing. Do you know Hughes's *In Hazard*, is it? It's very good, in some ways, about this terrific storm which takes this freighter apart, carries her right over a ridge – it saves her, you see. And the chief engineer is retiring after this voyage, and he hates the sea and he fears the sea, and he thinks he's going to be done by this storm. And when it dies away he works like hell, and they get a donkey engine running – you see, a big ship without power is a useless lump – nothing can be done – you can't even move the rudder – and they finally get a donkey engine working – it's very well described – and really get her clanking away; and he reckons he's beaten the sea, after all this work, and he goes up on deck, leans against the rail, wiping his head, and thinking, tomorrow I'm ashore, he falls asleep and goes over the rail. Hughes says: 'He floated for a long time'. Hughes has the same thing, you see. I don't claim to know the sea in the way Hughes did; he was a professional sailor, and I'm just an amateur sailor. But I know enough about it to hate it.

JC. I've only read Hughes's *A High Wind in Jamaica* – which is surprisingly penetrating about children . . .

WG. Ah, if you're going to ask me that question, may I say that I hadn't read *A High Wind in Jamaica* until after I had written *Lord of the Flies*.

JC. You talk in this last book, *An Egyptian Journal*, about a wartime incident at sea when – is this right? – a wave broke a helmsman's neck?

WG. It wasn't in the ship I was in, it was in the same convoy. It was what they used to call a corvette – a small ship – and it went up like that, and the bow came down crash, because of this big wave, and this bloke was thrown forward onto the wheel, and his neck was broken, just by the movement of the ship.

JC. Passing on now to something else that has influenced you – Greek poetry, Greek literature. You taught yourself Greek at Bishop Wordsworth's, didn't you? What is it that you think you get from the Greeks? I know you say you get a certain structure. Do you also get a view of the psyche?

WG. Possibly, yes. I think that the Greek view of the psyche was – this is dangerous, because if I say this I'm going to have everybody on my tail – but the Greek view of the psyche, I think, was relatively simple. Maybe I'm attracted by that, with a sense of relief, as though the explanation has been made simple, whereas part of me knows that it's not that simple. And I get structure from them, as you say. And also, I think, probably, the Greek language seems to me to lie closest to the object. The words, the Greek words, seem to me to lie nearer or perhaps even more *in* the thing they stand for, than those of any other language.

JC. That's Homeric Greek you're thinking of, is it?

WG. No – I'd take that on – Modern Greek perhaps not, because Modern Greek is very much a diminished language, I think . . .

JC. But you mean, then, in the tragedians you find this closeness? . . .

WG. In the tragedians, yes.

JC. Is there also in the Greeks a feeling of clarity behind their vision; so you have, as it were, an experiment – you say, what will happen when Agamemnon comes home, as you say, what will happen when there are boys on an island? Plans and plots are made and worked out. There's that Greek theoretic interest in how things will pan out?

WG. They were free to play 'supposing' in a way that Europe lost until the Renaissance. And if you add that to everything else, it's very attractive.

JC. Taking up that point about 'supposing'. You present yourself often as anti-scientific. You say that Piggy is meant to be a portrait of a naive optimistic scientist. What I have often felt, though, is that your imagination is really scientific. I mean, it's typical that when you're talking about *Treasure Island* you pick out the fact that the boat could not – the *Hispaniola* could not have anchored in nine feet of water, given the size. And that commitment to the actual – that seems to me a scientific viewpoint?

WG. That's because I'm a sailor, not because I'm a scientist.

JC. All right. But when you say, 'How would it be like to build a medieval cathedral spire?' or 'What was the life system of the neanderthals?' isn't your imagination working scientifically then?

WG. Well, I suppose the best kind of scientist works imaginatively. He says to himself, What would happen, if? But the sort of second class scientist goes on doing things until something happens. I would say that because I'm a human being – and whatever I have said about them in the past, scientists do tend to be human beings – we're bound to have things in common. The two cultures have an awful lot in common, and it's a kind of cultural chauvinism to attach oneself wholly to one or the other.

JC. And the question, What would happen, if? – a passage I've always greatly admired in *The Spire* is when the earth begins to creep and you write about the stones 'skittering' out of the columns like stones across ice – isn't that asking yourself, What would happen, if? Because you can never have seen that; and you're imagining what is a scientific phenomenon.

WG. I don't know about that. Because I think one has tucked away in one's mind such a vast store of happenings that can be transferred from one set of circumstances to another; and I think you do that, sometimes consciously, sometimes unconsciously. I know – I can't give you an example at the moment, but I know I've stored things I've seen, and thought they would come in handy.

JC.   You make the writer's mind, there, sound like a great metaphor factory – one thing merging into another; one experience becoming another – it's full of metaphoric potential.

WG.   I don't think there is any language but metaphor. If you start to try and find the language that is not metaphor, then what you're stuck with is mathematics. Mathematics is either one huge metaphor, or no metaphor at all. And if there starts being metaphor in mathematics then it goes haywire, or that's how I conceive it. I'm not a mathematician.

JC.   Another question besides, What would happen, if? that it seems to me you ask yourself a lot is What would it be like to be someone else? And that leads you to imagine – well, it leads you naturally to a kind of tolerance, and to help readers towards tolerance I think. The way you write about homosexuals, for example – about Father Watts-Watt in *Free Fall* – you write, 'Why should he not want to stroke and caress and kiss the enchanting, the more-than-vellum warmth and roundness of childhood?' Do you choose to gain imaginative sympathy for homosexuals, say, because they have been treated as victims? Does it tie in with what we were saying about children?

WG.   Yes. Wholly, I think. Because I would not wish to be among the people who persecute a minority – and I have deliberately given homosexuals every benefit, as it were, that I can, as one might have done, you know, to Jews or Negroes.

JC.   And then, women. I mean, imagining being a woman. That's something you've obviously thought about, when you make Sammy Mountjoy say 'How do they react in themselves, those soft, cloven creatures?' – and you do in a way answer him, don't you, in *Darkness Visible*, when you show Sophy washing herself out, and feeling inside herself. I was intrigued by one of your lesser known stories, 'Clonk, Clonk', when you show the women of the prehistoric tribe as being more intelligent than men – pretending to comply with the male rituals, but actually seeing through all their male conventions. Is that separateness and difference of women a challenge to your imaginative sympathy?

WG. It seemed to me that it would be rather fun – well, the men are a team I saw at Dartmouth, in America, a football team, going off to their match, and being played to the coach by the band, with lots of Ra-Ra-Ra, and all the rest of it. This was the most male thing you could imagine – and very funny, I thought. And – oh, there were all sorts of things about it – the band, for example – right in the middle of the band was a tiny boy who was quite clearly a Jew. He was about so high, and he was playing an instrument, and you could see he had got his place made. He was covered, as it were. In this huge male whatnot, nobody could say he wasn't contributing. He might very well have been a WASP and not a Jew. Because there he was, right in the middle of the band, playing a football team along. And that – those are these chaps coming back, you know, with their Ra-Ra-Ra and all the rest of it.

JC. The hunters?

WG. Yes, the hunters. And, of course, also it credits men with the kind of tearful excitement and vivid but imprecise speech which I suppose you can say, in a sense, is rhetoric. Women very seldom have rhetoric, I think, by nature. But I think men are by nature rhetorical. But then, you see, don't misunderstand me. This was a jape, this whole thing. And I wouldn't even pretend that the average human being doesn't have a lot of those women and a lot of those men in him or her. There is no such clear-cut division as all that.

JC. No. Now, another thing. Since you're committed to, or rather interested in switching viewpoints, seeing things from other angles, how women see it, and so on, it might be expected that you would ultimately be a relativist: that you would believe that nothing exists except as the sum of ways of seeing it. But you're not, are you? You've said that you believe that there is a moral foundation to the cosmos, so ultimately there is a right way of seeing something. And indeed you have said, 'What man *is*, whatever man is, under the eye of heaven, that I burn to know.' Do you feel, as a writer, that there's any kind of friction between those two, the imaginative creativity which multiplies viewpoints, and the moral absolutism which ultimately would want to cancel them out, and leave only one?

WG. I don't honestly know. I should think some sort of process would go on . . . I suppose one would be aware of a moral position, so to speak, and then piercing this moral position from different directions, different viewpoints. And they may not individually agree with the . . . they shouldn't agree with the moral position that the author has taken up. After all, Duncan, Macduff and Lady Macbeth, each of them shows different views of an action, and different moral stands, but you can't actually say to yourself that Shakespeare took one of those moral stands and said this is the root of the whole thing. What you can say, I think, is that he must have had a different one which enabled him to see all these as piercing this tremendous story of murder and intrigue from different directions.

JC. I see. So that the final viewpoint that you say you burn to know would be one that included all the others – an overview that saw all the other ways something could be seen?

WG. Yes. It's extremely difficult. Because it makes a man sound as though he's playing at God. But I'm afraid that is true – perhaps not so much on the stage, but I think in the novel the author is bound to play at God. Because all the time he says, this way, not that. And he is dealing with life, and dealing with the universe, so in a sense he does play at God. But I would prefer not to think I did, I suppose I have to accept that I do.

JC. You play at God too in that you decide what happens – the terrible things that happen – the deaths of the boys, say, in *Lord of the Flies* – writing that makes you into a kind of god, and a god who might well wish not to do what he has to do.

WG. Well, yes. I think it is true. I think if you are writing about one of the horrors of experience, and you can't very well write a story dealing with human beings without a horror component in it, then it is going to be very dreadful to have to write it. And yet it must be written – well, I say it *must* be

JOHN CAREY

written – I suppose we could do without novels. One doesn't want to make the whole thing sound too important.

JC. I've noticed, hearing writers talk about their work, that they often seem to have very particular habits, superstitions almost – they're attached to some particular kind of pen or particular grade of pencil, some texture of paper; they write at particular times of day or night. Are you a very routine person in that sense?

WG. Not really. In general I'm completely disorganized, as far as work's concerned. Except when I know I've got a book. Then I sit down and write 2000 words a day until it's finished. So many pages, you see. And that is routine. And I stop in the middle of a sentence when I've filled the right number of pages, and with great relief, you know. It becomes a chore, but it's a chore I must do, and I go through with it. And sometimes it's not a chore, and one's surprised to find how much one's written, as it were by accident. But then 2000 words is there. I have very seldom said to myself, this is so exciting, or this is a point at which I know I can do this – very seldom gone on beyond the 2000 words. I've almost always kept rigidly to the 2000; because it's made me feel that if I write another 2000 in the same day, next day there won't be anything to write. But if I stop bang at the 2000, then next day I know I can join the next 2000 onto the other half of the sentence, or whatever it is.

JC. Does that mean that you – when you start out to write your 2000 – and you've got the novel, as you say – does it change as you write those 2000; does the thing happen as you write? Or do you know at the start of the day roughly what . . .

WG. Well, I did to begin with. I knew about *Lord of the Flies*. I planned that very carefully. But I think that's got less and less, that careful planning, and it's been a sort of by guess and by God, quite a lot of the way. I've an idea where this is going, but no specific idea what I shall be writing the day after tomorrow.

JC. You said somewhere that one of the major influences on your novels was great works of poetry. Did you mean English poetry?

WG. Greek, Latin, English, French, I think, are the only four I can really claim to have got something from – from the kind of language laboratory that poetry seems to be.

187

JC. You also said somewhere that the book of poems you published, years ago, was influenced by Tennyson, and I notice you have Christopher Ricks's edition of Tennyson in your bookshelf. One of the bits I have always thought Tennysonian in your work is in *Lord of the Flies* where the sea sweeps Piggy's body off the rock – 'it breathed again in a long, slow sigh', you say – is Tennyson a writer you learn from?

WG. I wouldn't have thought he was a direct linguistic influence. What I think is much more to the point is that I have consciously at times taken up Tennyson's – and really Homer's – idea of the extended simile, and used it quite deliberately. I think I can give you two – no, I can give you one, the other one's not a simile. There's a point when Lok – Lok [*pronounces it to rhyme with Smoke*] I call him, but people call him Lok [*pronounces it to rhyme with Sock*] – when Lok falls asleep in the tree or is falling asleep in the tree, and sleep is like the seeds of some plant that blow away in the wind. And I think it goes on for a paragraph describing that; and this is absolutely deliberate; the way Homer does a simile which lifts you away from the story. And if it's a question of peace, a peaceful feeling, well, that may well be; but he may take a moment of terror, and the simile is nothing terrible at all, it just goes away. And the contrast between the two, the terror and the beauty of the simile, is really the literary art at that point. And here Lok is really sleeping, and he won't see Liku eaten, do you see, although Fa sees him eaten; and that is covered by this gentle simile that goes away, and takes him asleep. Only if the reader has any sense he knows what's going on. That's a deliberate Homeric pinch. Tennyson does wonderful things with the extended simile, doesn't he?

JC. Yes. And Arnold – the Victorians knew about that.

WG. Yes. Well, they knew their Homer.

JC. Before you made your name with *Lord of the Flies* you had written several – you've said that you had written three or four novels. I suppose that discarded work is not something you're likely to publish?

WG. I shouldn't think so. I'm sure there were two – pretty sure there were three – I'm not sure, I don't think there were ever four complete – well, wait a moment, yes, four, that's perfectly true. Four novels that at least had an end – you know, stretches of writing that came to an end. But of course I was always thinking to myself from the last novel I had read, Oh, so that's how you should write a novel, so my novels were splendid examples of other people's work. And it was only when I was so far from succeeding that I thought, well, to hell with that lot, I'll write my own book and devil take the hindmost. Then I wrote *Lord of the Flies*.

JC.   Huxley was one of the influences on the earlier attempts, wasn't he?

WG.   I took him very neat, you know. I was fascinated by him. And he was, I think, superb – but *clever*: it was cleverness raised to a very high power indeed. Never what Lawrence can sometimes produce – never that kind of mantic, inspired . . . I don't think Huxley was even inspired: almost too clear-sighted to be inspired.

JC.   Have you a novel on the boil now?

WG.   No novel on the boil. I've got a novel simmering. But it's only simmering. It'll be a hell of a time before it comes to the boil, I'd think.

JC.   Is that a time you like? The happy times are presumably when you've finished a novel?

WG.   Well. There's a happy month or two after you've finished it. And then there is the other period after that, in which you not only think, but you know, you will never write another novel. Never again.

ANTHONY BARRETT, 1930-1986. Educated at Bishop Wordsworth's School, Salisbury and Peterhouse, Cambridge. Apart from the years 1973 to 1979 he spent his working life at the House of Commons. He was the Clerk of Standing Committees.

JOHN BAYLEY, Warton Professor of English Literature at Oxford University, is known for his critical writing on English and Russian literature – most recently *An Essay on Hardy* (1978) and *Shakespeare and Tragedy* (1981). He has also published a novel, *In Another Country* (1955).

JOHN CAREY, Merton Professor of English Literature, Oxford University; author of studies of Donne, Milton, Dickens and Thackeray.

BARBARA EVERETT, Senior Research Fellow of Somerville College, Oxford, has edited *All's Well That Ends Well* and *Antony and Cleopatra*. *Poets in their Time* (1986), a selection of her essays (on Donne, Marvell, Rochester, Keats, Eliot and others) is published by Faber.

JOHN FOWLES, novelist, lives in Dorset. *A Maggot*, his last book, appeared in 1985.

PETER GREEN, English writer and translator, Dougherty Centennial Professor of Classics, University of Texas at Austin. His numerous books on classical and English culture include the standard biography of Kenneth Grahame and *A Concise History of Ancient Greece* (1973).

IAN GREGOR, Professor of English Literature in the University of Kent at Canterbury, and joint author with Mark Kinkead-Weekes of *William Golding, A Critical Study* (1967). He has also written on

Byron, the Brontës and Victorian fiction. His *The Great Web: the Form of Hardy's Major Fiction* appeared in 1974.

SEAMUS HEANEY, Irish poet, currently the Boylston Professor of Rhetoric and Oratory at Harvard University. His *Selected Poems* appeared in 1980, along with *Preoccupations: Selected Prose*. His latest collection is *Station Island* (1984).

TED HUGHES, appointed Poet Laureate 1985. His *Selected Poems 1957–81* was published by Faber in 1982.

MARK KINKEAD-WEEKES, Professor of English Literature in the University of Kent at Canterbury and joint author with Ian Gregor of *William Golding, a Critical Study* (1967). He has also published *Samuel Richardson: Dramatic Novelist* (1973).

IAN McEWAN, novelist and short-story writer, first became known with the publication of *First Love, Last Rites* (1975). Since then he has published *In Between the Sheets* (1978), *The Cement Garden* (1978) and *The Comfort of Strangers* (1981). He has also written for films and television.

STEPHEN MEDCALF, Reader in English in the School of European Studies, University of Sussex; author of the study of William Golding in the Writers and Their Work series (1975); has also written on P. G. Wodehouse, G. K. Chesterton, Virgil and the Later Middle Ages.

CHARLES MONTEITH, Former Chairman, Faber & Faber, Fellow of All Souls College, Oxford.

PETER MOSS, was at Marlborough School under Alec Albert Golding 1932–8. He taught English in various schools and colleges 1949–71. He is now a full-time writer and broadcaster.

CRAIG RAINE, poetry editor at Faber & Faber, has published four collections of poems, *The Onion, Memory* (1978), *A Martian Sends a Postcard Home* (1979), *A Free Translation* (1981) and *Rich* (1984).

ANTHONY STORR, writer and psychiatrist. Among his best-known books are *The Dynamics of Creation* (1972) and *The Art of Psychotherapy* (1979).